The
Bad Boy Sinner

by

Lynn Shurr

A Sinner's Legacy, Book 8

The Bad Boy Sinner

Contact Information: info@thewildrosepress.com

Cover Art by *Diana Carlile*

The Wild Rose Press, Inc.
PO Box 708
Adams Basin, NY 14410-0708
Visit us at www.thewildrosepress.com

Publishing History
First Edition, 2022
Trade Paperback ISBN 978-1-5092-3941-2
Digital ISBN 978-1-5092-3942-9

A Sinner's Legacy, Book 8
Published in the United States of America

Mack embraced her tight against his chest, whether because he wanted to or simply needed the support of her solid body against his. Other couples crowded the floor for the final dance of the evening. They had very little room to practice their routine but still managed to move around the floor. Once when an opening occurred, he spun her out quickly and drew her back just as fast to rest against him. She fought the urge to lay her head against his heartbeat and close her eyes as Nell had and drew herself up straight. He moved them gradually toward the wide windows overlooking the bayou with the reflection of a full moon rippling in the water.

As the final words sounded with the plea to stand by me, he whispered in her ear, "Dip."

"What?" She found herself draped over one strong arm and heading toward the floor, but did not reach it before he drew her up again and wrapped that arm hard around her waist. He turned her to the view beyond the glass. Fireworks exploded, sending out shooting stars of gold and silver, bursts of violet and green, and blazes of red, white, and blue against the dark sky, outshining that low hanging moon.

Mack tightened his grip. "You okay with fireworks? I forgot to ask. I know some soldiers aren't."

"They're beautiful and high up in the sky. I'm fine."

Praise for Lynn Shurr

"Shurr is a wonderful storyteller."

~The Romance Studio

~*~

"Lynn Shurr's delightful New Orleans Sinners series is sure to please both non-sports fans and sports fans alike. Do yourself a favor and dive into the world of the Sinners."

~Farrah Rochon, USA Today best-selling author of the New York Sabers football series

~*~

"The author has created a family full of surprises with the Billodeaux bunch. After reading just one book, I am eager to read more about this colorful family."

~Rachel's Willful Thoughts, The Romance Reviews

~*~

"Very easy reads, well written, combined with conflict, believable plots and secondary characters that make the plot come alive."

~Jane Lange, Romances, Reads and Reviews

Dedication

For Nurse Julie Hebert
and the staff of the Iberia Rehabilitation Hospital,
who took such good care of me after my surgery.

A SINNER'S LEGACY
The Children of Joe and Nell Billodeaux
who fulfilled the prophecy that they would have twelve offspring, this way, that way, all ways.

1. **Dean Joseph Billodeaux** — Joe's illegitimate son by a one-night stand with a woman who planned to shake him down for money. He is adopted by Nell who believes she cannot have children of her own. Current Sinners quarterback. (*Wish for a Sinner* and *Son of a Sinner*)

2. **Thomas Cassidy Billodeaux** — a redheaded son who enters the family through an open adoption with a teenage mother. His birth father is Joe's no-good cousin. He is a kicker for the Sinners. (*Wish for a Sinner, Kicks for a Sinner, She's a Sinner*)

3. **Jude Emily Billodeaux** — twin of Ann, conceived by in vitro fertilization using eggs purchased from Nell's sister, Emily. (*Wish for a Sinner*)

4. **Ann Marie Billodeaux (Annie)** — Jude's quiet twin. (*Wish for a Sinner* and *The Heart of a Sinner*)

5. **Lorena Renee Billodeaux (Lori)** — First of Nell's little frozen babies to be born, one of the triplets. (*Kicks for a Sinner* and *The Aussie Sinner*)

6. **Mack Coy Christopher Billodeaux** — Second of the triplets to be born. (*Kicks for a Sinner, The Bad Boy Sinner*)

7. **Trinity Billodeaux** — Youngest of the triplets and named for the Father, Son, and Holy Ghost, smallest of the three and in need of a powerful saintly help to survive. (*Kicks for a Sinner, Dream for a Sinner, Goals for a Sinner*)

8. **Xochi Maria Billodeaux** — child of Joe's no-good cousin by a young Mexican woman. She is Tom's half-sister and is adopted into the family after the terrifying deaths of her parents. Her name means "blossom" in Aztec. (*Kicks for a Sinner* and *Sister of a Sinner*)

9. **Teddy Wilkes Billodeaux** — a child with spina bifida abandoned by his mother at Nell's health care center and adopted by the family. He believed himself to be Joe's natural son. (*Paradise for a Sinner* and *Never A Sinner*)

10. **Anastasia Marya Polasky (Stacy)** — daughter of Nell's sister, Emily, and a bogus Polish prince. She becomes a ward of the Billodeauxs upon her parents' deaths but is never adopted by her own wish. She arrives on their doorstep the same day as Teddy. (*Paradise for a Sinner* and *Son of a Sinner*)

11. **Edith Patricia Billodeaux (Edie)** — a normally conceived child, twin of Rex. (*Love Letter for a Sinner*)

12. **Rex Worthy Billodeaux (T-Rex)** — Edie's twin brother and future Sinner's quarterback, maybe. (*Love Letter for a Sinner*)

Chapter One

Mack Billodeaux tucked the football tighter and raced toward the goal line. Another ten yards should take him close enough to go into his slide, short of scoring but safer than being crushed by the Sinners' cornerback, Junior Polk, his own brother-in-law. This season he needed to rack up one-thousand yards and come into free agency good and strong. Then just watch the high bids for his services materialize. He'd had a record like that his rookie year, sloughed off, partied too much and practiced too little the following season. But not now.

The earth trembled beneath Junior's weight as the distance between them closed. Junior launched. The air displacement gave Mack a warning to go down on his own or be crushed. He didn't see the danger coming from his blindside until the hit, sending him sideways exactly when Junior buried him into the ground. His right leg twisted going two ways at once it seemed. Snapped. The pain rocketed from the tips of his toes to the top of his skull. He heard a scream and prayed it came from somewhere in the crowd and not from his mouth. Football players did not scream. Mack clenched his teeth and rolled to his back as Junior and the other player moved off of him. Bad idea, bad, bad idea.

For a moment, he blacked out, but came to in the shadow of Junior, frantic, gesturing to the sidelines and calling for a medic. "You're gonna be okay, Mack. I'll help all I can."

"Get me up. I want to walk off the field."

Helmet off, regret showing all over his big brown face, Junior shook his head. "Bro, that would not be a good idea."

Beside him, kneeling in the turf, the other cornerback who should have been playing the right side, not the left of the field, spoke to him in that damned Aussie accent, "Lie still, mate. Don't look down."

Jesus God, his other brother-in-law, Jock Brown, new to the game of American football and already a terror to opposing players. Mack had been sure he could outrun Junior, ignoring that Jock had been put into the game to replace an injured Sinner. Of course, he looked down because Jock told him not to do it. White bone jutted from his stocking. Nausea coursed through him. He swallowed it down.

The EMT hustled, arrived, studied the situation for mere seconds. "I'm going to give you something for the pain, small prick. Don't try to move. Understand?" Even a slight nod of his head hurt. The agony receded but didn't go away. A team of medics transferred him to a gurney and stabilized the leg along with the rest of his body with straps, packed some ice around the wound. Next thing he knew he rode the meat wagon, watching the stadium lights pass overhead like stars of ill omen predicting the end to his season and maybe his career. As the doors closed and the siren sounded, Mack shut his eyes against the future and did not open them again until he came out of surgery.

****

He woke to another familiar face. Dr. Connor Bullock stood by the bed, chart in hand, perusing it through his wire-rimmed glasses. Son of another great cornerback, Rev Bullock, Connor had possessed the intelligence to become a doctor instead. His reputation as an outstanding orthopedic surgeon grew and grew. Though Mack would have asked for this family friend had he been able, he had a fuzzy thought he'd been lucky to be injured in New Orleans and transferred to Ochsner. Lucky? He couldn't feel his injured leg. The fear of amputation seized him. Again, he looked down. No, he could see his toes pointing upward under the cover of a sheet. Thank God for that. He could deal with the pain but not mutilation.

"Is this a Joe Theismann injury?" the first words out of his mouth.

Dr. Bullock nodded. He might be intellectual, but he'd been raised in a football family and owned a thorough knowledge of the career ending injury of an outstanding quarterback in 1985. "Yes, a compound fracture of the lower leg requiring ORIF surgery. That's open reduction and internal fixation."

Mack returned the nod as if he knew what that meant, but he did have a question. "Theismann's leg healed shorter than his other. He had to go into announcing. What about me?"

"Orthopedic surgery has come a long way since then. I've put you back together with plates, rods, screws, and pins. Your MRI showed a real mess in there, but your leg won't shorten or shouldn't. I'll give you a copy of the post-surgery X-ray. It's impressive work. We won't be putting on a cast immediately, but you must remain immobile. If you want anything, call for a nurse."

"What if I have to pee?"

"You have a catheter inserted. No need to worry about it. The nurses will keep an eye on your urine and measure every drop."

"Oh, joy. Any pretty ones?" He tried for some humor. It fell as flat as he had.

"Not that I've noticed, but they are all top notch. When you can tell me if they are attractive, I'll know you are healing." Dr. Bullock gave him a thin-lipped smile. He had the green eyes and light complexion of his mother, also a doctor, but a GP in their hometown of Chapelle, Louisiana. He lacked her warmth. "Your parents are here. I'll let you see them for a few minutes, then we'll make sure you get some rest. The nurse will explain the pain pump."

"I guess the whole family is watching the game in the waiting room."

"The game has been over for hours. Your surgery took five."

"Who won?"

"I'm not sure."

His sister, Jude, once a surgical nurse, now an intern, stepped up to the bedside. She kept her black curls cropped close as did the doctor, no nonsense, nothing in her way. "The Sinners, twenty-four to seven. I think your injury rattled the Cowboys."

"Always glad to take one for the other team," he answered.

"But you hardly ever did," Jude said, referring to his tendency to slide to avoid injury. Her dark eyes snapped at him as if this situation were all his fault and not the action of two brothers-in-law slamming him to the ground.

"Here's mom and dad. I'll be around all night if you want me." She stepped out trailing Dr. Bullock, her form as short as his was tall and lean.

Their parents entered. His mom took his hand, the one not pierced with the needle from the IV bag. Petite and dark-haired like Jude, her brown eyes brimmed with tears, not judgment. "How do you feel?"

"Don't know. Too doped up. Did Connor tell you how bad this is?"

"The important thing is that you will walk again." An evasive answer from Mama Nell as she rarely skirted an issue.

"Dad, will I play again?"

His father, a man who'd made the pro football hall of fame on his first nomination as an outstanding quarterback, towered over the bed. He didn't answer immediately, but raked his famous passing hand through thick iron gray hair that Mack figured he'd have one day if he lived long enough. "I think that will depend on you, how badly you want to return, how hard you work on your rehab. You could be back on the field next September or permanently retired. Either way, there is life after football."

Sure, but what life? He hadn't built a trust fund charity yet, not given it a thought in his first two years filled with women and booze and fast cars. He didn't have the winning personality of his handicapped brother, Teddy, who'd become a sought-after sports commentator and journalist. Not to mention his own mediocre efforts in English, just enough to keep him on the team in high school. No culinary skills like Junior who already owned a restaurant and the damned Aussie who'd invested in a winery. Twenty-four, and all he'd ever done was play football and enjoy the benefits it brought him except for the money his dad insisted he put away for a rainy day. This day couldn't get much wetter. Mack closed his eyes, not wanting to face the future.

His mom picked up on that right away. "You're too tired to think about this now. We'll be going. The rest of the family at the game wanted to be here, but I sent them home with the children when we learned the probable length of the surgery. I'll space out their visits tomorrow."

His dad evaded the IV lines and squeezed his shoulder. "Rest well, son."

As they left, he had the desire to ask them to stay the night in his room like a child would after a bad dream. Being a grown man, he'd have to cope with the nightmare by himself.

****

As promised, his siblings visited two by two, the elephant and the kangaroo. Loopy on drugs, the old Vacation Bible School song came back to him. Junior could sub for an elephant any day by his sheer size, but also for his great memory for plays and his gentle nature. He sat by the bedside with tears on his round, brown cheeks, while Xochi, his wife and Mack's adopted sister stood by his injured leg. Some thought Xo possessed healing powers, but he had his doubts. People believed what they wanted.

"Are you going to lay your hands on my injury and make me better, Xo?" he said in a mocking tone.

She shook her head. "I'll do what I can for you, but I can't mend broken bones. That's why we have doctors

6

like Connor Bullock."

She closed her eyes and ran her hands lightly over his surgical sutures, all the while whispering prayers in the old Cajun French. She'd studied with a *traiteur* to learn the mumbo-jumbo. He expected nothing—until his leg warmed and the warmth spread throughout his body clear to his heart. Pain momentarily vanished, replaced with the complete confidence that he would recover and play again, but when she stopped, his leg remained as immobile as before, no leaping out of bed and shouting, "Hallelujah, I'm cured." He started to say that, but held it in when he looked into her soft brown eyes, so full of empathy for his plight. Her face, the tawny color of her Mexican birth mother reputed to be a beauty, had the glow of a Madonna, one who already had two children.

Junior rose, smoothed her long, dark hair, and tucked her close to his side. "Sometimes, she feels a little weak after she's given someone her strength."

Glad he hadn't said anything sarcastic, Mack fell back on a few simple words. "Thanks for trying, Xo. I did feel a little better there for a moment."

She smiled, radiant. "It's a matter of faith. I tried to boost that, but the results might not show for some time."

No, they wouldn't because her powers weren't real. He wouldn't hurt her by saying so.

"I'm going to take her down to the cafeteria. She needs to recoup what she's given away in energy. Lori and Jock are waiting to see you." Junior escorted his wife out, keeping her close like a precious and much-loved treasure.

Lurking in the hallway, the kangaroo, Jock Brown,

waited with his sister, Lorena, a newlywed pair. He'd warned her not to marry the Aussie who would whisk her away to the bottom of the world, rarely to be seen again. As always, his triplet sister ignored him and appeared happy with her decision.

She spoke first since Jock, the hulk, stood behind her. "Did Xo work her magic on you?"

"She did her best, but I'm still lying right here."

"Sorry, mate, I didn't mean for this to happen. Every time I go out on an NFL field, I need to prove to myself that I'm up to the job and then some. But you'll recover, and I'll be chasing you down again next season." Jock punched his bicep lightly as if they'd just won a game together. He wanted to punch him back much harder, but Lori wouldn't forgive him.

"Next time, I'll outrun you. Look, I need to rest. Can you tell the others to hold off until tomorrow?"

"Anything we can do for you, Mack." Jock went into the hallway and announced in a voice that could be heard over the roar of a stadium crowd, "No more visitors until tomorrow. That's what he wants."

Lorena stayed only a moment longer. She planted a kiss on his cheek. "You need to forgive him."

"I'll try." He closed his eyes to make his point that he'd had enough family for today.

As Lori moved out of the hospital room, he drifted off thinking Xochi told him to have faith—in God or himself, he wasn't sure about either.

Chapter Two

Mack lay on his stomach on the exercise table that did double duty for massages, part of the amenities provided in the pool house at his family's ranch. He gazed across the array of athletic equipment better than many gyms people paid to use. Of course, he'd been forbidden to use most of it for the moment. Only the weights had seen any use since his accident. He'd managed to keep his upper body strength intact. Eight damned weeks in a wheelchair and then on crutches hauling that cast around probably helped, too, along with their housekeeper's meals. One mandate he could agree upon—eat plenty of protein and forgo the carbs since he no longer had hard workouts.

Now the cast had come off, and he hated looking at his right leg, pale, shriveled, and bearing a livid scar that ran from knee to ankle. He'd begun the recommended light exercises and still couldn't make his muscles raise his foot more than a few inches. To top that, pain coursed through him randomly, not only while stretching the injury. It came on worse at night when you'd think lying down would help.

Brooding, he watched a tape of his team's last game on the wall-mounted TV. His replacement ran as fast as he had and didn't do the slide, thus gaining a few extra yards. His hands weren't as good. A guy didn't grow up as a son of the renowned Joe Billodeaux without catching hundreds of footballs, always going long, when they played friendly family games, and later, benefited from the constant practice, middle school into high school. When his oldest brother, Dean, declared he would be a quarterback, Mack became his wide receiver. After a while, that's what he wanted to be, not competing with his brother or dad. He'd elected to go to the University of Alabama and play for the Crimson Tide rather than LSU just to be different. With his pro career in danger, his college years might turn into his few glory days. Regardless, he'd have stiff competition to get his old job again.

Now, his mom nagged him to do the supposedly easy home exercises when even the simple toe twirls pained. His dad had taken over with more bluff encouragement. "You want to play again or not?" He'd tried, but given up when the progress proved too slow to suit him.

His parents put their heads together. Should they ship him back to Dallas and let the team handle him? Doing his early rehab at the ranch seemed good at the time, but he wasn't responding as they wished. They'd stood there discussing him as if he weren't in the same room. At last, his mom said she knew a trainer she often recommended to people who came to her psychology practice. If this one didn't work, she didn't know who would. He awaited his new tormentor, due to start today.

A sharp slap on his behind jarred him from his depressing thoughts. Shit, what a stealthy approach. His trainer had arrived on little cat's feet, circled the table, and taken up a stance at parade rest directly in front of his face. Average height, dressed in the usual khakis, knit shirt, and athletic shoes as most people in the rehab business did. The clothes covered a toned body and a pair of high breasts, not particularly large. Yeah, they'd stuck him with a woman, most likely thinking he'd behave better, be more polite. *Right*.

"Hey, what you just did could be considered sexual harassment." He gave her one of his wicked, sexy smiles, rightly inherited from his daddy, and sure to melt the most callous heart.

Her expression didn't change one iota. A pair of the coldest gray eyes he'd ever encountered stared back at him from a heart-shaped face saved from being precious by a dent in the chin. She wore her hair, corn silk blonde same as his brother Teddy, very short, but a long swath brushed over her forehead kept it from being mannish. Her lips seemed locked in a straight line. She spoke. "Then get up off your duff and protect your ass, Slide."

"What did you call me?

"Slide, isn't that your nickname?"

"Only used by people who trash talk my performance." He'd show her. Pushing up with his arms, he used that impressive upper body strength to raise his torso and swung his legs, one on either side of the table. A twinge of pain traveled the length of his bad leg, but he forced another smile. "Call me Mack. I don't think we've been introduced."

"Susan Katherine Kozac."

He lowered his voice to sexy. "May I call you Suzy?"

"No, you may call me Sarge." No change in her expression.

"Ah, a military hard ass then."

"Some might say. I'm retired and here to get you through the first part of your rehab." Her face told him she had a mission and aimed to complete it.

"You seem young to be a sergeant."

"I enlisted in the army at the age of eighteen. I'm now twenty-seven. I earned promotion to sergeant at the age of twenty-five, but as I've said, now retired."

He tried that bad boy smile again. "Did you do something naughty? Were you drummed out?"

"That would be a court martial, and no, I did nothing wrong. My retirement was medical." She stepped back a few paces and raised her left pant leg. He saw the metal rod that replaced her ankle and disappeared into her shoe. "IED exploded under my truck. I lost a foot. Others lost their lives. I consider myself lucky. I retrained in physical therapy and specialize in working with injured veterans. I'll supply you with my resume if you want."

"Ah, no. If my mother recommended you, that's fine by me." He sat there still experiencing the pain in his leg, and up until a minute ago feeling very unlucky, victim of a freak hit by two cornerbacks. Could this uncomfortable sensation in his chest be shame?

"If there is nothing else you want to know, let's get started. That position is probably uncomfortable for you. Lay down on your back. Have you been doing your gluteal sets?"

"Yeah, my buttocks are rock hard. Do you want to see or did that swat on my rear tell you all you need to know?" Even that didn't get a rise out of her.

"No need. You appeared very firm. Let me take a few measurements before we get started." She retrieved a satchel she'd brought along, withdrew a tape measure, and proceeded to wrap it around the ankle, calf, and thigh of his bad leg, jotting down the results on a clipboard. She did the same to the good leg.

He couldn't resist another jab. "What do you think of my limbs?"

"You had a good surgeon. Nice clean scar, no lumps, and best of all, no flesh-eating bacteria in the wound like Alex Smith had to cope with after his compound fracture. That man lost so much tissue, he had to have a muscle transplant. Took him two years to recover, but he'll play again this year. That's admirable."

Was she putting him in his place again or simply stating the facts? "What about my other leg? It's prettier, don't you think."

"It's fine. We'll build it up as we go. Unless you want me to show you mine, we'll begin with twenty quad sets." She began to raise her pant leg again.

He had no idea how far her artificial limb went and didn't want to know. "Ah, no, twenty quad sets you said."

She nodded, booted up a laptop and entered her findings.

He lay down and bent his feet toward his head, tightened his thigh muscles, and held for the count of five. Relaxed and did the toe twirl thing. Again, nineteen more times. This one didn't pain him too much. They worked up to the straight leg raises, the one that made him believe he'd wouldn't play again. She asked him for ten inches. He could only give her three, and those made his forehead break out in sweat.

"Okay, do the left leg. We don't want to neglect it."

No sweat there, but it pulled on the injured leg some. "I could do better if I had my pain pump."

"You are done with the pain pump. No one wants a morphine addicted wide receiver."

"I guess I wouldn't pass the drug test."

"For sure. We'll take a break. Have lunch and repeat this afternoon."

"Two a days in early November. Who would have thunk it?" Did she ever smile?

"That's how you'll get back on the field. Your father gave me the keys to the golf cart if you want a lift back to the house."

How he wanted to reject the offer, but the truth was using the armband crutches for that distance wore him out. Sliding carefully from the table, he used the crutches to attain the passenger side of the cart as Sarge went ahead opening doors for him like a prom date. "I guess you're driving?"

"Until you can bear weight on the right foot. Since I lost my left foot, I'm good to drive."

"To think I have a Jag gathering dust in the barn." With all the demeaning things happening to him, he wanted to boast just a little, impress the lady a tiny bit.

"That's the best place for it right now. Once we start loaded exercises, I'll let you drive the golf cart. That's as fast as you should go for a while."

She didn't impress easily, not like other women who stood in line for a ride in his Cowboy blue Jaguar. A golf cart, a friggin' golf cart would be his next vehicle. His folks bought it to transport him back and forth to the gym, and he hated using it. To soften the blow, they said the Camp Love Letter families would get good use out of the vehicle next summer when the

Billodeauxs hosted children with serious illnesses on the ranch. That is, if he had no need for it anymore.

Sarge didn't initiate travel conversation, so he felt compelled to fill the dead air. Silence was not his thing. Passing one of the cottages where the camp families lived, he asked, "Are you staying in a guest house or with my family?"

"The main house, the room next to yours in case you need help in the night."

"I told my parents I don't need help anymore. I can get to the toilet with my crutches and do my own damn bath on the shower stool."

"I believe they wanted to convince your Nurse Shammy to move back into her home out by the gate. She wouldn't go unless someone else was on duty. I've seldom met a person more devoted to nursing—or to a family. You should be grateful."

"Grateful that a woman old enough to be my grandmother, who took care of me and my brother and sister as preemies, an ex-nun, brought me a urinal in the night and gave me sponge baths, all except my junk which she covered with a washcloth and let me do that part myself?"

"Yes," Sergeant Kozac said, a person of few words.

"It was humiliating. We could have hired a male nurse. I mean she's married to our butler now, and did he try to stop her? No." Mack put on a British accent and lifted his nose in the air. "In times of crisis, we must all do our duty. I will forego the company of my dearest Edith until Mr. Mack no longer needs the ministrations of her gentle hands."

"It must be nice to have so many people care about

your needs."

Sensing he dug the hole ever deeper the more he talked, he ended with, "I suppose so," as they pulled up beside the kitchen door. While he struggled with the crutches, Sarge beat him to the door again, holding it wide for his entrance, though from the sour expression on her face she might have preferred letting it slam on his ass.

Corazon bustled about setting out trays of cold cuts and condiments. Soup simmered on the stove, something rich and meaty. "Gumbo?" he asked with hope, though the early November day was temperate and not made for the spicy Cajun specialty.

"No, no. Is what they call bone broth now and full of fresh vegetables. Funny, my people always made soup from bones, but it had no fancy name. It is good for you. Sit, sit. I bring you a bowl."

Rather than express his disappointment in front of Sarge, Mack took an end seat in a chair with arms, easier push up on when he needed to get out. Eyeing his new keeper, he made a point of saying, "Thank you, Corazon. It smells delicious."

"That's a good boy. Eat it all. Maybe gumbo tomorrow. You make a sandwich you like. See how good you are doing, no more bed trays. Now I go visit my grandchildren." Corazon ruffled his hair, longer than ever since he hadn't had it cut before the accident and now held it back with a sweatband or leather thong. She bestowed a kiss on the cheek for good measure before whisking off her apron, grabbing purse and keys, and vanishing out the door.

"Corazon's son, Junior Polk, is married to my sister Xochi. She dotes on their baby son and little daughter."

"Appears she dotes on you, too." Sarge served herself from the simmering pot and took the seat next to him. Maybe she thought he couldn't make a sandwich.

"I'm not her favorite. I'm no one's favorite." He grabbed two slices of rye, slathered on hot mustard, and piled it with Cajun-seasoned turkey and Swiss cheese.

"Why do you think that is?" Sarge concentrated on the bone broth, but she sounded awfully like his mother talking to one of her psychology patients. Think of an angel and in she flew. His mom entered the kitchen.

"Anything I can get for you, Mack, before I sit down?"

He poured some iced tea from a nearby pitcher into his glass. "Nope."

His mom persisted. "You should have milk. Did you take your calcium and vitamin D pills today? We've got to build strong bones."

"Yes, I did." As she set the milk in front of him, he had the urge to urge to knock it over, but Sarge pinned him with a penetrating glance as if she read his mind. He spun his frustration into a joke. "It's great when I'm swallowing the same pills my mother and grandmother take to prevent osteoporosis."

"They're good for both, rebuilding bone and preventing bone loss." Not even a hint of a smile because Sarge took everything seriously. She finished her soup and constructed a sandwich from whole wheat bread, turkey, tomato, and lettuce plus the lightest smear of mayo while his mother concocted a salad from all the veggies on the tray and added a few turkey strips on top. Sarge didn't eat like a man, but not girly like his mom.

His dad came in from the barn where he'd either been grooming the horses or mucking the stalls. Whichever, he gave his hands a good washing before filling a bowl with soup and laying layers of thin roast beef on a po-boy roll, dressing it out with the vegetables and several dashes of hot sauce.

"How did our boy do this morning, Sarge? He giving you any trouble?" While stated low-key, Joe made it clear he expected a report.

"He did what I asked of him. If he keeps it up, he'll be doing loaded exercises soon."

"He give you any lip?"

His dad eked a slight smile from her stern mouth. "Some lip. Nothing I can't handle."

His father chuckled. "I asked if I should introduce you two this morning, and she said, 'No, I prefer to sneak up on the enemy.' Glad you are getting along okay."

Mack chose not to agree with that, but no one sassed his dad. Instead, he snatched a couple of oatmeal cookies from a dish and dunked them in the milk. If he had to drink the stuff, he might as well put it to good use.

"He might benefit from an Antigravity Treadmill fairly soon. The equipment unweights the body up to eighty percent and offers a high intensity workout without putting too much stress on an injury of this nature. Kevin Ware, the basketball player, used one in his rehab for a similar injury. The trouble is those professional machines cost $75,000. Some smaller models run about $35,000. Possibly, you could rent one for a few months. We might have Mack up and running on his own early next year."

Never indecisive, his father said, "We'll buy one. I'll bet some of our Camp Love Letter kids would benefit from using it and maybe Teddy."

Mack watched his trainer's light brows rise and fall back into place in an expression of wonder, but she declined to say anything more about the expense. Instead, Sarge gathered up both her dishes and his and carried them to the sink.

"Tell Corazon I loved the soup. Mack, take an hour's rest and be ready again at two. If you need a pain pill, go ahead." Sarge settled back at the table with a cup of coffee and a cookie while his mother felt the need to explain about Corazon rushing off to see her grandkids.

"During football season, Xochi and the children usually stay in New Orleans, but they came home for a few days to see her."

"Aren't they your grandchildren, too?" Sarge questioned.

"Yes, but we'll see them on Sunday when we go to see the Sinners play. We like to let Corazon have alone time with them since she won't travel to New Orleans. She fears she'll see Junior get hurt like Mack. Her husband is our ranch manager, and he watches on the TV since he hates to leave the care of the property to anyone else. I understand he shouts out the score to his wife in the other room. By the way, you are more than welcome to come to the game with us and sit in our sky box or down on the fifty-yard line with Joe. We'll put Mack in his wheelchair, and away we'll go."

"No. I am not going to be seen in a wheelchair. Someone will take pictures and sell them to the tabloids. I don't want to be an object of pity." Mack pushed away from the table and grasped his crutches. "I'm going to rest."

"I don't mind staying with my patient. He'll be tempted to do things he shouldn't if he's left alone. Let me help with the dishes." Sarge also rose, but to be helpful, not lazy.

"I'll clean up the kitchen. Then, I'm off to work. You might like to take some free time."

Away from me, Mack added in his mind. He rose, positioning the crutches for the walk down the corridor to the elevator that deposited him by Teddy's old bedroom designed for a handicapped kid—the place where *he* stayed now. Fiddling with the doorknob, he went inside and glanced through the adjoining bathroom to his sister Lorena's lavender and lace female lair. She stayed in New Orleans with her husband, Jock Brown, the man more than half responsible for his injury. Resting against the frilly dust ruffle sat an olive drab duffel bag so very out of place, Sarge's only luggage.

Down the hall his adolescent space went unused. Athletic trophies covered the shelves on the walls also bedecked with posters of sports figures he'd idolized back then like his dad's best friend and wide receiver, Connor Riley. Inside his closet, Connor's wife, Stevie, posed on a foldout taken in her prime and wearing nothing but sand. Both he and his brother, Trinity, had harbored huge crushes on her. Deeper in its recesses, the *Playboy* magazines were stacked high. The pain pills dulled his urges right now, but he longed for the large, high bed where a man could stretch out, not the single maybe two feet off the floor that made it easier for him to get on and off the mattress.

Stowing his crutches, he helped himself to a pain pill, washing it down with a slug of warmish water from a carafe on the night table. Using a grabber presented to him in the hospital, Mack maneuvered out of his athletic shoes thanks to Velcro closures and peeled off his white socks. He shucked his sleeveless gym shirt, his sweat-soaked shorts and briefs, the headband that kept his long locks out of his face, and lowered himself onto the bedspread, giving his bum leg an assist from his hands. It throbbed from the morning's exertions.

Waiting for the medicine to kick in, he stared at the ceiling. He'd always pitied Teddy, born with spina bifida and abandoned by his mother, unable to participate in sports. The guy always had a smile on his face and worked hard at becoming independent. Everyone loved Teddy, often away fulfilling his contract as a network sports commentator, but welcomed back every time to his home on the ranch by a pretty wife and two adoring daughters. No sportscars, no gorgeous women, no outsized paycheck, no chance of recovering from his condition despite multiple surgeries. Teddy had nothing compared to Mack and yet he had everything. On that bleak thought, his eyes closed, giving him some respite until Sarge took over his life again.

Chapter Three

At fourteen-hundred hours precisely, Sarge appeared in the open doorway of the adjoining bathroom. Mack Billodeaux slept hard, his broad chest rising and falling in a regular rhythm, an Adonis among men, the god of fertility and desire. Yeah, she'd once immersed herself in Greek mythology during middle school, a secret only a few of her sisters knew since her strict Catholic family did not approve of reading about other gods, even fictional ones. She surveyed his body from top to bottom. His wild, slightly curly black hair, as long as many women wore theirs, splayed out on the pillow. He had thick, dark lashes a girl would envy, but didn't come across as the least bit feminine. Sensual lips rested amid the scruff of his beard, not shaven in several days.

Great shoulders, well-muscled chest with just the right amount of hair for masculinity that arrowed down to his privates well suited for a fertility god, impressive when flaccid and most likely spectacular when aroused. She already knew his glutes were firm and well-rounded, the legs beyond them long and strong, only marred by the scar of his injury. Once he got back on his feet that wouldn't interfere with his very active sex life.

Preferring to know all she could about her clients, she'd spent some time researching Mack Billodeaux.

The Adonis of myth had been a renowned hunter who died when gored by a wild boar either to be resurrected as a beautiful flower or a god depending on which version a person read. Mack, once fleet of foot, and he did have large ones with long toes, fell more into the category of desirable prey that could not be caught.

The deep, dark eyes she'd peered into at the gym while trying to get a read on him seemed to be thinking perpetual naughty thoughts. Add the wicked smile which backed them up, and he was a bad boy type irresistible to some women who thought they could tame him and be his one and only. While she admired his form, she found no appeal in his character. She'd worked with real men who put their lives on the line daily and suffered more grievous injuries than either of them. No, he wasn't her type of man, and she most certainly wasn't his type of woman, though he appeared to flirt with any female nearby.

Still, she hated to wake him. Rest contributed to recovery as well as physical therapy. But they had to develop a schedule. It would not do to let him slack off when he felt like doing so. Sarge slid the bathroom door closed and rapped on it hard enough to awaken the sleeping god. "Up and at it," she shouted.

She got a groan as a response. "Minute. Not dressed. Need a quick shower."

"I'm A-Okay with that, but don't take too long. We have work to do." She retreated into her room and shut that door as well. In a minute, she heard the thud of his crutches, the opening of the walk-in shower, and the drum of hot water against the tiles. She used the time to pack her blade prosthesis in a gym bag. Might as well get some exercise herself while she supervised Mack.

Too bad if he found it unattractive.

The water stopped. She gave him time to dry and get into fresh workout clothes before tapping on the inner door again. A string of muttered oaths answered her. She cracked the door open. "Need some help?"

"No. I'm just putting on my damned, shittin' shoes and socks. There, got it." Mack bent over from the waist and secured the Velcro closures. "I can't wait to get back to laces. These are no good for running."

"You won't be running for a while, and these are easier. Let's go."

She rode down in the elevator and escorted him to the golf cart. His parents were gone from the kitchen, Miss Nell to the clinic and Mr. Joe back to ranch duties. She suspected the Billodeauxs were seldom idle, hard workers all despite their wealth, though she wasn't too sure about Mack yet. Would he tread the long and painful path to full recovery or give up when he'd mastered walking again?

Positioning the exercise table next to one of the treadmills, she offered Mack a hand to mount it, but he pulled himself up using only his arms and appeared proud of it. "You know the routine. Get started."

She sat on a bench and opened her gym bag, took out the prosthetic blade foot, and laid it beside her. Yes, she noticed Mack wince and not from his gluteal sets. "If this bothers you, I'll turn around, but I plan to get some running time."

"Uh, no, go right ahead."

She removed her stump from the socket of her artificial limb and repositioned it inside the more complicated blade apparatus. Her shoe with the metal pylon jutting out of it sat beside her like a gruesome

Halloween prank. Let him get used to it and realize that he had it good no matter how much his leg hurt at the moment. She walked to the treadmill with a spring in her step and set it on low to warm up, then gradually picked up her pace while keeping an eye on Mack, making sure he followed the exercises in order and did not cheat on his reps. A few times, she thought he'd done more than necessary because he couldn't stop staring at her prosthetic feet, both of them. Wouldn't hurt him any.

He wasn't too worn out to talk. "I'll bet you're the favorite in your family being a war hero and all."

"Having your foot blown off and losing half your squad doesn't make a person a hero. It makes you a liability to the military and your family. The army got me through my rehab and paid for my first foot. I guess I could have stayed on in a desk job but thought it better to take advantage of some of the programs for retraining. I saved up for the blade." She turned up the speed on the treadmill, hoping that would shut him up.

"Your parents didn't help?" He continued his quad sets.

"My parents don't have $75,000 lying around for fancy equipment. I'm the fifth of eleven children. Some are still at home. Life is a little easier for the younger ones now that oldest are out and on their own. Most of us went into the army to help earn college tuition. I decided to make it a career. I overstayed." She snapped her mouth shut. The end.

He segued into his next exercise. "My parents have twelve, so I know something about large families. You seldom get enough individual attention. My parents are big on doing things as a family."

"At least, your family could afford twelve kids. Attention wasn't the problem. Buying clothes at thrift shops, relying on food banks when the groceries ran out, and always being pointed out by the priest as a model Catholic family, one that didn't practice birth control, that's what rankled. We got a free education at the parochial school because my dad worked as a janitor there. My mother used to teach English and fell for the line that he intended to be a noted playwright someday. Having a job that didn't require much mental effort let his mind free to compose deathless prose." She had to stop now or start frothing at the mouth with anger toward her parents.

Mack kept right on asking questions, very personal questions. "Did he write plays? I know guys who would use that as a pickup line."

"Yes, he did, plenty of them. A few were published in catalogs that went out to high school drama clubs and were purchased and performed. He did skits for the school for free, and sometimes he'd get a little royalty check for the use of others. He's still writing them even though he's lost most of his teeth because he can't afford dental care and won't take charity for himself. My mother took the rest of us to a free clinic like the one your mother gives her time to or we'd be toothless as well. Mom has dentures, nursing too many kids and not enough calcium. She's as worn out as one of dad's mops. The best dental and medical care I've had was in the army."

"I won't miss another calcium pill, I swear."

She didn't appreciate the levity. "Your mom looks great considering she had twelve. I'll bet she didn't nurse."

"Well, she only gave birth to seven, two sets of twins and one time, triplets, me, Lorena, and Trinity. The rest are adopted. As for nursing, I don't think so since we were all preemies and multiples. I suspect she's had one of those mommy makeovers they advertise on TV, but I'll never in hell ask her that. Yours had them one at time?"

"Yep." Maybe a short answer would shut him down for a while. She felt herself letting too much out.

Sarge turned down the pace, a half hour on the machine about all she could handle with the blade, and cooled down. Taking a place on the bench again, she removed the blade and the sweat damp sock that had provided some buffer against the impact. Her stump appeared to be okay, a little red but no blisters. Drying it thoroughly, she put on a fresh sock and lowered it into her serviceable everyday prosthesis.

Mack had gone into his leg lifts, adding an inch to what he'd done in the morning. He continued asking questions, more personal questions. "How do you keep that on without straps?"

"Suction."

"Ah, suc—tion," he repeated, pursing his lips and making the word sound dirty.

"Grow up."

"Sorry. Talking makes the time go faster and distracts me from the pain. Do you have any more feet, I mean ones that look like real feet?"

"I have another on order. They must be custom made so it takes a while. I can pay it off over time."

"How much?"

"Around ten thousand dollars. Depends on what you want them to do and how real they look." At a

27

minimum, he was getting an education on what his life would have been if he'd lost his limb. That kept him away from her private world.

He finished his leg lifts and wiped his face with a towel. "What do you want your new foot to do?"

"Dance. I used to love to dance." She noted the skeptical glance he gave her.

"Okay. Save a dance for me—because I will dance again one day—and so will you."

Not sure if what he said constituted flirting, encouragement, or a dare, she didn't give him a yes or a no. "How about some light upper body work before we go back to the house?"

"Great. I'm fairly sure I can out lift you."

"It's not going to be a contest."

"Right now, I could probably lift you over my head."

Compensating for his injury, she guessed. "We won't be trying that. I'm heavier than I look. I think compact is the word used to describe me most often."

Mack sized up her body as he used the crutches and moved himself to the weights. "Yeah, compact would be right, no extra weight but not skinny either."

"Thanks for that assessment." She retrieved an ice pack from the freezer for his leg before selecting a set of five-pound weights for free exercises. As she'd figured, he took a set quite a few notches higher. They both started with bicep curls, and she did give him a fleeting glance of admiration that she hoped went unnoticed.

"You know, I thought I'd love to have my parents' undivided attention. Sick as it sounds, I was jealous of all the attention Teddy got every time he had another spina bifida surgery. My mom stayed with him, and Nurse Shammy didn't leave his side. My dad visited when he didn't have a game, and my sisters played board games with him endlessly. With my youngest brother and sister, Rex and Edie, off at college, all the scrutiny is on me. It's not so great at all. I've been on my own for almost three years, and it's kind of hard to take. I can't wait to get back to my penthouse in Dallas."

"That will be some day, but hey, you had a psychological breakthrough."

"You sound like my mom."

"I work with injured vets, lots of them with PTSD. I studied some psychology, too, hoping to help them."

"What about yourself? You got that also?"

Again, getting too personal, but she answered. "Some. I didn't see much combat. Mostly our platoon escorted convoys. Sometimes, we drew fire and shot back, not knowing if we hit anybody. The enemy always disappeared into the dust, hit and run. I lost my foot in the worst incident. You might experience it as well from your traumatic injury."

Mack set aside the ice pack and transferred himself to an apparatus with a seat and weights lifted by pulleys. Again, he selected a higher amount than she would have assigned, but as he handled it well, she kept her mouth shut.

"Have any of your brothers been in combat?"

"Yes." She dearly wanted to change the subject. "My oldest brother evaded all that by feigning an interest in becoming a priest. Oh, so pious, always going to church, helping with charitable affairs, carrying a Bible everywhere he went. I used to laugh with my sisters, betting Eddie wouldn't go through with it. We knew he had lots of interest in girls and not much self-restraint, but he did get an excellent education compliments of The Church before he backed out. He married within a year and made up for his deception by cranking out kids of his own. I think they are up to number five by now and more to come."

"Did you consider pretending to have a vocation? Sarge, the nun." He squinted his eyes at her. "No, I can't see that, though some of them are pretty mean."

"Not any more than I can see you being a priest."

He laughed outright at her comeback. "The nuns at school had me figured out from the time I hit adolescence. They told my dad I had far too much interest in girls and to speak with me about respect for women and waiting for marriage."

"Did your father do that?"

"I got his usual talk for the boys, maybe a little sooner than most of my brothers. Let the woman go first and always remember to wear your rubber raincoat. A rubber raincoat is a condom. I guess you know about going first."

"Of course." She hoped she hadn't pinked up under the scrutiny of his dark, lascivious eyes. Exertion could account for that. She pumped her weights a little harder.

"I guess it's difficult to get a date when you have only one foot."

So clueless, she didn't want to answer. "I've been out a few times since I broke up with my fiancé. He couldn't handle the situation. Many loved ones can't. Alex Smith is fortunate to have such a devoted wife."

"Yeah, he is. Something I don't have." Mack glanced away, embarrassed at last. "Sorry your fiancé was such a douche."

"I should have known better than to get mixed up with a supply sergeant. Over and done. Between rehab and retraining, I didn't have much time to grieve over it. I miss my foot more than I do him."

"Good for you," he said in an overly enthusiastic voice, still not looking at her.

"I think we've done enough for today. Before your mother went to work, she said Corazon left us a Mexican lasagna for dinner. Sounds good. Let's hit the showers."

"We could save water and shower together." And the old Mack had returned.

"The shower stool isn't big enough for two." She would not let him get the best of her again.

"Yeah, you'd have to sit on my lap. Well, then, as my dad would say, ladies first." He gathered his crutches and headed for the golf cart.

She retrieved her gym bag and the keys, making a mental note to be sure to lock both the bathroom doors before turning on the shower. Ladies first, indeed.

Chapter Four

He'd shunned her help in getting ready for bed, but Sarge waited until he slept before opening the two connecting doors a tad in case he called out in the night for assistance. No calls, but pathetic moans aroused her around 0300 hours. She pushed from her bed and hopped on one leg through the bathroom to his door. She took a quick peek. Wearing boxer briefs, he lay on top of the covers. "Are you okay, Mack?"

"Leg pain. It's always worse at night. I took a pill, but it hasn't kicked in yet. Sorry I woke you. Go back to bed."

"Yes, that's called a diurnal pattern. The inflammation kicks up in the evening. Here, roll over on your stomach so I can reach your right leg. A massage will help."

She hopped to his side, rested on the bed near his feet, and dug her fingers into the injured calf, loosening the muscles, and warming the leg. He groaned again.

"Am I hurting you?"

"No, it feels great. The pain is receding. Do you still have pain at night?"

"Day and night, except I have no foot to massage, and sometimes, I want to scratch it so bad but nothing is there."

"You're really fast on one leg."

"You should see me jump rope."

"Can I call you Bunny or maybe Hop-Along?"

With his face in the pillow, she couldn't tell if he joked or really meant it. She suspected the first and retorted with her standard answer. "No, you may call me Sarge."

She felt his hand move to the sleeve of her pajamas. He fingered the cloth. "White silk PJs. I had you figured for boxer shorts and a camo T-shirt."

"I had you figured for sleeping in the nude." She shot a quick glance to his black boxer briefs.

"Usually I do, but having Nurse Shammy walking in on me made me more modest. Now, I have you bunny hopping around in silk pajamas. Bet they feel nice against the skin."

"They do. A gift from my ex-fiancé. The pants covered my stump which he couldn't bear to see. Nice try, but it didn't help in the end. Still, why throw out something this luxurious that I wouldn't have bought for myself."

"That's practical. Did you give back the ring?"

"I did. Army sergeants don't make the kind of money that ring cost. I would have felt guilty keeping it."

"Compassionate, too. I'd bet if I had given any woman an engagement ring, she'd keep it and finance her next wedding with it."

"I think that ring would have to be a great deal larger than mine."

"Leslie at Schifferman's might have helped me pick it out."

"Huh?"

"Family joke. The Billodeauxs always buy rings from him because he has exquisite taste, and we don't."

"I can tell you're feeling better. I'm hopping off to my bed now."

He tugged on her sleeve. "Would you stay a while until I get back to sleep? This time of night I tend to relive the accident and conjure up dread of the future."

"Get under the covers." She tucked him in as she had her younger brothers and sisters and lay down beside him on top of the duvet, a tight fit but she wasn't as big as him.

"You do that well."

"Lots of practice in my family."

"What are the names of your brothers and sisters?"

"Edward after my dad, Mark, Mathew, Luke…"

"Let me guess, John."

"No, Susan after my mother. I broke their streak of sons. The next one turned out to be John." She hesitated a moment. "Johnny, just eighteen months younger than me. We were close because the older boys didn't want to play with a baby."

"That wasn't right. I mean, Trinity was a complete wimp, and we always let him play with us."

"I doubt your mother would have had it any other way. Mine was too distracted trying to manage all of us while my dad wrote his plays." She stopped and made a motion to leave.

"You haven't finished," he prompted.

"Okay. Along came the rest of the girls, Mary, Margaret, Theresa, Claire, and Bernadette."

"Recite them again slowly without pausing."

Before she finished the second listing, the hand resting on her sleeve loosened, and he slept. She eased out of the bed, got her balance on the back of a nearby desk chair, and made her way back to her own nightmare, the explosion and death all around.

Chapter Five

The weeks passed. Sarge raised his reps to forty, added loaded exercises, squats and lunges, inching sideways the length of the parallel bars, or simply walking while holding onto the rails. She allowed Mack a walker in lieu of his crutches to get those feet moving, but he hated it big time. "Like I'm in a frickin' nursing home," he said of his assistive device with the yellow tennis balls on the rear legs.

"Keep doing so well, and you'll soon have your very own cane," she promised as they ended with the weights as usual, sitting side by side.

"Exciting. If I must use a cane, I want a cool one."

"I'll see what I can do."

"You know, outside of my mom and sisters, I've never talked so much to a woman."

"Is that so? I would have thought you had plenty of opportunities if the tabloids are correct." She attempted to keep the derision from her voice, but he didn't appear to notice.

"They aren't far off the mark, but we didn't spend much time talking. As soon as they started yapping, I knew enough to get out because the topic always became engagement rings and marriage."

"Women do have their expectations."

"Not you, though. I feel like I really know and understand you."

"You don't. My expectations are based on your performance."

"Well, so were theirs."

Sarge shook her head. He couldn't seem to help himself. "Mine begin and end here in the gym."

He conjured up his devilish grin. "Lots of mats lying around unused."

"If you have so much excess energy how about we raise all your reps to fifty."

"I'd be happy to do that for you. I like the way you don't put up with my bull."

"And never will. You flirt with me because I'm the only woman you see who isn't related to you. However, I can tell you're feeling better if you joke about it."

"True, but maybe not the sole reason."

The days when he teased her weren't the real problem. At night if his leg pained him, he called her instead of taking a pill and toughing it out. She massaged until he got relief. Then in what had become a little ritual, she recited the names of her siblings similar to counting sheep until he rested. She didn't mind. His recovery lay in her hands, day or night. If she could help, she would.

One evening, she'd cried out, the damned combat dream again. He'd grabbed the nearby crutches and showed up in her doorway. He looked so splendid in the faint glow of the nightlight they kept on to prevent either of them from tripping in the dark, an adult Cupid come to call, but she didn't appreciate it fully at the time, lying there sweating and shaking.

"Sarge, are you okay? Can I do something to help?"

"Only a nightmare. Go back to sleep." She sat up

and sipped water from a glass she kept bedside, slopping the liquid over the edge because her hand shook. Instead of returning to his side of the suite, Mack moved forward and sat beside her.

He grasped the glass and held it to her lips. "Does that help?"

"Yes, thank you. You can leave now."

"I don't think so. You're still shaking."

"I'll turn on the light and read a little. That will help me get over it."

"I have a better idea. Lie down." He tucked covers she'd loosened by thrashing around her and lay down close enough to warm her body. "Let me recite the names of my brothers and sisters. There's Dean, the quarterback, Tom, the kicker, Jude, the doctor, Annie, the nurse, Lorena, the athlete, Trinity, the geek, Xochi, the healer, Teddy, the handicapped, Stacy, the princess, Edie, the sweetheart, T-Rex, another quarterback, and me, Mack Coy Christopher Billodeaux. Bored and sleepy yet?"

"No, wide awake and curious. What does Xochi's name mean?

"Blossom in Aztec. It suits her."

"Shouldn't Teddy be the sports announcer? You are defining him by his disability, not his ability."

"Good point. I know I don't want to be referred to as Mack, the crippled former football player. I was winging it and got careless." He slung an arm behind her shoulders and drew her closer. "There, the shakes are gone."

"Why do you have three forenames? Is it a family custom?"

"No, I'm the only one. Dad wanted to name me for

his friend, Howard "Howdy" McCoy, but Mom didn't like Howard and wouldn't have Howdy—so Mack Coy."

Too alert, too aware of his arm cradling her, she asked, "Then why add the Christopher?"

"Because my very Catholic grandmother insisted that I needed a saint to look after me. Fat lot of good he did." Mack shifted his bad leg to a better position. "I was pretty mischievous as a kid, and when I reached my teens, Mawmaw claimed I'd have gone completely to the devil without the protection of St. Chris. She commented that my injury was his way of slowing me down to think about my life. That old lady shows no mercy."

"Could be she's right. Who knows?" She'd feigned a yawn. "I'm fine now. Thanks. Go away and let me sleep." But she hadn't. Long after he'd gone leaving both doors open a crack, she'd couldn't banish the feel of his arm around her, his body heat pressed against her side.

Then, there had been last night when she'd gone to his rescue for leg pain again. She'd massaged the scar, recited the soothing mantra of her siblings rather plain names until he slept, and dozed off herself on top of the duvet. She woke before dawn to find his hand had worked its way under her pajama top and rested on her breast. Since he remained deep in slumber, she'd removed it carefully and made her way back to her own mattress. Like the arm around her shoulder, like her missing foot, she continued to feel its warmth and weight long after it was gone.

She drew in a deep breath. "About the other evening, we can't let that happen again."

"You mean no more nighttime massages and your dulcet voice helping me to sleep. I'll have to get back on the pain pills without you."

She snorted. No one described her voice as dulcet, more like a bark when giving orders or a monotonous drone when reciting the names. "Not that. I'm happy to help you. I, um, dozed off myself and found your hand—ah, inside my pajamas."

"Force of habit, I guess, when a woman sleeps next to me. What, are you embarrassed because you haven't waxed lately?"

"That is none of your business. No, your hand lay on my breast." Damn, she should have noticed the twinkle in his eyes.

"I apologize, but I really don't remember doing that. To think I got to second base without being awake enough to appreciate it. Next time, you can tie my arms to the bedstead with a scarf. That might be fun." His devilish grin suggested she should not have mentioned it at all.

"I accept what you did to be accidental. We won't discuss it again."

"Sure, whatever you want. I can't be held responsible for what I do in my sleep, right?"

"Right. If you want to do some bench presses, not too heavy now, I'll spot you." She couldn't leave it at that and added, "Heavier exercise might keep your unconscious libido in check."

"Doubtful, but we'll give it a try."

Good thing Thanksgiving approached and Nell insisted she take a few days off to visit her family in Texas. By the time she returned, they both would have forgotten about it.

Chapter Six

Sarge set her alarm for 0500 Wednesday morning. Mack heard its sound followed by the patter of a brief, brisk shower after she'd closed the access to his room. He pulled on sweatpants and a hoodie since jeans still presented a dressing problem, and slipped barefoot downstairs in the elevator to head her off in the kitchen. She appeared with her short, pale hair still darkened by the bath water, stripped of the very light makeup she usually wore, and lugging her duffle bag.

"I can make coffee," he offered. "You won't be able to find any this early before you get to Lafayette."

"Don't bother. I'll find a fast-food place somewhere before I get on I-10."

As if conjured by the comment, Corazon bustled in through the kitchen door. "No, no, no, you don't leave without a hot breakfast." She removed a bulky, handknit sweater she'd put on against a chill and frosty early morning and got to work on scrambled eggs and ham slices after plugging in the coffeemaker she'd prepared the night before. As she poured orange juice, Corazon added, "I get up early to bake the pies for tomorrow, and I have these to take for your family." She delivered four, small foil-wrapped loaves to Sarge's place. "Pumpkin bread. You can freeze if you don't eat it all."

"Oh, we'll eat it all, no doubt about that. Thank

you for going to so much trouble."

"Is no trouble. This time of year, I bake, bake, bake." The housekeeper poured the coffee for all three of them.

Sarge took a grateful swallow of the strong brew. "This should get me as far as Houston. It's a long day's drive to west Texas."

"I put the rest in a thermos for you."

"I know when I'm being spoiled, but thanks again." Then, she eyed Mack sitting next to her. "I was going to leave without waking anybody, but since we're doing this, I might as well go over your schedule for while I'm gone."

He groaned. "No interesting breakfast chit chat? No vacation for me? I only came down to see you on your way."

Sarge ignored his remarks and dove right into her list. "You do have tomorrow off, but your dad will oversee your exercises on Friday and Saturday. Nurse Shammy will sleep in my room in case you need a leg massage or other help in my absence."

"It won't be the same," he pouted. "I guess you want to be with your family for Thanksgiving, but you could have stayed. Tons of people and food here, too."

"Not so many people at our house now. Eddie stays in Indiana with his family. The rest of the boys will be eating turkey in a mess hall overseas, Mark in Germany, Matthew in South Korea, and Luke in Iraq. My five sisters will be there with Mary home from college."

Corazon slid full plates in front of them and added her own, all topped with whole wheat toast. She sat, taking a break before starting the baking. "We will have turkey, one stuffed with cornbread dressing and one with oysters. Many, many sides. What does your family make?"

"If they still get the charity boxes, and I suppose they do, a large turkey, canned yams and green beans, cornbread mix and rice, a dozen heat-and-serve rolls, and two store-bought pumpkin pies. We always came up one roll short, and mom gave the last to my father. She'd carve up those pies to make sure everyone got a piece. Only eight for dinner now, so there will be bigger slices and maybe even leftovers."

"You left out Johnny, your favorite brother," Mack prompted.

"He won't be there. John enlisted two years after me and died halfway through his first tour in an ambush."

"*Pobrecito*," Corazon murmured.

Mack hadn't kept up with his Spanish, but he remembered that word, one Corazon used to comfort children with skinned knees, poor little one. He knew Sarge wouldn't take pity well and hoped she didn't understand. If she did, she ignored it.

"I sent them a ham, and I'm bringing ten pounds of fresh shrimp Joe picked up for me as a special treat. I told him to take it out of my salary, but we'll probably have to argue about it."

"*Si*," said Corazon, nodding her head in agreement.

"Well, I need to get on the road." Sarge went to the refrigerator and pulled out a small cooler. The ice covering the shrimp shifted and crackled as she hauled it to the door where her Jeep waited. Her transportation appeared old and beat up enough to be real WWII surplus, but wasn't, Mack thought. Still, it suited her the way a Jaguar would not.

"Sorry I can't help you with that," he said, standing.

"Don't you dare. No patient of mine is going to risk injury moving ten pounds of shrimp and ice."

"In Cajun country, it could happen, just saying."

She'd loaded her duffel also but came inside again to accept a bag with the pumpkin bread and the thermos from Corazon. Mack made his way over to them in time for Corazon to plant a kiss on Sarge's cheek and wish her a *Vaya con Dios*. He took advantage of the situation and brushed his lips over the other cheek. She froze and that pale skin of hers pinked a little.

Happy with the effect, he continued, "Happy Thanksgiving, Sarge. Be careful and call when you get there." The kiss had been brotherly, and what followed sounded like his mother.

Sarge went into action again. She turned to face him. "I've served two tours in Afghanistan. I guess I can find my way home."

"It's those Texas drivers. I know because I'm one of them—when I'm allowed to drive again. I'm not so sure your vehicle will get you there."

"It may be beat up on the outside, but the engine is fine. A friend of mine rebuilt it for me."

"Wish I could have helped with that, too." He sent her off with his most appealing grin and closed the door.

"Was nice, you give her a little kiss. She do you lots of good," Corazon said, lowering his head with her broad, brown hands and giving him a smooch as well. "Now, you peel apples for me until the rest get up. Your *papi* always wants the fresh apple pie. This don't strain your leg."

She placed a sack of Granny Smiths on the table along with two bowls and a paring knife at his place. As he created spirals of green peel and dumped them into one of the bowls, he wondered if Sarge had done KP with potatoes early in her career the way the cartoons always showed. He admitted to himself alone that he enjoyed yanking her chain. It made the monotonous and often painful PT more bearable.

As for the hand on her breast the other night, no accident, but not any more sexual than the kiss he'd just given her. He'd wanted the warm comfort of touching a female body, the solace of feeling the beat of her heart. He'd gone three months without a woman in his bed and missed that even if he couldn't perform adequately at the moment. Doubted if he'd gone without sex less than once a week in years, but seldom appreciated what else a woman had to offer. After two or three times, he grew bored and moved on to another, never getting to know them.

On the other hand, he was becoming acquainted with Sarge and knew if he'd gone south into her silken bottoms instead of north with that hand, she'd have awakened with military alertness and twisted his balls. She'd given him a pass on the fondling, well, not actually fondling as that would have stirred her at once, just the laying on of a hand in an intimate place. Whether she'd believed or not, he remained unsure, an odd emotion for him. He took what he wanted when he wanted it and prided himself on never having to force a woman as they came to him on their own volition, just as they had to his father in his raucous heyday before he met Mom and he transformed into Daddy Joe. Well, he wasn't ready for that.

A hand covered in flour and Crisco grasped his wrist. "Look what you doing."

He'd peeled the last apple into a spiral clear down to the core and dumped all of it in the bowl for waste. Deep thoughts didn't pay in the long run. He should just keep skimming the surface and run as fast as he could. "Sorry."

"I cannot use this in a pie, too thin." Fishing out the flesh of the apple, Corazon placed it in front of him. "You eat this. Is good for you."

"Sure, an apple a day keeps the doctor away and maybe the PT trainer." He stuck one end of the coil into his mouth and ate it bit by bit as he prepared another to take its place.

"Such bad manners." Corazon snapped off the strip of apple and broke it into pieces before going back to the preparation of pastry to fill the six pie pans she had lined up in a row.

When he'd finished the chore to her liking, she put him on slicing the cored apples into pieces of equal thickness and after a squeeze of lemon juice, tossing them with a mixture of cinnamon, sugar, and cornstarch. By the time his mom and dad arrived for breakfast, the scent of baking apple pies filled the air, and he'd rewarded himself with another cup of strong coffee before his mother switched the pot to decaf.

For her efforts, Corazon received a hug from Daddy Joe. "My favorite pie. Thanks for making it for me. Yours are the best."

"Oh, Mack helped me, saved me lots of time."

"Here I thought I'd have to blow a whistle to get him out bed for his exercises, but he's up bright and early." His dad hastened to pour the last drop of coffee into his mug as his mom began filling the filter with a better-for-you brew.

"I got up to see Sarge on her way at five a.m. You'd think she was still in the military. The woman never sleeps in."

His mama raised her brows. "Nice of you, and also helping Corazon. I keep telling her we can buy the pies, but she insists on homemade." She framed her words as a compliment, but her tone said he didn't put himself out for anyone often. "I'll make Joe his fried eggs unless he wants oatmeal on this chilly morning. You don't have to interrupt your pie making, Corazon."

"*Bueno*." Their housekeeper, cook, and in-law began dumping the ingredients for pumpkin pies into the mixing bowl.

Why he couldn't accept his mother's comment and let it go, he did not know. "Yeah, I'm training to be a pastry chef in case I can't get my old job back. Maybe Junior will hire me since he's partly responsible for my bum leg. I don't think the army will take me with this disability."

"Self-pity won't get you back on the team. Put your shoes on. We'll go to the gym as soon as I've eaten," his dad said. "No oatmeal for me, Tink. You know how I feel about that gray stuff."

"It lowers your cholesterol and eggs don't," his mother retorted with affection in her voice. She took the time to plant a kiss on his father's cheek. "I want you to live a long, long time."

The man still called her Tink, after all these years, a tribute to her petite size and spunk. You'd think Sarge would appreciate a pet name like Suzy Q or Bunny, but she didn't, not from her patient. Before he hopped down that road full of pitfalls, Mack pushed up from his chair. "Going for my gym shoes."

What used to take no time at all would now take him a half hour to get upstairs in the elevator, fight with the shoes, and return again, but at least they weren't babying him anymore since Sarge arrived. She must have put in a word. Corazon turned on the mixer diverting his parents and Sarge's scrutiny of him, and drowning out both conversation and thought.

Chapter Seven

Thanksgiving remained the same as always, too much food and too many people stuffed into the house. The single change as far as Mack was concerned involved having to tell Edie what he wanted on his plate because he couldn't handle both that and the walker. At least, she didn't lecture him like medical intern Jude who had traded Thanksgiving leave for Christmas at the hospital.

Instead, his curly-haired sprite of a baby sister prattled on and on about life on the LSU campus, all the activities she'd signed up for, and the new friends she'd made. He hadn't done that at college. All he needed to get attention was to play outstanding football for Ole Miss and keep up half decent grades in Kinesiology. People wanted to know him, and his major caused him less sweat than workouts. That his choice of schools ranked seventh as a party school hadn't hurt at all.

He'd finished his mounded plate full of dark meat and gravy, cornbread dressing because he hated oysters, a heaping spoonful each of green beans and candied yams, one French bread pistolette roll, and some mac and cheese. The salad he didn't particularly want came in a separate bowl. Now, he awaited his dessert service, a piece of that apple pie he'd helped to make and a small serving of Mawmaw Nadine's meringue-topped bread pudding. No wine for him during the meal because of his meds, but he requested a cup of the real coffee. His server had morphed from petite freshman college girl into a hulking cornerback.

Junior Polk pushed the walker aside and took up the space he'd made as he placed the sweet course in front of him with the true flourish of an experienced waiter, which he had been at one time while learning the culinary arts. So far, most of the family members had made a short visit and moved on, no sympathy or pity expressed. Word must have spread. He hoped Junior wouldn't cry again as he had at the hospital bedside right after the accident.

"Um-umm, my mama makes the best pies. Look how she cut those autumn leaves out of pastry and glazed them with milk to make them pretty. The pumpkin and pecan pies have the crust cut to make them seem like sunflowers. I wish she'd do dessert trays for the restaurant, but she keeps saying no. As for that bread pudding, I only hope Mawmaw don't pass without giving me the recipe." Junior finished his opening and went straight to another apology. "How's the leg? I wish I could have stopped myself in midair before coming down on you so hard."

"Just doing your job, man. Not your fault." Mack glanced around and spotted Jock Brown sipping wine from his own Australian vineyard paired with the pumpkin pie piled high with whipped cream. "It was his. So new to the game he didn't stay on his own side of the field. You had everything under control. We both did until he crossed the field in that showboat move and got in our way."

"Yeah, I knew you were going into your slide, but he didn't. New to being a cornerback and hasn't played that position since. He's too dangerous. He wants to speak with you if that's all right."

"I can't stop him. You've moved my walker too far away."

"I'll tell him to put it back. See you in the theater when the games start." Yes, all but the small children and some of the women would spend the afternoon immersed in college football and the Cowboys traditional Thanksgiving game. He would rather have been sitting on the bench with his team. Junior gave Jock a nod and moved away as the other huge man approached much more slowly than he had on that fateful day.

"G'day, Mack. How you going?"

"Going nowhere. Doing nothing. But only today. My trainer will be back Sunday."

"I've said my sorries before, but I wanted you to know I've asked the Sinners to make me permanent on offense. I'd rather take my knocks than hurt another man the way I did you."

"Yeah. I noticed you're playing tight end now. Fast becoming quarterback Dean Billodeaux's favorite receiver all the commentators are saying. You still have to block some of the time."

"Block, not tackle. Next year when we play Dallas again, we won't be on the field at the same time, so no worries."

"If I'm back on the field."

"I have no doubt about it, mate. Shake on it." Jock held out a hand just as intimidating as the rest of his six-foot-six frame, but his grip remained firm and cordial.

"Do me a favor and sneak me a glass of that wine." He might as well take advantage of his brother-in-law's guilt because no one else would do that for him.

"Righty-O, but just the one."

When Jock returned, remorse still showing in his green eyes, and handed over the glass, Mack chugged it down. Oh, it went well with apple pie, not so much with the very sweet bread pudding. "Thanks, I needed that."

However, when he attempted to rise on his walker a half hour later to make his painful way to the theater, he found he wobbled, almost lost his balance a time or two. The fact that Jock Brown trailed him made him nervous, afraid of falling again.

"No worries, mate, I've got your back," Jock said.

Great, another babysitter, and one he had no fondness for at all.

At last, he reached the darkness where the first game already in progress showed on the screen. Relieved, he took a seat in the front row where no one would trip over the walker beside him and went to sleep pondering how Sarge had spent her Thanksgiving Day. The text message he'd found on his phone simply read, "Home safe" with a time stamp past midnight. Not quite phone sex or the repartee he'd hoped to have. One thing for sure, that glass of wine would not have gotten past her vigilance.

Chapter Eight

Fewer sat 'round the table and far more to eat, Sarge or Suze as the family called her, assessed. She'd arrived at the two-story frame farmhouse that once belonged to her grandparents past midnight and intended to sneak inside, go up to the girls' dormitory style room, and slip into any empty bed, but her mother had waited up to make sure she arrived safely and didn't need any help unloading the Jeep. Her mom looked as careworn as always, more so as her once blonde hair, never cut, had gone white, and she'd screwed the long braid into a bun, both making her seem older than her age. Sarge dispensed a hug and gave her the offering of shrimp to put in the fridge and the sack of pumpkin bread. She toted her own duffel upstairs.

Her dad had knocked the walls out of several small bedrooms as the family grew and the girls started showing up regularly, creating two larger spaces to hold a single bed and a nightstand for each child across from a wardrobe for their clothes. Strange that no one occupied the boys' dorm anymore and not as much need to fight over the single upstairs bathroom.

Her parents had taken over the downstairs room by the kitchen meant for the elderly or sick and added another small bath sticking out of the side of the square building like a cow shed. It often came in handy, though the rules said the parents bathed first. Things that hadn't changed in a century—the constant whining of the wind and the dust it shoveled under the doors and windowsills.

Only her sister, Mary, sat up reading as always while the other four sisters barely opened an eye before pulling their covers over their heads and going back to sleep. She'd gone from this to sleeping in a barracks, not much difference. Giving Mary a nod, Sarge went to the wardrobe that once belonged to her and found a granny-style flannel nightgown. Nights got cold out here on the plains and silk would not do. In fact, she'd left her favorite pajamas at Lorena Ranch. As she shed her clothes and draped the nightie over her body, she smiled at the thought she might take this one back with her and surprise Mack with its primness one night when he called out for her attention. It covered her stump every bit as well as the PJs.

"You seem happy to be home," Mary remarked, shutting the book and placing it on her nightstand along with her glasses. Her brown eyes seemed smaller without them, but the way she'd bobbed her long brunette hair immediately after leaving for college suited her very well.

"Not so much. I can tell you the Billodeauxs do big families better. But I brought shrimp for cocktails to start off the meal. We dine like the rich and famous this year."

"Yeah, we received your ham and the charity box. Two entrees, pretty fancy. As soon as I get my teaching degree next spring, I'm going away from here just like the rest of you. I'll turn out the light as soon as you're tucked in."

Tucked in, that exact phrase brought Mack to mind again, arranging his blankets and then lying on top of them at his side until he slept. The hand on her breast, intentional or not, she had to shove it aside. Sitting on the side of her bed, she unfastened her prosthetic foot, drew a pair of heavy socks from her duffel to cover the stump and remaining foot, and swung her body into bed. She typed out a terse message to Mack in case he'd meant what he said, which she doubted. He always tried to get a rise out of her, and that concern and kiss on the cheek constituted just another prank to unsettle her. She gave Mary the nod and sank into darkness on ice cold sheets.

****

Up earlier than her sisters, Sarge seized the first shower. Cold water clanged through the pipes for some time before it heated enough to bathe. Old habits die hard. Leaning against a wall, no shower chair here, she made the bath as brief as possible to conserve hot water for the others. Because her mother would insist, she put on a somewhat wrinkled dark green wool dress, midi length that covered most of her prosthesis, with a large collar of lace tatted by her grandmother and passed along to the eldest daughter, black flats on both feet, real and imaginary. She'd vowed she wouldn't be defiant or snarky this year. If Mom wanted them dressed up for the holiday, she could oblige her. It wasn't a big thing to ask.

In the kitchen, the coffee pot simmered on the stove. The turkey sat in the oven but hadn't roasted enough to send up delicious aromas from its still pimply white skin. Her mom shoveled cornbread dressing from a large bowl into a Pyrex casserole dish to be heated later. No oysters for the Kozacs, too dear and too far from the coast. Sarge stuck her finger into a small bowl of red glop and sucked it off.

Her mother, hands freed, slapped her lightly with a wooden spoon. "It's cocktail sauce. I made it myself with ketchup, horseradish, and Worcestershire sauce. For the shrimp."

"It's good," Sarge acknowledged. When they had the makings, her mother knew how to cook. "Do you want me to boil the shrimp, devein, and chill it."

"Oh, you're too dressed up for that and should be treated as a guest since you come home so seldom. There's a pot of grits on the back burner and sliced pumpkin bread on the table."

"I'll put on an apron. I'm only family." She wouldn't be lured into promising to come home more often.

Grits, breakfast for most of her life. How lavish a Billodeaux breakfast seemed or even a military one with several choices that included eggs. She filled a mug, a misshaped thing one of her sisters made in a middle school pottery class, to the brim with coffee. Not to judge, but she'd gotten used to the dark roast of Cajun Country and this brew seemed weak as the dishwater in the sink. Helping herself to a bowl of grits, she put a substantial pat of butter on top and dug in, saving a piece of pumpkin bread for last. When the grits were gone, she bit into the sweet bread redolent of cinnamon, ginger, and nutmeg—and surprise— chocolate chips, not raisins. The very taste reminded her of the warmth of Corazon and the chocolate color of Mack's deep brown eyes. She grabbed another piece before the rest of the horde came downstairs.

Mary arrived first, not dressed but showered judging by the dampness of her brown hair. She wore a heavy robe and handknit slippers, her mother's work. Without a word, she got her coffee and grits and plopped down on one of the long benches that ringed a trestle table made by their father. He was handy that way. Probably should have become a carpenter rather than a janitor and failed playwright. Mary finished off the bowl of mushy white grits and bit into a piece of pumpkin bread. The coffee had aroused her enough to say, "Wow, this is so good. Did you make it Suze?"

"Me in a kitchen? No. The Billodeaux's housekeeper, Corazon, did. She's also the mother-in-law to one of Mack's sisters and very much a part of the family."

"Must be nice having someone to do for you," her mother said as she dumped two cans of yams into a pan to be candied. "I did try to teach you to cook."

"Since I was destined for the army like the boys, I had no use for cooking my own food."

"Well, you would have been a great help to me if you had." Her mom dotted butter over the yams and sprinkled brown sugar over the top. Into the oven it went to cook on the rack beneath the turkey.

Mary, who had learned to cook, remarked, "What, no marshmallows on top?"

"I'll put them on when I reheat the dish while the turkey is resting. I want to get ahead so we can talk and take phone calls from the boys." She took out another casserole dish, put the two cans of drained green beans into it, vigorously stirred in the obligatory mushroom soup and milk, then folded in the crunchy fried onions, saving half the container for the topping.

Margaret, almost always called Maggie, wandered in dressed similarly to Mary. "Claire beat me to the shower. Can I use yours?" She flipped her blonde-streaked brown hair cut to a reasonable length over her shoulders and rubbed the cinders from her brown eyes as near-sighted as Mary's, but she'd paid for her own contacts. Her hand dipped into the can of crispy fried onions. She snagged only a few before their mother whisked them away.

"Those are for the green beans. No, you'll wake your dad. Wait your turn. The grits are on the stove."

Her dad, who didn't believe in birth control, had spent entirely too much time in bed, Sarge thought but didn't say. To give him some credit, he'd always been a hard worker who took on woodworking jobs when his janitorial duties allowed. The only thing that kept them poor was of course the size of the family.

"Always grits for breakfast. Usually, I buy a Cinnabon before I go to work," Maggie griped. Twenty and working at a retail clothing shop in a Lubbock mall, she paid for her own small luxuries, but Sarge was certain part of her salary went to the support of the family. Some of her own military pay had been sent home to Texas. She hadn't bothered since losing her foot.

"I like your hair, Mags," she offered.

Her second sister flipped her locks again. "Sam loves it this way, but it is a lot of work. I always wished I had your hair, but a cut like that wouldn't look good on my big head. I had to take after dad, and you got Mom's high cheekbones and delicate features, plus the light eyes."

"I only wish she hadn't cut it so short and boyish,"

their mother said. "Men do prefer long hair. It attracts them. That's why Muslim women have to keep theirs covered."

Sarge couldn't hold back a very juvenile eye roll. "Yeah, long hair would distract them from my lack of a foot."

Her resentment bubbled like the yams in the oven. She'd had good grades and decent SAT scores but not high enough to impress a college into giving her a scholarship. In elementary school, she'd excelled in sports, soccer and juvenile races around the track, but with more babies on the way, Mom needed her at home to help. No time in middle school and high school to go to practices and try to earn an athletic scholarship. Once, she'd naively asked for dance lessons. No money for that, plus the expensive costumes. Instead, she'd learned some moves from Dancing with the Stars, enjoying the romantic, stately waltzes the most. Though her dad disapproved of the skimpy costumes, her mother let her watch and dream on. When her new foot came, perhaps she'd dance again.

She took note of her mother's sad gray eyes and added in haste, "Are you and Sam any closer to getting married?"

"She's working hard on getting that Mrs. degree," quipped Mary.

"Maggie is only twenty. No need to hurry. She has plenty of time to marry and start a family. I was twenty-three when I met your father and had Eddie at twenty-four." Their mother poured a cup of coffee and sat down in the armchair at the end of the table.

Unnecessary to make dessert. The two pumpkin pies from the charity basket sat on the counter awaiting a dollop of Cool Whip. They tasted all right, but what Sarge wouldn't give for some of Corazon's fresh apple. Well aware of her Sunday school teachings about being thankful for what she did have, she shifted her mind again when Claire led the way with her youngest sisters yammering behind about all the hot water being gone.

With a weary sigh, their mother said, "Have your breakfast, then I'll wake your father. After he showers, our little water heater should have enough for one more person and the other might have recharged by then."

Claire, not the most generous of her sisters, snatched up the last piece of pumpkin bread and took a bite before Theresa, aged sixteen, and Bernadette, fourteen, could protest.

"Hey, what was that?" Terry demanded.

"The best pumpkin bread in the world," said Mary. "You snooze, you lose." All that remained on the plate were crumbs and a single chocolate chip.

"I brought three more loaves from Lorena Ranch. Slice another one." Sarge put an end to the bickering with her authoritative voice in place. Maybe she'd always been destined to be a sergeant.

"See, that's why I'm enlisting as soon as I finish my senior year. I want to boss people around like you do, Suze," Claire said. "First thing I'll do is ask them to shave off all my hair. I'm tired of being mistaken for a Pentecostal."

Their mother, who had gotten up to cut more pumpkin bread since no one else did, gasped. "You'll break your father's heart."

"By joining the army or cutting my hair?"

"Both."

"Once I'm eighteen, he has nothing to say about it

anymore."

"Do what you want with your hair, but don't enlist. This family has given enough to the army, three sons in for life, my foot, and Johnny's death. Do anything but. Besides, if you don't want to take orders, you'll be miserable for years before you gain enough rank to give them to others." Sarge finished her coffee and tried to ignore her mother's tears being wiped on the edge of her apron. Any mention of Johnny brought them on.

"Give me that apron, and I'll cook the shrimp. That's one handy thing I've learned in Louisiana." She removed the pumpkin bread platter from her mother's hands and put it on the table, shoving Claire's greedy hand away as it reached for another piece. "Let the shrimps of our family have some first." She offered it to Terry and Bernie, last products of a worn-out womb and both much smaller than the rest of the family at five-two and five feet. They did not hesitate to dive into the treat.

"Mom, why don't you go wake Dad and then take a rest yourself? I'll take over here." Sarge claimed the apron and shooed her mom from the kitchen. She found the big soup pot, filled it halfway with water and a liberal amount of salt, and placed it on the biggest burner to heat. Taking the cooler from the fridge, she drained off the water and ice and began beheading crustaceans with a neat twist between their head and body just as she'd been taught in survival training to kill a chicken.

"Oooh, nasty looking things," Bernie claimed as she poured milk to wash down the quick bread, being of an age when still denied coffee.

"Some say they are more flavorful when cooked

with the heads on, but I like to get that part out of the way. Believe me, you won't recognize them when I'm done, but you don't have to eat them if you don't want." She scooped the whiskery heads into a plastic bag and tied it tight to keep in the odor.

"More for me," Maggie said. "But I like them fried better."

"Because you've never had shrimp cocktails." Her family, she just had to shake her head. The water came to a boil, and she scraped the shrimp from the cutting board into the pot, watched it carefully while stirring with a slotted spoon, and then took them off the moment they curled up like the ones seen hanging from cocktail glasses in fancy gourmet magazines. Draining the shrimp into a colander, she ran cold water to cool them down.

Her dad wandered in wearing a ratty bathrobe all the children had chipped in for years ago on Father's Day and men's scuffs on his big feet. He enveloped his first-born daughter in a big hug. Yes, he was damp from a shower, but hadn't shaved off the prickly silver stubble or brushed what remained of his teeth yet. "There's my Suzy Q and she's cooking shrimp. Wonders upon wonders."

"Grits are on the back of the stove."

"Your mother didn't make an egg for me? She usually does."

"Sorry about that, but I have to deal with these shrimp. There's some great pumpkin bread on the table. Who is going to help me peel and devein them?"

The youngest three disappeared to get dressed. Maggie demurred as she didn't want to ruin her expensive manicure, but Mary took a seat and began removing the shells. For each she peeled, Sarge hooked one of her short nails under the back vein, really an intestine, and stripped it out. Into a bowl of ice water they went to be ready for pairing with the cocktail sauce as an appetizer or first course unheard of in the Kozac household. That's why Mary remained her favorite sister, always willing to help, plus she'd broken the chain of military service through hard work on her grades. Sarge had to admire that.

Their father sat slurping his coffee in the larger armchair at the farther end of the long table, ever his throne, and downing his grits without eggs, keeping the remaining slices of pumpkin bread near at hand. The only man she allowed to call her Suzy even though she'd asked repeatedly to be known as Suze, brief and hard like Sarge, ate his breakfast oblivious as always to the emotions in the room. She wondered if that was why he so often failed with his plays, good enough with light comedy but lacking in feeling. She couldn't change him, not now, too late.

She removed the apron and hung it on a peg. "You know, I think I'll take a nap in the boys' dorm where it will be quiet. I arrived late and got up early. Call me around dinner time or if the Cowboys game comes on, whichever is first."

"Hear that, Mary," her dad said. "Remember to wake Suzy."

Did he never take responsibility for anything? Sarge made her way to the second floor and entered the boys' area, silent, the beds made up with military precision. She chose Johnny's bed and lay down feeling close to him, missing him, and let herself drift away from Texas and back to the Billodeaux ranch where once Mack's hand had rested on her breast.

Chapter Nine

She'd gotten through the holiday okay without causing major arguments or upsets that would always be attributed to the loss of her foot but had roots far longer than that. She only wished other family members had been more forbearing. Managing to get out of the plains and through hill country before dark, Sarge drove in darkness along the flat stretch of I-10 lined with rice paddies and cane fields that crossed Louisiana. Nothing to see, she assessed her family visit instead.

She'd gotten up early enough to make lettuce cups in her grandmother's green glass dessert dishes and arrange the shrimp in a ring around a red pool of the sauce. Needless to say, the Kozacs did not own cocktail glasses, nor had their granny. One of the other girls had set the table with the good china, also inherited from the same source. She swore if her grandparents hadn't been able to afford small luxuries, they would have had none in their lives, not even a paid off roof over their heads.

Seeing how things were going, her widowed mom's mom left all she had to the growing Kozac family who took care of her for the remaining days of her life. Sarge had only vague memories of Granny in her rocker, holding one of the babies or reading to an insistent child. Thank God, she'd taken care of them, or by now her dad would have dreamed away what little they had. The house, she'd learned not too long ago, had been put in her mother's name only. From time to time, heirlooms disappeared, an old clock or a knickknack. Some returned from the pawnshop. Others did not, but they still had the china.

Sarge placed the shrimp bowls at each place. Then, she made herself useful heating the rolls in the microwave as her mother stirred the gravy while the turkey rested on the cutting board awaiting her father's hand with the knife. In the oven, the yams now puffy with marshmallows, and the green beans topped with crispy onions warmed. The ham, sliced cold, was ready to go. All got to the table on time but cooled as her father gave a lengthy prayer of thanksgiving. Plenty for everyone this year and all the boys gone, so no grabbing to get hands on a dish first.

They carried their pie, more generously apportioned than usual, into the living room with its shabby sofa, antique rocker, and a recliner, once spewing its stuffing and salvaged from the roadside, positioned around a TV of no great size and a coffee table made by her dad out of oak beams salvaged from a house being torn down. His writer's area, nothing but a tiny desk with a computer and piles of loose papers occupied a corner. The announcers were still commenting about various players who exercised on the field below.

"That's Mack's brother, Teddy, the one in the wheelchair. I guess he won't have his dinner at the ranch," Sarge offered by way of conversation from where she sat on the sofa with Mary, Maggie, and Claire since game play hadn't started. Bernie and Terry lounged on floor cushions their mom had made. Dad, as always, stretched out in his duct-taped recliner and her mom in the rocking chair knitting yet another pair of slippers.

Her father patted his distended belly. "They couldn't have had a finer meal than us. Thank you, Susan." Her mother nodded and kept on knitting.

"I think it's sad he isn't with his family today," Bernie said, forgetting her three brothers at army bases abroad.

"He's well paid for his job," Sarge pointed out. "I'm also sure dinner will be waiting for him at home."

"Do you think Mack will play again?" asked Terry. "He's so dreamy."

"Yeah, give us the skinny, Suzy, since you're taking care of him," her dad added. "We want to be the first to know."

"I'm doing rehab with him, not taking care of him. He's coming along well and might play again next year." On the TV screen, Teddy Billodeaux said the same thing which caused them to laugh.

"Is it weird putting your hands on such a gorgeous guy, Suze? What is he really like?" Claire asked.

"Not weird. He's only another client."

"Yeah, right," Mary said.

"Look, he can be as petulant as a child and wants recovery to move faster than it does, but if he has the will and puts in the time, he can come back."

"But I mean, it must be hot touching him, running your fingers through his dark mane, being on the receiving end of that sexy smile," Maggie insinuated.

"I've yet to run my fingers through his hair, though he could use a good cut right now. That smile is lethal and must be ignored because he uses it to get his way, and the only part of him I touch is his injured leg." No way would she admit to lying by his side at night on top of the covers as if performing some kind of Puritan courtship.

"I don't like the way this conversation is going. The game is starting. You know the silence rule is in effect," her father stated. They could cheer, boo, hiss, make brief comments related to the game, or leave the room. Dad took his football seriously, and she suspected, bet on the games from time to time. Fortunately, the Cowboys were a strong team and didn't lose often. They triumphed in this one big time. She wondered if Mack fretted over his replacement making three touchdowns in a high scoring game. Now, she'd bet on that and win.

Later in the day, the big and potentially upsetting news arrived during Mark's Facetime call from Germany. As they crowded around the small screen, her oldest brother drew a slim, blonde woman next to him. "This is my fiancée, Roswitha Meier. We're going to be married over here next month. Sorry you won't be with us."

Their mother gasped. "Who is going to marry you? Is she Catholic?"

"One of the army chaplains will do the deed."

The woman spoke up for herself in good but heavily accented English. "No, I am Lutheraner, but named for an abbess who wrote poetry and the dramas."

"Isn't that great, Dad? Rose, I call her Rose, writes plays, too. When we are stationed stateside, you'll have a lot to talk about. Maybe you could write a play together. And Mom, she's currently a teacher."

In the gap of silence, Sarge spoke up. "I'm very

happy for the both of you. Can't wait to meet you in person, Rose."

She meant it sincerely. A high school romance between Mark and a protestant girl had been stamped out like live coals about to set the house on fire by her parents shortly before he'd left for basic training. Over the years, Mark had worked his way up the ranks, been tapped for officers' training school, and now wore a captain's bars. There must have been other women, but he'd mentioned none. Good for him, standing up to their parents at last.

The call ended with many Happy Thanksgivings expressed, and the debate began. "I just know she's pregnant or why the rush?" her mother started in on it. "And a Lutheran, too."

"Calm down. Lutherans aren't far off from Catholics in liturgy. You should be happy she didn't have an abortion and will give you a grandchild—if she is pregnant. I'm only glad he finally found someone to replace Holly," Sarge argued.

"Don't mention that little slut's name to me. We shipped Mark off to basic training just in time. I am sure she planned to get pregnant and trap him that way, sneaky Baptist."

"Now, Susan. Maybe this Rose will convert. Wouldn't that be nice?" her father soothed.

"What if Matt and Luke bring home foreign girls with heathen religions?"

"Mom, you know the army looks out for their men. They do background checks on the families. There are all sorts of rigmarole and paperwork. If they are getting married next week, she and Mark have been together for a while. Give the woman a chance," Sarge reasoned.

There was no reasoning with her mother, and she soon gave up. Glancing at her watch, she counted the hours until her return to Lorena Ranch.

The call from Matt seemed anticlimactic, but he lost points with the parents when he said, "Good for Mark." As for Luke, they didn't hear from him. He probably ate his MRE turkey and gravy somewhere in the field and would get in touch when he returned. Eddie's large family talked all at once, but yes, as Sarge figured, another child was on the way.

Copious leftovers for dinner and more football topped off the day. How would she get through more hours of this Sarge did not know.

"Tough it out, kiddo," she told herself, and she had despite her mom finding birth control pills in Maggie's purse the next morning when she rummaged around looking for a small loan, she claimed.

"What do you want me to do? Get pregnant before I marry Sam?" Maggie shouted.

"You are supposed to practice abstinence until you are married."

"Yeah, like that worked for you. I can count backward nine months. Where did you and Dad do it? In the janitorial closet?"

Oooh, a low blow but an unspoken truth in the family. Sarge had never dared to mention it. Maggie, slated to work Black Friday, drove off in a fury. Their dad offered to "talk to the boy." A lot of good that would do. Sarge washed dishes, helped make meals, and let her mother rant all weekend which reached a crescendo when Maggie packed her bags and moved in with her Sam, slamming the door on the way out. On Sunday morning, Sarge made herself a ham sandwich and refilled the borrowed thermos with coffee, escaped at dawn again well before being bulldozed into going to Mass.

All these years she'd pitied her mother, a victim of her father's inability to practice abstinence. Instead, he diddled around pushing his mop and writing plays clean enough for high school kids to perform. Abstinence, hell, most of her Catholic friends had no more than two or three children. She doubted they didn't use birth control. Now, she suspected her mother ran the show, choosing to be an ultimate Catholic and leading her easy-going husband along by his cock. Perhaps, her mom punished herself for conceiving before marriage to a man with far less status than a teacher. Even Maggie's choice of Sam Hoover, always described as a "nice Catholic boy" until this weekend when he'd become the devil incarnate, seemed a wiser choice. Sam had a decent job repairing computers, and Sarge would bet, used condoms to protect himself.

She turned off I-10 at the Lafayette exit. In thirty minutes, she'd be back at the comparative sanity of the ranch. They'd entrusted her with a fob to open the gate and a key to get in the mansion. As she approached, the lights in the oak tree alley winked on and illuminated her way. While most of the house sat veiled in darkness, a lamp burned in Mack's room. Was he having a difficult night? It better be an emergency because she wasn't in the mood for any of his crap.

Chapter Ten

Mack, waiting up for Sarge's return, hit the elevator button and made his way to the kitchen entry before she'd parked by the barn and followed the low-lit pathway to the house. The automatic lighting that came on when the gate to the compound opened had given her approach away even if the noise of the Jeep engine had not. He'd stayed dressed in his sweats to await her safe arrival. His parents shrugged and went to bed after some debate when he said that he would.

"She seems like a very competent person," his father said. "I'm sure she'll call if she has any trouble."

"Yes," his mom agreed. "Sarge might not appreciate being worried over. It implies she's weak." His mother, the psychologist, speaking.

"You always waited up for me when I lived at home, even when I asked you not to do that. I said I wouldn't total my truck."

"And yet you did your senior year in high school."

"Right, but I wore my seat belt and wasn't hurt. A dog ran into the road, so not reckless driving." Why did he bring that up at all? Oh, yeah. "Everybody needs someone to wait up for them. You said so yourself."

He watched his mother's brows raise. She turned to his dad and said, "It's happening."

'What's happening, Tink?"

"He's growing up."

"No, I'm not. I mean I'm grown up already."

His mom's big brown eyes leveled on him even though she had to look way up to get his attention. "Perhaps I should have said you are starting to care about others which is a sign of maturity."

"I care about people. You and Dad, the whole family. I tried to keep Lorena from marrying Jock Brown, but she didn't listen to me."

"That might just have been butting in where you didn't belong," his dad, who'd wanted Jock to join the Sinners, said.

"Whatever."

Then came the shrug and off they went to their suite at the far end of the hall from his current room. If they had sex, he wouldn't hear it. Their flame never seemed to falter.

But here came Sarge, unlocking the door with her own key and lugging the duffel inside on her back. He couldn't help her with that, so he offered, "Welcome back. Can I get you anything? A glass of milk, a sandwich? I can make a sandwich though it will probably be turkey. I know it's a long drive. I only go back and forth as far as Dallas and put in close to eight hours each time, big state, Texas."

She didn't take him up on any of his offers, but instead nailed him with that same steely gaze she'd had when they'd first met. "Why in hell are you up? We have PT first thing in the morning. Go to bed. I'm going to do the same.

"What, no thanks for caring?" He added his signature grin.

Sarge stalked to the far side of the kitchen and put her hand on the light switch. "Let's go." She waited for him to catch up using his walker, and they rode up in the elevator together in silence.

He tried again before entering his room. "Bad holiday?"

"You could say that. How about you? Any night pain while I was gone? Did Nurse Shammy take care of it?" She appeared to soften the tiniest bit.

"Once, but I pounded down a couple of pills. No way I want my baby nurse giving me a massage."

"She probably massaged you as an infant. It's good for preemies, and you would have been better for letting her do it instead of taking medication."

"Look, that's not all I did. I got dumb Jock Brown to bring me a glass of wine. It had more effect than I thought it would, but he followed me around until I got into a chair and fell asleep. I missed most of the Cowboys game. Maybe it's good I did. The new guy is running hot."

"Yes, I saw."

"I need to get off this walker and make real progress soon." He hoped he didn't sound too needy.

"Thank God you were on the walker. If you'd stumbled and fallen, that might have been a big setback. Sounds like Jock has more sense than you do."

He winced. She'd struck at a sore spot. He'd hoped his confession would earn him points before she heard it from someone else, but Jock got all the credit.

"Sarge, I need you to keep me in line, not let me fall back. Will you stay here for Christmas, please? It's crowded and noisy and maybe you'd rather go home, but I'm not good at resisting temptations."

"You're a grown man and should be able to practice self-restraint—but I'll think about it. Perhaps, we can have you on a cane by Christmas. Goodnight."

Sarge moved her duffle into her room and left him in the hall. Might be she did understand his desperation after all.

****

Sitting at the kitchen table, Sarge enjoyed a good-sized portion of scrambled eggs flecked with red and green peppers and covered with lots of cheese. Two plump sausages flanked the mound. She'd made her own whole wheat toast and poured the high-octane coffee before the pot got switched to decaf. No grits in sight. Best of all, she could eat in peace with only Corazon humming at the stove because she'd showered and dressed before Mack woke. He hadn't called for her in the night, and she wasn't sure if she felt sorrow or relief. As for staying at the ranch for Christmas, she'd like nothing better, but he didn't need to know that.

Joe had finished eating and fueled a travel mug with his brew before heading to the barn as usual just after her entrance. Nell hadn't come down yet.

Corazon remarked again about the nice note her mom had sent thanking her for the pumpkin bread. "Most people, they don't know how to do a good letter anymore and have no manners—not the children I help raised, but most of them."

All the Kozacs knew about writing thank you letters—to St. Vincent de Paul for the winter coats, to the Rotary Club for the food basket, to anyone who gave them anything. Pens and paper were cheap and gratitude cost nothing, her mother often said. She couldn't image what the Billodeaux kids needed to be thankful for that they did not already have. On that thought, Nell walked in and scooped a small portion of eggs out of the skillet, poured juice, and popped bread into the toaster.

"So quiet here after all the children have gone to their homes again, but the Sinners played on Sunday and most cleared out on Saturday morning. Edie and Rex couldn't wait to get back to campus. But that's the way it goes when they grow up," Nell mused.

She brought her breakfast to the table and continued talking to Sarge. "Nice of Mack to wait up for you, don't you think? He seemed very concerned about your safety. It's good to see him growing in that way." Nell's voice held a silvery note of hope.

Sarge shook her head and said, "I think he only wanted to confess to getting drunk at Thanksgiving before someone else told me. He asked me to stay for Christmas to keep him in line."

"We'd love to have you celebrate with us—and watch out for him. You told us not to coddle him while you were gone, and we didn't. Edie fetched his food for him, but the wine got by us. I'm grateful Jock didn't let him fall."

"Since Jock supplied him, that was only fair. Some of the pills Mack takes for pain and to keep infections at bay turn the alcohol from one drink into five. He knows this."

"Bad behavior to get attention?" Nell's disappointment wrung her heart.

"In this case, it seems more like feeling sorry for himself. This setback in his career could be a good learning experience in patience if he lets it be. Will the Antigravity Treadmill be here by Christmas? I think he'll make fast progress once he starts using it."

"Best they could promise is delivery between

Christmas and New Year's Eve, but we'll put a picture of it in a box to surprise him."

"Talking about me?" Mack moved into the room with his damp, black hair hugging his shoulders, a dark scruff shadowing his perfect jaw, and a tight tee showing off the expanse of his chest, far more attractive than any man should be.

"If we said we were, it would go right to your head. Eat and get ready to go to work." Sarge finished her coffee. Mack missed out as his mom offered the last cup to Corazon and started the decaf.

"Yes, sir, Sergeant, sir."

"That's the respect I like to hear." She carried her dishes to the sink and waited at the counter until he ate as she jiggled the keys to the golf cart.

The morning passed as it usually did as if she'd never been gone. She collected new measurements on both legs, assuring him that he had gained muscle mass, and ran on the treadmill while he did his many reps. They didn't talk much until they worked with the free weights.

No sense in keeping him waiting anymore. "I'll stay for Christmas."

"Great. Your Thanksgiving was miserable, right?"

Could he be gaining perception and empathy? Big egos seldom did, but then, life-changing accidents such as his could be transforming. Why not tell him? No one else cared.

"Yeah, even with plenty of food we managed to pick fights. They thought the shrimp I brought was great but would rather have had it fried. My dad didn't get his egg for breakfast because my mom went to lie down for a while. Those were the little things. My brothers try to call home every year no matter where they are. Luke didn't manage it, so we knew he'd been deployed somewhere dangerous. But Mark dropped the big bunker buster bomb. He's engaged to a German woman—and she's a Lutheran. Dad hopes she'll convert. My guess is Mark won't bring her home for a good long time after they marry and have a grandchild or two to offer."

"Your family has your very own Mawmaw Nadine, our grandmother. The first question she asks any girl we bring home is 'you Cat'lic?' Have you met her yet?"

"I haven't had the honor, though she's told Corazon to bring me to Mass. I'd rather sleep in on my Sundays off."

"You and me both. I've been claiming I'm in too much pain to go and do all that standing and kneeling. For sure, you'll meet her at Christmas."

She had to laugh and shouldn't have said, "We'd make a fine pair with our mutual avoidance of The Church."

"Hey, it's a start. Spot me on the bench press."

What did he mean by a start, start what? She might as well expose the rest of the mess. "I haven't told you the worst. My mother found birth control pills in my second sister Maggie's purse. What did she expect? Maggie and Sam have been together for two years. Big row. Maggie moved out of the family home and right into Sam's apartment."

"I can't see how person's sex life or how many kids a person wants is anybody else's business. Of course, my mother wouldn't have so many if Mawmaw hadn't constantly bothered her about her little frozen babies. Mom had trouble conceiving, went the in vitro route, and gave birth to twin girls. I don't know if she planned to use the rest of those fertilized eggs or not. She won't say, but the next time she had babies, Lorena, Trinity, and I came into the world. I guess I owe Mawmaw a thanks."

A fair exchange of family secrets, she guessed. "At least, those births were planned. Maggie brought up that my mother came to the altar pregnant."

"So do lots of women."

"Not usually a teacher who did it with the janitor. Must have been quite the scandal at the parochial school. End of her career because women always bear the shame. She's spent the rest of her life dropping children they couldn't afford every two years as some kind of penance, I believe."

"I can't see you doing that."

"Absolutely not."

"Well, I don't intend to turn into my father either, dad to a dozen. I think I need to start those bench presses now to get the idea out of my mind."

"Sounds like a good plan." She'd gotten her relief already, simply telling someone how she'd felt all these years and not shared outside the family.

Chapter Eleven

Christmas thudded closer in its big, black Santa boots. Sarge had broken the news to her family, telling them she would not be home for this holiday. She softened it with a little white lie, that her client had asked her to stay, true, because he expected a new piece of equipment for his rehab and needed her to learn to use it, somewhat false. Mack didn't know about the impending arrival of the Antigravity Treadmill, or he'd be annoying her about it every second like a kid who wanted a new toy.

Nor did he suspect she'd ordered a cane made for his height and weight with a little more style than most. The gilded brass head had an engraved design and shaft custom made to her specifications. He wouldn't mind being seen in public with it, she hoped, unlike the walker or a more practical apparatus. It set her back fifty dollars, so not that much.

The real dent in her bank account occurred from buying overly generous gift cards for each person in her family. Guilt was a real bugger sometimes. She'd had to tell the prosthetics people she'd be a month behind in making her payment for her new foot, her dancing foot real enough to fool people from a distance. She'd sort of hoped to have it for the fancy Christmas gathering with the Billodeauxs, but what the heck, by now they all knew about her disability.

She'd shelled out for a red velvet pant suit that covered her metal rod and a necklace of enameled holly leaves and berries from a local craft shop to fit in better with the gathering. Nell did tell her not to buy gifts for the family because it had grown to such a size that the adults simply drew one name from a hat now. Since she'd told about the cane, Nell suggested she be Mack's Secret Santa. Her son was hard to buy for at the best of times.

Rarely jumpy, she found herself nervous about the coming festivities. Mack had been up to his old tricks, flirting with her and calling for her at night, not always because of pain. At times, he couldn't sleep, full of anxiety about his future, reliving that hard hit on the football field. He asked for the mantra of her siblings' names and sometimes repeated those of his own. She sometimes fell asleep first, right there on top of the covers, but she'd prepared her deterrent for any more straying hands.

Going to bed in her underwear of plain cotton bikini pants and sports bra, she kept the old flannel granny gown under her pillow. When she hopped across the bathroom to attend him, the worn floral fabric, as attractive as a feed sack, covered her from neck to the toes on her only foot. A row of tiny buttons denied him entry from the top, and she doubted if he'd try work his way up from the bottom. The first time she'd worn it, he'd exclaimed, "What the hell happened to your silk pajamas?"

"In the wash," she claimed. "This gown is warmer."

He'd turned that around fast. "If you're cold, you can snuggle under the covers with me."

"Oh, I don't think so."

Feeling quite invulnerable, she'd dozed off on top of the duvet in a room always well-heated on chilly nights. When she woke, his roving hand rested at her midriff on top of the flannel. Knowing how comforting a single human touch could be when bad dreams rode in on nightmares, she'd removed it tenderly and tucked it in beside him.

However, she suspected he worked on a scheme to get under the nightie and had to be vigilant. Even with her on guard a week before Christmas, his hand lay on her midriff again under the flannel this time, aware only of the warmth of his touch when she woke. With cunning, he'd covered her lower half with part of the top sheet to keep her from noticing a change of temperature when he lifted her gown. How carefully he must have moved that hand up her body in order not to disturb her.

She groped for her panties—still on, though riding a little lower than usual, perhaps. She half thought he might have claimed them and put them under his pillow. This had to stop. After removing his hand, lowering the nightie, and flipping off the sheet, she shook him awake.

"What, what? Did the fire alarm go off? Save yourself. I'll have to use the elevator."

Good acting job, but she was fairly sure he'd been waiting for her reaction to his little trick. His hand still lay by her side. She picked it up and let it fall back to the mattress. "This hand somehow found its way under my nightgown and up to my waist."

"The drugs I'm using cause some pretty weird dreams. You occupy my mind a lot. I guess my hand picked up on that and went where it wanted to go." He put the fingers of his right hand against his ear. "It's telling me you don't wax."

"You don't know that for sure."

In the dim illumination from the nightlight in the bathroom, she saw the white of his teeth as he smiled his devilish grin. "Maybe, maybe not."

"If this happens again, I won't come when you call."

"Is my need for a human touch less of an emergency than a leg cramp? You know you could help me out with a hand job, and I'd do the same for you. Give us both some relief. Your turn first, or I could just watch. It turns me on."

"I don't imagine it takes much to turn you on, or maybe you're always on. Use your big boy words and say masturbation. Thanks, but I can take care of my own needs. As for you, both of your hands work just fine. Use one of them. If that's not enough, maybe your father could bring in a hooker for you."

"Madame Mystique's House of Pleasure just across the parish line does offer a high-quality takeout service, and I could call myself. Hey, that's how they got the name call girls, I'll bet. But my mom would flip out and probably blame my dad, so no. I guess I'll have to wait until I can drive again in the interest of marital tranquility."

"If you get any ideas about hiring an Uber, be sure to tell your partner she'll have to be on top. Your leg isn't ready for missionary position yet." She settled herself on the edge of the mattress and pushed up for her hop back to her own bed.

"Thanks for the advice. I have no trouble with that.

Say, I'll bet your thighs are really strong. That's another possibility." His wayward hand brushed her thigh and made her jump, nearly upending herself.

"Sorry, didn't mean to startle you." She heard the laughter behind his words.

"Yes, you did. Last straw. I am not coming in here again at night."

"Come on. Just teasing."

She hopped to the doorway and got a grip on its edge. "You're hitting on me because I'm the only woman available."

"Not so. You're a strong woman, a challenge, and like I said, always on my mind."

"Keep dreaming."

She shut that door and made her way to the next, secured it, and finally lay down more shaken than she wanted to admit. Sweating, she shucked off her flannel gown.

Any woman who'd gone without sex for a long time and been dumped by her fiancé knew how to take care of her needs. Taking her own advice, she worked her hands under the covers and handled the matter. With fantasies of Mack in her mind, it didn't take her long. Relief, temporary relief.

She'd ceased believing she'd go to hell for a little self-pleasuring and waited for the drowsy aftermath to kick in, but it didn't. Her heart still pounded, and her mind wouldn't release its hold on its vision of Mack. With her pale complexion, the dark circles of a sleepless night would show in the morning, and he would know he'd gotten to her. Damn Mack Billodeaux.

Chapter Twelve

Not having availed himself of any kind of relief, Mack tossed most of the night. He gave up trying for sleep around five a.m. No sound from Sarge's room, no alarm going off. He tried the bathroom door as he pushed by, locked from the inside. He'd wait to shower and use the powder room downstairs. She deserved some rest—mostly from him. He headed out, barefooted, wearing only the sagging pajama bottoms covered in a hound dog print, last year's birthday gift from Trin he'd put on with the weather getting cooler.

The darkness of the corridor to the kitchen reminded him of how close they were to the longest night of the year which he'd now have to endure alone, a fitting punishment for treating Sarge like any woman he might have invited into his bed and making the same kind of lewd suggestions they'd been happy to accommodate. She wasn't just any woman, but stronger, tougher, and more complex than any he'd met before his injury. He'd worked to gain her trust, going slowly, and now blown it in a single evening because of the challenge of that frickin' flannel nightgown.

He turned on the lights in the kitchen and flipped the switch on the coffeemaker. Foraging in the refrigerator for breakfast, he found a bag of raisin bagels and a tub of low-fat cream cheese. After popping the bagel into the toaster, he placed a mug under the drip from the coffeemaker and waited for it to fill with the high octane he'd need to get through the morning. Sarge had added harder leg strengthening exercises with more reps lately, a good sign that he'd soon be off the walker. Today, he especially wanted to impress her with his diligence and no added bullshit.

If he had a cane now, he could use it to rake his Christmas gift for her out from under the gigantic tree in the den where he'd thrown it behind the mound of gifts, only one each, for the Billodeaux grandchildren, but it still made quite a pile. The Victoria's Secret box was too distinctive. Ordering it had been no problem. He had an established account he let his bed partners use if he enjoyed their company. "Get yourself a little something, baby, and wear it for me later."

It wasn't that bad, but under the circumstances, a big mistake. Maybe his understanding mom would help him out of this jam, though she'd brought the package in with the mail and at the time, questioned him about it. "Are you sure about getting Sarge something from this place? It doesn't seem like her style."

"She doesn't have many nice things. Besides, it's only PJs, very modest ones."

"If you're sure she won't be embarrassed."

"Nothing to be embarrassed about, though I did spot some stuff I wouldn't mind seeing her wear."

"Don't toy with her, Mack. I mean it." When Mom said that she meant consequences. He already suffered from those thanks to last night.

The bagel popped. He smeared it with cream cheese. He thought he might eat standing at the counter since handling the coffee and a plate became a pain in the ass when using a walker. He had the leg strength to move without it. He knew he did. Balancing his food, he took one step forward without assistance.

"Let me take those things." Not Sarge but his dad. No sense in arguing with him. Or either of them for that matter.

Joe, fully dressed in boots, jeans, and chambray shirt, deposited the mug and dish on the table, poured his own coffee, and eyed the empty stovetop. "I guess all the ladies are sleeping in today."

"It isn't six yet. We've got bagels."

"I think I'll wait to see what Corazon cooks up. I thought I heard you moving around downstairs. The clunk of that walker gave you away."

"And you came to rescue me from myself."

"You wouldn't be the first person I've rescued. Have just a little more patience. Sarge says you're doing great."

"Truth? She doesn't tell me that. It's always you skipped a rep or aren't getting those legs high enough."

"You expect her to be soft on you because she's a woman. That's not what you need."

"I know, I know." Mack gulped some black coffee. Rare he had his dad all to himself. "Say, when did you get tired of fooling around and decide to settle down with Mom?"

Joe delved into old memories. "I bedded over a hundred women and proud of it. Believed I left none unsatisfied. But they began to play me. Articles in scandal magazines and then Dean's mother getting pregnant on purpose in a plot with her lawyer who I also took to bed. Not that I'm unhappy about how Dean came into my life. He was the reason your mother finally married me. I got two great gifts for one. When I think back on it, I became tired of being the bad boy. Once I moved off the bench and started as the Sinners quarterback, I wanted something better. It's a miracle I got it considering how I carried on back then. If you are trying to imitate me, son, I don't recommend it."

He tried to make a joke of it. "I'd like to think I have a style of dissipation all my own."

"Not something to boast about." Damn it, his mother had crept in on them. Up earlier than usual as well, she wore a fuzzy red robe and scuffs. Her pixie haircut had a tousled look. She greeted his father with a smile and a kiss. "I got cold in bed without you. Let me start breakfast. French toast okay?"

"I never turn down *pain perdu*," his dad said.

"Me, neither. This bagel won't hold me until noon." Mack swallowed the last bite and cleared his plate for something better.

His mom took down a mixing bowl, cracked a half dozen eggs into it, added some milk, and raided the spice rack for cinnamon. A few drops of vanilla added and she beat the ingredients together. She heated the griddle while cutting a loaf of slightly stale French bread into generous portions. As the first pieces hit the hot pan, Corazon bustled in well-wrapped in her long, bulky sweater.

"What, I am late? No, no, only a few minutes past six, and you make your own breakfast. You need butter in there," she chided Nell.

"You aren't late. We're all early today." Because she'd never hear the end of it if she didn't, Nell added the butter.

Corazon rattled some cookware together like a disturbed nesting hen who'd gotten her feathers ruffled.

"I make the bacon. See what Miss Sarge give me, but not for Christmas, just because. A special bacon pan that makes a whole pound at one time and drains the grease—as seen on TV." She lined up strip after strip on its top grid and placed it in the oven.

Nell surrendered her spatula to Corazon and went to make her decaf after emptying the remains of the pot into her husband's travel mug. He'd do it if she didn't, they all knew.

"Miss Sarge, where is she? I want to show her how well this new pan works. Usually, she is here by now. *Enferma*? I take her some tea and toast."

"No, we don't think she's ill." But his mom gave him a questioning stare.

"Only tired, I believe. I had several leg cramps last night and kept her up." He ducked his head and took in more deep, dark brew.

"You, you go upstairs and see. Put on a shirt. No half-naked men at my table." Corazon waved the spatula at him.

His mom intervened. "I'll go. If she's ill she might not want Mack to see. I'll bring you a sweatshirt."

He knew what ran through her mind, that he'd gotten Sarge pregnant, slim chance of that. "Maybe flu, nothing else," he suggested simply to ease her mind.

"We'll see." Mama Nell marched away and returned fast enough with his old 'Bama sweatshirt and a brief report. "She's in the shower, so I expect she'll soon be down." She tossed Mack his chest cover. "Save her two pieces of the French toast and some bacon."

Still suspicious and riled, she sat down to a plate holding a single portion of *pain perdu* and a couple of strips of bacon. Corazon handed her a cup of coffee and continued to work the grill until everyone had a serving, two each for the men and extra bacon. Syrup made its way around the table, and they ate in silence.

Sarge appeared in her regular trainer's gear, hair still damp as usual. The only change Mack noticed was the blue smudges under her eyes from lack of sleep. He'd put them there, and she hadn't bothered to cover them with makeup which she wore lightly anyhow. Her pale face could use some color, but otherwise, she possessed one of the finest complexions he'd seen on a woman, unmarred by her tours in Afghanistan.

Corazon fussed, "You don't go outside in the cold with wet hair."

"No, ma'am. I don't want to be sick for Christmas." Corazon's fussing seemed to relieve the tension around her lips, fading away as Mack watched her tuck into the French toast with a good appetite. She accepted coffee, frowned a little at the weakness, but said nothing.

"Here, take Dad's travel mug. I know you like it stronger." He shoved the offering her way.

"Hey," his dad exclaimed.

"No, it's all right. The decaf is fine." She returned the mug to Joe, refusing Mack's small gift. He owed her a real apology, but not here in front of so many family members.

Joe rose, placed his dishes in the sink, and pulled on a denim barn jacket from a hook by the door. Not quite light yet, but he glanced out the window at a frost-covered yard revealed by the footpath lights. "Lots of Cajun snow out there today. I'd better get to work. Lil is missing her kibble, and the horses will want oats to stave off the cold." He seized his covered mug as if someone else might try to expropriate it and headed to the barn.

"You try the bacon," Corazon insisted, giving Sarge more though she hadn't eaten the first yet. "The new pan, it works very good."

Sarge ate a piece with her fingers. "Nice and crisp. I hope it makes your work easier with so many to feed."

"*Si*, it does."

Sarge licked her fingertips, either as a tribute to Corazon's bacon or to drive him crazy. He had to escape before the smudges under her eyes made him feel guiltier. "I'll get showered and ready to go. Won't be long."

She studied his long bare feet, the ones that let him pivot so well on the field and dig in when he ran. "You must be cold."

"No, not cold at all. I'll be ready when you are." There, a double entendre, he couldn't seem to help himself. Maybe, she hadn't noticed.

"Fifteen minutes or you use the walker to get to the gym." She ate more bacon with obvious enjoyment. Perhaps, she had understood and covered it well.

He showered in ten, blew off shaving, put on sweats, and hassled with his shoes for the rest of the time. Regardless, Sarge sat outside in the golf cart wearing a worn army jacket and checking her no-nonsense watch. As soon as he slid in beside her, he conjured up the words he hoped might make a difference.

"Look, I'm sorry about last night. I shouldn't have spoken to you that way. You aren't some woman I picked up at a party. You deserve better treatment."

Never taking her gaze off the path, she said, "All

women deserve better treatment, but if you think I haven't heard worse propositions after years in the service, you'd be wrong. I think your renewed interest in sex is good. I just happen to be the only woman nearby right now. Some men after a traumatic incident can't get it up for years."

"That's a scary thought. Do you forgive me?"

"Nothing to forgive." She parked the golf cart by the pool house and waited to hold the door open for him and the walker. "Start your warmups."

"Say, did you hear from your brother, the one who didn't call at Thanksgiving?" He tried to show he listened to more than her orders when she spoke.

"Yes, he's fine. He was out on patrol as we figured. He's getting leave for Christmas."

"If you really want to go home for the holidays, I'll manage without you."

She snorted as if skeptical. "I've already told the family I'm not coming and sent the gifts. Let Luke have all the attention this time around."

"I know our Christmas celebration is over the top sometimes—that immense tree and the poinsettia extravaganza, kids running around, and the excess food."

His mom hired Beau's Blooms to dress the house for the occasion. The custom-ordered tree in the den stood within an inch or two of the high ceiling. Beau's crew used ladders to string a multitude of white twinkle lights and swags of red garlands interspersed with the large ornaments so in style at the moment. Every spare inch of space held a poinsettia, red in the den, pink in the formal dining room. All of it had sprung to life one afternoon while he labored in the gym. After their return, Sarge, wonderstruck at the transformation, had murmured, "Gorgeous."

"How do the Kozacs celebrate Christmas?" See, he did care about her life and not only his.

"Oh, we don't decorate until Christmas Eve, not so much a custom as the best time to get a cheap tree. Dad loaded us up into the old van and drove around to the lots to see what they had left. Sometimes, we got one for free with all our pathetic faces pressed against the glass waiting for him to cut a deal. We had my grandmother's old ornaments for decorations and made paper chains and strings of popcorn to wrap the tree. The charity baskets arrived with plenty of food, and gifts came from various organizations. My parents managed a present for each of us. Actually, it was the best time of the year—but I like yours better, the way your father went up the ladder after the decorators left and hung every homemade ornament his children ever made handed up one by one by your mother, and all the reminiscing as they did."

"Now they're collecting the ones from all the grandchildren and hang them low so they can see them. I'm sure old Beau would have a hissy fit if he saw what they did to his tree."

"I think it's wonderful." She paused, thoughtful. "Why so much interest in a Kozac Christmas? Are you trying to delay those new exercises I gave you? I know they hurt, but we need to stretch the scar tissue. Get back to work."

"But we're good about the other thing?"

Her face a blank white sheet, she answered, "What other thing?"

Chapter Thirteen

Okay, Sarge admitted to herself, a Billodeaux Christmas awed her, and not only because they could afford decorations as nice as Macy's department store. Their tree exuded the scent of real evergreens, filling the house with its aroma. Sure, decorators put it up, but the homemade ornaments brought the whole affair down to earth. That Joe and Nell limited everyone, even the grandchildren to one gift, spoke of their values. They had wealth but did not use it to spoil family members. Perhaps, Mack's present of a seventy-five-thousand dollar Antigravity Treadmill seemed excessive, but she'd been asked to order smaller support slings to accommodate the handicapped children who attended their Camp Love Letter each summer. The machine would be put to good use for years after Mack healed.

She did try her best to evade midnight Mass at the historic Ste. Jeanne d'Arc Catholic church in Chapelle, but found herself loaded into Teddy's red handicap van along with a sullen Mack and his despised walker, two wheelchairs, and the adults who used them. Their two small children remained behind in the loving care of Nurse Shammy and her husband, Brinsley, the butler. She'd offered to babysit at the main house, but the girl who lived with Annie and Matt Keaton claimed that position. No help for it, she put on the green wool dress, pressed for the occasion, and the lacy collar, wanting to save that lipstick red pantsuit for tomorrow.

As it turned out, the service was ecumenical with a large choir singing the Christmas story with readings in between from *Away in the Manger* to *Hark the Herald Angels Sing* and ending with one and all lighting candles in the darkened church to finish with *Silent Night.* In the end, she didn't hate it, but Mack by her side grumbled the entire time. Unable to fit the wheelchairs into the old box pews recreated after the church burned and was resurrected from the original plans, he'd had to sit in plain view with Teddy, his wife Jessie, and their grandmother in the very front of the sanctuary after wheeling in through a side door. He hated being on display. She knew the feeling, especially since the legendary Mawmaw Nadine in her own chair had used a grabber attached to the armrest to prod her leg.

"You the one wit' a metal foot, Mack's trainer. I hear good about you. You Cat'lic, girl?

She took a deep breath and answered, "Born and raised." That seemed a satisfactory answer because the old lady let her alone after receiving it.

They exited the service through the same side door near Teddy's special parking space. She had to admire their driver, the deft way he switched to armband crutches, helped his wife into the front seat and got the two chairs stowed before taking charge of the hand controls, all with a smile on his face despite Mack's griping, his pale blond hair so much like hers falling down over his brow. But then, Teddy Billodeaux had been born with spina bifida and lived crippled all his life. He'd made the best of it and often said he'd landed in clover to be taken into his adoptive family. His knowledge of football and genial personality had landed him a job as a commentator on national television, but his contract contained a clause that he would always be home for Christmas.

Waiting in the chilly air, Mack showed no gratitude at all while waiting for his brother to finish loading the van. He fidgeted and leaned against the van, facing away from other parishioners. That did him no good. An attractive brunette woman about his age appeared to track him down. Dressed in a festive red suit with no under blouse to prevent a little cleavage from showing, she towed along a prosperous looking older husband and two school-age children, maybe five and six. Her color ran high, fanned by the breeze. Both her eyelashes and ruby lips appeared enhanced to Sarge, there was just so much of them. She attacked Mack with a hug and two air kisses that set him off balance. Sarge grabbed his elbow to steady him again, and he shook off her aid.

"Why, Mack Billodeaux, I haven't seen you around here in ages, not since you took off for Dallas. Such a sad ending to your football career. We all saw it played over and over again on the sports channels. Terrible, just terrible—and taken down by your own kin."

"My career isn't over yet, Brooke. I'm rehabbing right now. I'll be back in the fall." He said it with a confidence Sarge knew he didn't possess.

She added her support in another way. "Yes, he's progressing rapidly."

Brooke turned toward her with a smile as cool as the atmosphere surrounding them. She did a brief study of her homely dress and lack of makeup, maybe missed the piece of metal descending into her shoe in the dark. "And you are?"

"Susan Kozac, his trainer." She failed to return the smile or offer a hand.

"Leave it to Mack to get a woman to do all that touchy-feely stuff."

"I hurt him every day to make him stronger. Lesser men couldn't endure it."

"Can we go now?" whined one of the children. The boy got seconded by his dad who wore a business suit with muffler and hat. "Yes, dear, it's late and cold outside."

Brooke wrapped it up with false warmth. "When you are recovered, you'll have to come to dinner. We've renovated the old Duchamp mansion. You know where it is."

"Sure, right around the corner. You better get moving before y'all catch the flu." He coughed as if he might be contagious, and Brooke drew back, gathered her family, and went away with a wave that was more of a dismissal.

"Speaking of getting going," Teddy said. "We're ready."

"Step up using your good foot," Sarge prompted.

"I know which damned foot to use." Mack pulled himself onto the seat and slid over to make room for her.

"Be glad you have one," Sarge retorted. Whatever joy and calm she'd absorbed from the service had flown away like the many illuminated angels that hung in the boughs of the live oak trees surrounding the church. He'd been pissy all evening. When Nell, out of kindness, admired the lace collar, telling her it looked like snowflakes draping her shoulders, Mack had to spoil the moment by saying "or dandruff." When she'd replied her grandmother had made it, he'd drawn back a little and said sorry as his mother stared him into better manners.

"Do you want to tell me about your friend?"

"Old girlfriend, head cheerleader in high school and meanest of the mean girls, but what a body for someone seventeen. She thought I'd marry her because she put out right up until she found out half her squad did the same for me. The best way to get rid of a woman you no longer want is to cheat on her with other women. She did all right for herself. Never finished college, married a divorced banker, now likes to lord it over one and all, Mawmaw says. For a while I thought that first kid might be mine, but the numbers didn't add up, and I always took care. I think the old dude knocked her up and did the honorable thing by her."

"If you are here long enough, you'll run into lots of his old girlfriends. We think that's why he hides out at the ranch and rarely goes into town when he visits." She could hear the smile in Teddy's words as they made their way in the dark to the ranch turned magical by the addition of tiny white lights in the branches of the oak alley, wreaths with big red bows on the doors, and a single electric candle in each window.

Inside the mansion, family members already made inroads into trays of Christmas cookies and helped themselves to eggnog from a punch bowl. A bottle of rum stood nearby for those who wanted it. Sarge tried to match the names to those Mack sometimes recited at night when she made him take a turn at their mantra.

The Sinners players were easy to pick out. She'd

seen them all on TV. Dean resembled his dad in good looks. The married kickers, Tom and Alix, one redheaded, the other a fit blond, huge Junior Polk, the cornerback and Corazon's son who'd married Xochi, the Billodeaux's adopted Mexican daughter sat nearby. She'd heard plenty about the Aussie Sinner, Jock Brown, who poured a shot into his nog and stood by tall, dark Lorena, the volleyball player, his wife. Two gorgeous blondes, one of them the famous model, Josee Riley who'd married the nerd brother, Trinity, at her side, stood together. The other must be Stacy, Dean's wife. Both dressed in designer clothes, or what she guessed were designer clothes, and wore them well. Then, two short, dark-haired women, the twins, one leaning against her husband, the Sinner Matt Keaton, and the other close by, solo, wearing the same kind of no-nonsense expression Sarge often saw on her own face when reflected in the mirror. The two college students Edie and Rex, also twins, home for the holidays, stoked up on cookies and added a dash of rum to their drinks when Mama Nell wasn't looking. Teddy and Jessie she knew already.

Nell brought them both eggnog and a plate of cookies to share where they sat slightly outside of the large group on a couple of the dining room chairs. "Overwhelming, I know, but you'll nail down who's who tomorrow. Did you enjoy the service?"

"Very beautiful." Sarge took a sip of eggnog and passed the cup to Mack, then tasted the other. Both passed the alcohol-free inspection.

"Hey, what are you, my poison taster?" Mack objected.

"Yes," she answered and watched the devilment

enter his sinfully dark eyes.

He placed his lips exactly where hers had been and drank. "Sweet, so sweet."

Since his apology, he hadn't called to her in the night or attempted anymore flirtation, though she knew he had restless nights as did she. Theirs was a strange relationship, alone most of the day in the gym, only meals taken with Nell, Joe, and Corazon, usually both so tired they went to bed early and woke in the night only one room apart. A cord of tension connected them even though she knew his interest in her grew out of boredom, restlessness, and proximity. She could not give in to impulse. All she had to do was ignore his innuendos and worse until March when her work ended, and she turned Mack over to the team's trainers in Dallas. Not so long a time, but even sullen as he was tonight, the man tempted more than the plate of gingerbread and Mexican wedding cookies on the plate before her.

She finished her eggnog and ate a gingerbread man, first taking off a leg, then an arm, until he'd vanished. Mack polished off the rest of the sweets. He should sleep in a sugar coma tonight. She noticed Jock and Lorena leaving with Xo and Junior to stay at their large Victorian home on the bayou, maybe because she occupied Lorena's space in the mansion. Others retired to their old bedrooms with beds big enough for couples. A little white dog named Brody followed Edie toward the stairs as both were having a visit from college in Baton Rouge and New Orleans where the pup now dwelled with Lori.

"I'm turning in, too. Do you need anything before I go?" she asked Mack.

"Yeah, but you won't give it to me."

She ignored his remark. "You only had a half day of exercises and are off tomorrow. Take a pill if you can't sleep. Merry Christmas."

"Yeah, sure. Take a pill."

She let him find his own way to bed.

Chapter Fourteen

Christmas Day began with the demanding cries of young children eager to open presents around six a.m., Dean and Stacy's two across the hall she figured. Somehow, they were placated, and Sarge let herself doze again, a rare occurrence. She rose after Mack showered and went downstairs. Taking extra care with her appearance, she bathed, blew her hair dry, and applied just a bit of makeup, some blush on her cheeks, a swipe of a mascara wand to darken her light lashes, and a slash of red lipstick across her lips. She put on the red pantsuit and holly necklace, checked herself in the mirror on the back of the bedroom door, and assured her inner self that she'd fit in with the Billodeauxs. Best of all the shaft of her prosthetic foot did not show. She had no desire to terrify the small children.

Proceeding toward the uproar of many people downstairs, she found herself overdressed amid a crowd still in nightwear which applied to all of the children or covered with robes and sweats. They gorged on cinnamon buns, croissants and danish, coffee, milk, and juice. Nell in the red robe and scuffs she usually wore early in the morning hurried forward to where Sarge stood frozen in the doorway.

"I should have told you we don't bother to dress until before dinner. The children are so eager to get to their presents and sticky from breakfast before we get that far. But you do look wonderful. Please help yourself. We start opening the gifts once Teddy and his family and Xo with hers arrives."

Mack leered at her over his mug of coffee. "You look hot, Sarge."

She knew her cheeks turned redder than the blush she'd applied to them. "I was trying for festive, but thanks. Um, I'll have orange juice and a croissant. I don't want to hold up the party."

"Eat fast. I hear Teddy's van coming down the lane." Mack poked at her again.

"Do no such thing. Xo and the rest haven't left their house in town yet. Here, sit by Mack and make him behave," Nell said. "If he keeps this up, he'll only get coal for Christmas."

She wasn't sure if she could assert her authority over him dressed as she was when he wore those hound dog pajama bottoms with a fitted brown tee that showed off his pecs and a small patch of black chest hair in its vee. Instead, she ate the flaky croissant, tearing it into small pieces to take a bite at a time.

"Say, how come you tell my parents I'm doing great and stand up for me in front of Brooke but never give my any compliments in the gym." Mack stole a small piece of her roll just to annoy her, she was certain.

"I'll get one of these for you if you want it."

"Already had two and a cinnamon bun. Dinner isn't usually until one on Christmas. Answer my question."

"Because your head would get so big you wouldn't be able to raise your leg." She moved her plate before he snatched more of her breakfast.

"Do you really think I'm bearing the pain well?" He wasn't going to give up.

"Yes. We've reached the hardest part, when I have to stretch your scar tissue for you to regain maximum mobility. You don't whine when I throw my whole body into it, and believe me, I have made grown men cry."

Instead of puffing up with pride as she expected or making an off-color remark about throwing herself on him, he said, "It's the Billodeaux way. You grit your teeth and swallow that pain. Even Trinity handled his gunshot wound pretty well, and he's a computer geek. So what do you think your Secret Santa got just for you?"

The change of subject caught her off guard. "I have no idea. I shouldn't have been included since I'm not family." She sipped her juice and studied her plain short nails. She should have painted them red for the occasion and shocked him.

He laughed loud enough to draw attention to their corner of the room. "Stay here long enough, and you become family."

"Does that apply to everyone?"

"Most. If they don't like a person they're gone way before that happens. The trouble is my parents like nearly everybody and are big into second chances or Jock Brown wouldn't be walking in the door right now.

"Good thing for you, also."

He had no time to retort. Xo had arrived with Junior, Lorena, and Jock, plus her children, Pilar and KC. They'd picked up Mawmaw Nadine on the way. In case she'd forgotten, Mack supplied her with the names. The family moved into the den where Joe seated himself, an extraordinarily handsome, fit, and beardless Santa, in the big lounger nearest the tree. The others spread themselves out on the floor and whatever seating remained.

"Mama Nell, the first present, please."

Nell, serving as his Christmas elf all dressed in red, took a package off the children's stack and handed it over.

"I see this is for Wynn."

Dean's little blonde daughter stepped up, ripped off the wrapping, and exclaimed, "A unicorn." She ran her hand over the plastic flank of the toy, and it played music and lit up in colors. "Thank you, Pawpaw and Mama Nell." She sat down immediately and began brushing its mane and tail. DJ stood to receive the next gift.

Sarge and Mack again sat on the edge of the group. He whispered in her ear, "This goes on forever. What was your favorite gift as a child?"

"Well, we were given two, one from a charity, one from our parents. The charity ones came marked for a boy or girl. Usually my brothers got balls: footballs, baseballs, basketballs, soccer balls. One year, they fought over a GI Joe. The girls received dolls, mostly baby dolls—as if we didn't have enough babies in the family. Getting a Barbie was a big deal. The Barbies had to share clothes just like us. Me, I stole the soccer ball more than once."

"Tomboy?"

"I wasn't permitted to be. Long hair down my back, always made to wear dresses or the parochial school jumpers."

"I wish I could see you in that uniform with your

hair long."

"Only in your dreams. I could wear my fatigues for you. As the oldest girl, they expected me to help with the house and younger children. My mother sewed doll clothes, and my dad made wooden toys. I appreciate them more now than I did at the time. The best were the unclaimed bicycles from the police department which meant freedom and mobility. How about you?"

"My first Sinners football because my dad would throw it to me. Of course, all the guys got those, even Trin and Teddy. One year, a mare dropped a foal close to Christmas. I had to share her with Lori and Trin, but it was great even though we had to do all the work in taking care of her."

"Everyone wants a pony for Christmas."

"A horse, not a pony, and in Lazy Angel's case, a racehorse. I tell you she was a thrill to ride exactly like my Jaguar."

"What happened to her?"

"Life. We grew up and went off to college. Dad got an offer for her he couldn't refuse. Her racing days were over, but she was prime breeding stock. She's living out her days on the bull rider Bodey Landrum's ranch. We can visit if we want."

"Have you?"

Seeming a bit ashamed to admit it, he answered, "Yeah, a few times. She's well taken care of."

The presentation of gifts to the children came to an abrupt end as Joe called, "Beck, where is Beck?"

"I'll take it for him," Dean said. "Ilsa took him to Germany for Christmas without my permission. She's trying to negotiate a new custody arrangement where I'll agree to let Prince Dobbs adopt him. She says she's tired of having babies to give him a son. Little Countess is only nine months old, and Ilsa is already expecting another girl. But I won't let her have sole custody."

"We'll back you on that all the way." Joe changed the game by drawing out a set of cards he'd tucked away. He showed them to the grandchildren gathered at his feet. "How many ponies do we have?"

"Four," shouted Wynn.

"And what color are they?" He splayed out the cards like a winning hand.

"White, my princess pony is white," Wynn answered.

"Okay, but let someone else answer. Which is your favorite, DJ?"

"The pinto."

"Right. Pilar, do you know what this one is called?"

"Mino." Her mother whispered in her ear. "Palomino."

"Right again. This last one is a Welsh pony. What color is he, Lizzie?"

"Brown, he's brown," Teddy's adopted daughter answered, with the curly black hair and lively personality.

"Very good. What color pony don't we have yet?"

Mama Nell moaned, "Oh, Joe, you didn't."

Joe flashed another card he'd stowed in the side of the recliner, and Lizzie shouted with joy, "Black with a little white mark on his face."

"We call that a star, baby. Yes, he's our newest pony."

"Oh, I want him," Lizzie cried.

"You must share with your sister. All the ponies

are to share. We'll go visit him after dinner." Joe appealed to Nell. "We have ten grandchildren and Drew. This way the smallest five may have a pony ride first, then the oldest five can ride around the ring by themselves."

"Sure, that makes perfect sense. No more ponies, do you hear me, Joe?" That drew laughter from the audience who knew Pawpaw Joe well.

They moved on to the adult gifts with the difference being each came up to the tree, found their own gift one by one, and opened it to be shared and admired by the others. She understood she'd gone wrong again. Most of the presents cost around twenty dollars, favorite books, a new game, or a gag gift. Jock Brown received a new supply of Vegemite, the Aussie spread that was definitely an acquired taste. Some were homemade. One lucky person got Corazon's pumpkin bread. She'd gone overboard with the fancy cane, but it couldn't be helped now.

"I'll get yours when I pick up mine," Sarge volunteered.

"Ah, maybe that's not such a good idea." Why the objection she wondered?

Somehow, she'd been called last. Three gifts remained under the tree, two for Mack and one for her. She jolted a bit when she recognized the well-known Victoria's Secret wrapping though she'd never bought anything there. Maggie often dragged her through the store in the mall when she picked out sexy underwear to entice Sam. All watched them with great anticipation as she made her way back to Mack and placed the long, slim box in his lap first. She put hers under the chair hoping it would be forgotten.

"From you, Sarge?"

She nodded.

He tore the paper away as eagerly as the children had and ripped through the tissue to expose the cane, elegant and gold-handled.

"Does this mean I'm through with the walker?"

"Yes. Open the other."

Mack kicked aside his walker first. Annie's three toddler boys deserted their new toys and began pushing it down a hallway. He shook the small box as lightweight as air. "Well, it's from Dad and Mom and not a football or a pony."

"Just open it, you showboat. I'm getting hungry," Trinity, his triplet brother, said.

Mack pried up the taped down lid and withdrew a folded piece of paper. Intrigued, he opened it up. "The Antigravity Treadmill, it's here."

"Not yet, but sometime this week," his dad said.

"If you think I'm working you hard now, wait until you start on that. Okay, how can I help with dinner?" Sarge offered.

She did her best to avoid opening hers, but Stacy immediately said, "What about yours? I can tell it's something nice by the box. Who is it from?" As if all of them didn't know.

Trapped, she leaned down and retrieved the package she'd hoped to open in the privacy of her room. The lid came off easily. She parted the black tissue and forced her fingers to hold up silk pajamas very like her own but pink and piped in black.

"Pink is so your color," Josee, the model, raved as she sat there garbed in an elegant turquoise peignoir, every inch of her beautiful. "Really any pastel would look good on you. Not that you don't wear bright red well, too."

She did hope pink became her because surely her entire face flooded with that shade. "Thank you, Mack. You shouldn't have." Her very embarrassment made the family chuckle—or perhaps they laughed at Mack who studied the floor like a shy schoolboy.

"Yeah, I know."

Leave it to Mama Nell to handle another sticky situation. "We do have one more gift for Sarge from the whole family to show our gratitude for her work with Mack." Big Jock Brown carried in the cumbersome box and set it in front of her.

She began taking out the extensive packing material and finally withdrew the present. DJ who had approached it with curiosity shouted in awe, "It's a foot."

"Oh." She pressed her hand against her mouth and closed her eyes to hold back her emotions. "It's perfect." And it was, a dynamic response foot with a split-toe design. "Thank you so much."

"Your foot for dancing. Mom and Dad asked me what you'd really enjoy. I found your payment slips in your room, and we contacted the manufacturer who put a rush on finishing it." Mack raised his face and locked a potent gaze on her.

"What were you doing in my room in the first place?"

"Looking for the size of your silk pajamas." Under the clamor of the small children crowding in to see the foot, he whispered, "I hope this makes up for the PJs," and then as if he couldn't help himself, "You'll look great in pink."

"It's the color I hate most."

"Should have guessed that."

Joe clapped his hands, as he often did when sending his team into action, and issued an audible over the din. "Everyone get dressed. Let's help Corazon put dinner on the table."

Xochi and Lorena, who had come dressed, headed for the kitchen tailed by their spouses. Annie and Dre corralled the grandchildren in the den to keep them out from underfoot and doled them out to their mothers for the exchange from pajamas to Christmas clothes. The crowd moved around Sarge, still overcome by her presents, both of them.

Mack pushed up using his new cane. "It's the perfect height and weight."

"Yes, I had it made to your measurements, and you can use it as a fashion accessory. No one must know you need it right now—which is the real reason I think you don't like to go out in public no matter how many ex-girlfriends you have here."

"That transparent, huh?"

"No one wants to appear needy. And Mack, my new foot is better than a soccer ball or a bicycle, my best Christmas gift of all time."

Chapter Fifteen

The Antigravity Treadmill arrived two days after Christmas along with a technician to train Sarge in its use. She worked with him all afternoon, taking a turn in the mechanism herself. Mack lurked nearby like a jealous lover until she sent him back to the house in order to concentrate better, sweetening the deal by letting him drive the golf cart. Now the machine sat, taking up a chunk of the gym, a clear inflatable plastic bag mounted over a treadmill and possessing a complex control panel that adjusted the electromagnetic field moving the lifters.

Nervous, Sarge helped Mack into the black compression shorts with what appeared to be a skirt around the waist. He stepped into the running machine. She fastened the Velcro around his waist and zipped him into the cockpit. She calibrated his weight. The plastic bag inflated as she raised the level of his body with his toes barely touching the treadmill and set the controls to a walking pace and twenty percent gravity.

"Do a few heel raises first. Are you comfortable? We don't want to overdo the first time. Only twenty minutes walking to start out. Try for a natural gait."

"When do I get to run?"

"As soon as I am convinced you can walk."

She sat on a nearby bench and traded out her usual foot for the glamourous one. Fitting a pair of low heels on both the prosthesis and her actual foot, she walked around and around the gym as slowly as Mack paced.

"Trying it on for size?" he asked, not breathing the least bit hard.

"It was made to my measurements, but like a new shoe, you have to watch out for tight spots and break it in. The feel is different from either of the others. If I have a problem, I'll have to take it in for adjustments. There's always a chance my stump might have changed in configuration, too."

"You know, your stump isn't all that bad. Sure, I flinched a little the first time I saw it, but I'm over that. I don't know what was wrong with your fiancé."

"Believe me, my leg was swollen and fairly ugly as it healed. He tried and failed to accept it—but I did get a nice pair of pajamas out of it."

"How about my gift. Do they fit?"

"The size is right." Did he really expect her to admit to wearing them? She had tried them on, but not taken the chance that he'd test her again by calling her name in the night and went back to the plain white ones. So far, he'd left her alone, but she kept waiting for him to break and make another try. She did a few dance steps, clumsy and ill-formed, but she'd practice and practice as she had with the others until she could gain a natural grace.

"How does it feel, your new foot?"

"Like dragging a weight about on the bottom of my leg, but it will improve."

"From the first, the fact that you walked without a limp impressed me."

"If you're worried, I'm sure you won't end up with a limp."

Conversation outside the gym interrupted her. Nell peeked into the room. "May we come in? We wanted to see how Mack likes the new treadmill."

"It's terrific. Can't wait to go longer and faster."

"That describes you to a tee," his dad said. "And you, *cher*, how's that new foot?"

"Getting used to it gradually. Like the treadmill, it takes time. Really, you are too generous. The original price was fifteen-thousand dollars, and I only had it half paid off."

"Our pleasure," said Nell. "You are doing all sorts of wonders for our boy."

"He's done all the work."

Another commotion by the door caught their attention. Teddy entered in his wheelchair with Lizzie holding the door open for him. "We wanted to see how well the new machine worked. 'We' might be too strong a word. Lizzie needed some exercise since her nursery school is closed for a week's vacation."

A timer dinged. The treadmill stopped.

"Do a few more heel raises as you go back to regular gravity." Sarge unzipped Mack as the plastic tent deflated.

He backed out and took up his cane again with reluctance. "I want to run."

"I want to run." Lizzie copied his words and took off around the gym.

"I want to run," said Teddy in imitation, a teasing smile on his ever-pleasant face.

"Sure," said Sarge. "I see you have your athletic shoes on. We can wheel you right into the machine."

"No kidding?"

"I do not kid."

"Believe me, she doesn't," Mack said as he took a seat, unhappy to be denied. "I guess you'll want to get into my pants now."

"Mack, please," his mother said.

"I meant Teddy."

But probably not, Sarge figured. "We will need the compression shorts. Come on, you have gym clothes on underneath."

They made the exchange on the bench with Sarge helping. Beside Mack's scarred leg, Teddy's limbs, momentarily exposed, resembled frail sticks next to a solid log. Not bothering to compare, he wheeled into the deflated machine, pushed up to be zipped into place as Sarge removed his chair and fiddled with the settings again.

"Give me some heel raises if you can."

"I can." He hung on and did the requested exercise.

"Twenty percent gravity, as low as it can go, and a slow jog. Move your arms and feet as if you are running."

"I am. I'm running—and I've never run before. It's amazing."

Lizzie stopped to watch the dad she'd seldom seen without crutches or a wheelchair. "Go, daddy, go fast as you can. Then it will be my turn."

Joe, father of many, sensed an oncoming tantrum. "We don't have shorts in your size yet, Lizzie. But I'll tell you what we do have—ponies. Let's go to the big house and get some carrots to feed them. Maybe Black Star will want to give you a ride."

"We won't go in the bull pen," the child assured her father, taking her grandfather's hand.

Before her own father backed out of the

contraption, Pawpaw Joe and Lizzie were gone in their quest for horse snacks. Nell shook her head. "He is good with children. Who would have thought so when I first met him? People can surprise you, Sarge. We'll bring Lizzie home before dinner. Teddy, maybe you can get some writing done this afternoon."

"I'd appreciate that. Love my kid, but she is a handful." He sat by Mack again to remove the compression shorts. "I'll bet that's the first time you've envied me since I got to run and you didn't."

"No, I told you before I used to be jealous of all the time Mom and Dad spent with you after your surgeries. I already know that's not fun. Then, you have a job you can do forever, a house, the wife, the kids who adore you. I'm not sure I'd be good with children."

"Won't know until you try. You still have plenty of time for all that."

"So I keep telling myself. An accident like this changes your viewpoint. Football is all I've got. What if I can't play again?"

Sarge put a hand on his shoulder. "Alex Smith is going to practice with his team this summer, and you will also. I'll make sure of it. Enough for today. You can drive me back to the house."

"Right, throw me a bone."

She shook a finger at him. "Not one word about boners because I can sense it coming."

Teddy laughed, low but long. "She certainly knows you, Mack. I better get home. Jessie will wonder what happened to us—and she always worries it's something bad if Lizzie gets away from me."

Nell, who had been silently observing the trio, asked, "Will you give me a ride home? You know all of us look out for Lizzie, Teddy. That's why you live on the ranch."

"True. I'll be on my way. I'd like to come back and run a little faster."

Returning to business, Sarge said, "We should order more of the compression shorts in various sizes if you plan to use the machine with others, but that would be fine. We're here every morning and afternoon."

The last one out, she shut off the lights. "I'll let you ride up front with Mack. Fair warning, he speeds."

Nell took her seat. "Typical. I worry about him when he drives back to Dallas."

"Aw, Mom."

"But he does call when he gets there."

They hit a bump in the path and jolted up and down. From the back seat, Sarge said, "I gather Lizzie has had an encounter with a bull."

"Oh, yes, at our Camp Love Letter rodeo the other year. Bodey Landrum did a bucking bull demonstration. After he dismounted, Lizzie climbed in the corral, but Trinity was helping out and saved her."

"The bullfighter saved her. Trin only tossed her to him, but it made him look like a hero to Josee," Mack said with a little sulk in his voice.

"He also saved a child from drowning and later, Josee's life. I've always said Trinity has as much heart as any of the Sinners players."

"I could have done the same," Mack insisted.

"If you'd been around."

"She gave me the old heave-ho long before that."

Nell turned her heard toward Sarge who listened with quiet interest. "He took her out dancing, got too drunk to drive, and Josee drove him home in the Jag.

Good thing she knew how to handle a car like that. Evidently, she'd dated a racecar driver in the past."

So Mack had once desired the beautiful and intelligent Josee who ran her own businesses as well as modeling. Sarge counted herself in good company even if he only toyed with her for the moment. All the more reason to resist.

"I'm not drinking now and don't plan to do that much in the future." Mack caught the edge of a wheel in the grass and nearly overturned them.

"But still a reckless driver. I think it will help your chances with the Cowboys if you mean it," Sarge offered. "Your rival for the position is a Mormon. Doesn't drink, is married, and has four kids. He's Mr. Clean. Your reputation has been less pure. If they have to choose…"

"They only care that I can play ball like I used to do. And I will." He slowed the golf cart as if to prove a point.

"Good." She'd given him another incentive to train hard and come all the way back.

****

It seemed to Mack that Sarge intentionally withheld the use of the Anti-Gravity Treadmill until he'd completed all of his other exercises. Fine if Teddy wandered in and wanted to try it again. Her admiration for him was clear. She let him run longer and with a little more pressure, but he'd gone back to work as had all the rest of the family involved in football plus the college kids. Just the two of them again. Or maybe he should say the four of them because his parents lingered around the gym since the machine arrived and were present at every meal. How he wished to be back in

Dallas, taking Sarge with him.

Just as Sarge finished zipping him into the contraption and prompting him to do the heel lifts, his parents strolled in and made themselves at home amid the kettlebells and free weights. They watched his legs move inside the transparent sack. He did his only trick for them, walking backward for a few minutes before resuming his forward plod. If no one else was around, Sarge practiced dancing, sometimes with an unseen partner from the way she held her arms. Within days, she'd improved a great deal. If only he could go faster.

"We've been thinking that you've both been working very hard and deserve a special treat," his mom said. An opening remark like that never boded well. Her idea of something special usually involved a charity. His dad's, always football, and he didn't want to attend a Sinners' game or event.

"We reserved a table for four at the Hilton on New Year's Eve, a nice meal, music, fireworks over the bayou. Been a long time since I took your mother dancing," his dad said.

Sarge made the first objection. "I really don't have anything to wear."

"Oh, the red outfit you wore Christmas day will do fine. Lafayette isn't as fancy as New Orleans," his mom assured her. "We might get Mack into a suit again. It seems all he wears are sweats and gym clothes."

"Yeah, because all I do is PT and sit on my butt Sundays watching football." He should have kept his mouth shut.

"Exactly. Sarge uses her day off visiting wounded veterans. You both need some fun."

So that's where she went, returning for dinner, and

then taking in the evening game with him in the theater since his parents would be wherever the Sinners played.

"I put us all down for the prime rib with stuffed potatoes." Obviously, his dad had ordered the meal or it would have been broiled fish and baked potatoes. Nell shot Joe a look. "Of course, we'll have salad and some kind of vegetable—and cheesecake for dessert. I can change it if you want."

He intervened as fast as he could. "Sounds great to me."

"Sarge?"

"I'm no vegetarian. I'm sure it will be fine."

"We're all set then. Carry on. I think Mack is eager to do his running."

"If she'd let me."

"Soon," Sarge promised as she always did. She put in the setting and started the treadmill before going into her dance routine.

"I guess we should work on our dancing for the special occasion." That stopped her in mid-twirl.

"Sure, practicing dance steps would help me with my footwork. Before this mess happened to me, I did a mean Cajun waltz and a fast two-step. Picked up the Cotton-eyed Joe in Texas. All the Billodeaux men dance except Trinity who came into the world with a great big brain and two clumsy left feet, but he's improved since he has Josee in his life. You wouldn't suspect it, but Dean does a hot salsa. I've seen Teddy give Jess a whirl on his lap. Tom just makes it up as he goes along like a mating whooping crane. Dad is certain to ask you, and he's better than all of us."

"Oh, no, I'm not ready, not ready at all."

The treadmill slowed and stopped, his all too brief

time expired. "Come on and get me out of here. We'll see what we can manage."

Though she moved to deflate the tent and unzip him from the apparatus, Sarge kept shaking her head. "Too soon for you to do that."

"I can lean on you. As you've frequently pointed out, you aren't a delicate flower."

"Get your cane and…"

He snaked his arm around her waist and grabbed an arm. "Here we go, one, two, three, one two three." Leaning heavily on her and holding her close, they made their way around the gym. After one circuit, he planted his feet, spun her out of his arms and brought her back, then toppled onto a nearby mat still gripping her tight.

"See, you aren't ready yet. Let me up!" Sarge tried to wriggle from her place on top of his body which only put a happy smile on his face.

"Do you really believe I didn't do this intentionally? I know how to fall when fall I must."

"Lot of good it did you when you got this injury."

"A fluke. I intended to slide when the damned Aussie hit me blindside and then Junior piled on. This is the most joy I've had in months. We have to do it again."

Sarge wrested free of his embrace. "Let me check your leg."

"Which one? Both are stiff at the moment." Oh, how he enjoyed her outrage.

"I'm surprised you can get it up in those compression shorts. Very well then, stand."

Sitting came easily enough as he used his arms, the rest not so much. "Ah, give me my cane."

She brought it to him, stood back to watch him struggle. "I might need a hand up, too."

She grasped him around the wrist and threw her weight back. Between that and the cane, he got to his feet. Then, the embarrassment set in big time.

"I guess you were right. No more dancing."

"Actually, I was thinking no more fake falling. I see your point about dancing being good for your footwork. We'll try again tomorrow. Let me see your leg." She felt up and down its scarred length as if he were a lame racehorse. "Any new pain?"

"Nope."

Rising, she fetched her bag and the keys to the golf cart. "Here, want to drive?"

"No, not today."

"Are you really hurt and not telling me?"

"Only my pride. I've got lots of that for all the good it does me."

"It will serve you well later. Fine, I'll pamper you and drive. Imagine I'm your limousine chauffeur taking you and some starlet to a special occasion this time next year. It will happen, I swear."

"If Sarge says so, it will come true, right?" He tried to keep the doubt of his voice.

"Absolutely."

Chapter Sixteen

They stood before the mirror on the back of the door in the lavender and lace bedroom. Sarge had to admit they made an interesting couple with her so pale and dressed in bright red and him so dark in a bespoke black suit with a pale gray shirt and black and silver-striped tie. Of course, he outshone her like the sun did lesser stars.

Mack fussed with his jacket. "I pay for custom tailoring, and this coat is loose." He leaned on his cane which made him seem rakish rather than handicapped.

"You have lost some weight and muscle mass, but it is coming back. When you get into regular athletic training, you'll bulk up some more. Regardless, you'll be the second most handsome man at the Hilton's New Year's Eve party," she lied.

With his thick dark hair combed straight back and its length gathered at his nape in a black leather thong, his strong jaw, clean-shaven tonight, and high cheekbones, he appeared to be chiseled from granite. Add in the bittersweet chocolate eyes and those lush lashes, the sculpted lips, and her companion would make other women salivate for the chance to be with him.

"Only the second?"

"Well, your father will be with us this evening. Older men in great condition with a full head of iron gray hair, a charming smile, and a twinkle in the eyes have a great deal of appeal."

"We've got the same smile. It's usually described as wicked and the eyes as sexy—though the Hilton does draw an older crowd."

She patted his arm. "Believe whatever you want."

From the bottom of the stairs and all the way down the hall, Joe shouted, "Our ride has come."

"Here goes," Sarge said. She didn't add the nothing. They'd practiced slow dancing for a couple of afternoons and did well enough in the gym. A dance floor would be another matter.

"Remember, the last dance is mine."

"I won't forget if you really want to go through with it. I doubt my dance card will be filled." She started to lead the way to the elevator, but in an unexpected act of gallantry, Mack offered his free arm which gave her a small thrill she'd never admit.

Their driver had parked in front of the mansion. He opened the doors on a small black limousine of the type used for family at funerals, no long white stretch vehicles tonight, but still assurance that if the passengers wanted to drink, they could safely. Nell and Joe had already taken their seats. As if to keep her company, Nell had worn a deeper shade of red in the form of a dress with a knee-length full skirt and matching shoes that boosted her height a couple of inches but would neither trip her up nor pinch her toes for the duration of the evening. She had ruby studs in her ears and a modest string of them around her neck.

"Lovely ruby necklace," Sarge complimented as she fingered her own of enameled holly leaves.

"Garnets, actually. You look very pretty tonight."

She saw the small nudge Nell gave her husband. "*Mais oui, cher*. You will turn heads."

Not true, but beautifully said. She hadn't gone to her prom and not missed it. Like Mark, she'd been loaded on the bus for basic training just days afterward. Tonight rather made up for that. The Christmas lights still glittered in the oaks, and she rode in a limo, not in a freshly washed pickup truck most of the boys she'd known owned. Nor did her escort expect her to put out in the truck bed under the Texas stars following the dance. Not a terribly long ride, they barely talked except to point out exceptional holiday displays along the way.

No using up her leg strength hiking in from the crowded parking lot as their driver pulled the limo under the entryway canopy and sprang out to open the doors and hand the ladies down. Easy to find the second-floor ballroom by following the mass of people festively dressed heading that way. Without making it awkward, Joe summoned an elevator for his group, and they crammed in among the elderly also going to the event.

The ballroom, illuminated brightly, allowed people to wander and find their places already set with salads and desserts and the complimentary bottle of champagne. A centerpiece of decorative glass containers filled with tiny lights hinted at a more intimate atmosphere to come. The Billodeaux table sat very near the dance floor by luck or design. Sarge suspected the latter. The music hadn't started, but the stage was set up for a live band, not a DJ.

They took their seats. Mack immediately griped about his strawberry topped cheesecake upon noticing two of the other slices dripping with chocolate sauce and pecans. "Anyone want to trade?"

Sarge shook her head. "I do not share anything chocolate."

"Neither do I," Joe said.

"Eat the fruit. It's good for you," Nell ordered.

"See, this is what happens when you go out with parents." Mack tossed a roll onto his bread plate and passed the basket. "If I were on a real date, any other woman would switch with me with in a minute."

"Good thing I'm not any other woman." Sarge selected a roll and passed the basket to Nell who failed to hide her amusement.

Joe worked the cork out of the champagne bottle and filled three glasses. "I guess it's iced tea for you, son."

"We have a limo. Wouldn't matter if I got a little drunk."

"Go ahead and do that, but don't expect me to save the last dance for you. I won't hold up two-hundred pounds of inebriated football player," Sarge said.

"Okay, okay. Iced tea for me." He passed the bowl of ranch dressing for the salads. "Can we eat now?"

"I don't see why not. They like to remove the salad dishes before they bring the entrée." Nell buttered her roll and picked up her salad fork.

Eating curtailed the conversation until the rare prime ribs arrived accompanied by large potatoes stuffed with cheese, bacon bits, and chives and whole green beans wrapped in bacon strips and broiled. Sarge judged it to be the nicest meal she'd had in a long time, not to fault the food at the ranch, but this stood as special occasion dining even if she wasn't special. The waiters came around with coffee as they started dessert.

"I guess I can have coffee, right?" Mack asked with as much sarcasm as he could manage.

"Sure, as long as you don't need help getting to the bathroom." Sarge, taunting, licked the chocolate topping from her spoon.

"Decaf would be better for you," Nell suggested, her lips bowed in amusement again.

"Screw decaf," Mack said.

"Watch the language in front of the ladies," his father directed.

Sarge laughed hard enough to make blotting her lightly made-up eyes with her napkin necessary. "I swear worse than that when the occasion calls for it."

The house lights dimmed. The emcee mounted the stage. "Music tonight compliments of the Blue Bayou Orchestra and our chanteuse for the evening, the highly talented Caressa." The husky singer dressed in bold gold swayed toward the mic. She tossed her braids festively interspersed with multicolored beads and cued the band.

"She sang at Trin's wedding and is pretty good," Mack said.

"I'm surprised you noticed since you disappeared when she and X-avier Hopkins were doing their duets," his mother stated.

"I had other amusements keeping me busy."

"Bridesmaids," muttered Nell.

Sarge suspected as much from him and made no comment. Caressa possessed one of those voices that wrapped the listener in warm emotions. She planned to sit, relax, and enjoy. Joe stood and offered his hand to his petite wife. Within seconds the couple whirled around others, Nell's full skirt flaring as her husband spun her out and brought her back close to his chest. Because of the skill that came with many years dancing together, their size disparity hardly seemed to matter. What a pleasure to watch.

Mack sat back in his chair eyeing the unattended champagne bottle. Without looking his way, she said, "Don't do it," surprised when he obeyed.

A pair moving from the back of the room jostled their table as they made for the floor. She could have done without their pause to apologize or their greeting.

"Why, Mack Billodeaux, I never expected to see you here. Did you park your walker outside? I saw several in the hallway." Though Mack leaned away, Brooke bent over far enough to give him a good look at her breasts encased in a low-cut but classic black dress topped by a triple strand of equally classic pearls. She air-kissed both of his cheeks though got close enough to leave a small red smear of her lipstick on one.

"I'm using a cane now." His tone hinted that he'd like to hit her with it but restrained.

"Well, I surely hope you'll dance again. Hollis, I swear Mack was the only high school boy who could keep off a girl's feet." Her gaze strayed to Sarge's shoes, so perhaps the woman had noticed on Christmas Eve or heard local gossip, then rose slowly up to her face, making her feel cheaply garbed. Not a bit of metal showed tonight. Good for her pantsuit and the maker of her prosthetic.

"One of my many precocious talents," Mack said, distracting Brooke from her study of Sarge.

Brooke flushed a little and tugged her patient husband's arm. "We'll miss the next dance, too, if we don't move along, honey. Nice seeing you again, ah, Suzy, was it. Have a nice evening."

However, her husband stayed put and offered his hand to Mack. "I was and still am a member of the Boosters Club for the Ste. Jeanne d'Arc football team. I remember your exploits on the field very well. You won many a game for the team."

Sarge noted that Mack appeared gratified by the attention, or maybe the shot he'd gotten off at Brooke. It couldn't be that he meant to defend her from the woman.

"Loved doing it," Mack replied with a glance at Brooke who grew more insistent that they get out on the floor by snatching her husband's hand away and leading him if not by the nose, then by the fingers. From the rear, Hollis' bald spot showed along with his broad rear end.

"No competition with your being the best-looking man here," Sarge remarked. "Good of you not to outright call her a slut."

"Yes, I amazed myself, but poor Hollis, pussy-whipped if I ever saw a guy. I didn't like the way she called you Suzy because you hate that, and there is nothing wrong with what you're wearing."

Could it be that Mack Billodeaux was becoming less self-centered, even perceptive? She explored the idea further. "So, her comment about the walker didn't bother you?"

"I'm used to trash talk whether it bothers me or not."

"She marked you while shoving her boobs in your face." Sarge picked up her napkin and removed the red smear from his cheek

"I've seen better. Thanks for getting rid of that."

His parents passed by again, tightly pressed against each other for a slow dance. Nell's head rested on Joe's chest. Her eyes fluttered shut as she trusted him to guide them around the floor.

"Your parents, just wow, after all these years of marriage and raising so many kids."

"I know. They used to embarrass us, but now I kind of envy them. It's hard to find a perfect fit like that. But your parents are still together, right?"

"Not like that. When I was younger, I only prayed they wouldn't make another baby. I think they just live side by side now, no passion if there ever was any."

"They did have eleven children."

"They didn't practice birth control, and my dad had no constraint."

Brooke and Hollis went by maintaining a proper distance from each other as if her husband knew she wouldn't want her dress wrinkled by close contact. Easy to pick out the truly happy couples by the way they danced. Some of the very elderly gave off the same vibe as Joe and Nell, but not many of them. The music segued into another fast number. Joe and Nell glided by again, but many left the floor in favor of sipping champagne or ordering other drinks. Brooke and her husband avoided their table on the way out.

When the music stopped for a break between sets, Joe and Nell returned to the table. Joe refilled the three champagne glasses but downed a glass of iced tea before touching his. "Thirsty work and good exercise, dancing, but always a pleasure with my Tink. You're next, Sarge, if I might have that pleasure."

"Oh, I'm not so sure…I mean I can't dance like

Nell."

"We are a well-oiled machine, but I am certain you can hold your own, *cher.*"

"She can," Mack agreed.

"That's settled, then."

When the music started, Joe escorted her to the dance floor and kept her there for all three dances, but didn't hold her nearly as tight as he did his wife, which she expected but vaguely regretted. More an unanswered yearning than a real desire. All in all, she enjoyed being out there with her new foot performing wonderfully.

Upon their return during the next break, they finished off the champagne but passed on ordering another bottle. Both the iced tea and water pitchers were drained. Only one more set before midnight and the promised fireworks. As Caressa took to the stage once more, she leaned into the mic and breathed. "Let's make this last set for all the lovers out there. If I could have a little help from that gentleman in the audience, Mr. X-avier Hopkins, running back for the New Orleans Sinners."

Mention the Sinners, and it always brought a round of applause. X passed their table, pausing to slap hands with Joe and offer a "good to see you up and out, man," to Mack, before bounding up the steps to the stage. The two singers faced each other mics in hand and began *Unforgettable.*

"That seems to be their signature song. I heard them at the wedding. I wasn't upstairs with Catriona the whole time," Mack remarked, as if that gave him some kind of credibility. "I see he's kept the cornrows."

"Hush," said Sarge. "This is so beautiful."

His parents wafted by wrapped around each other, not caring what anyone thought. Brooke, who had hauled her hubby out again, fired off a look of disapproval worthy of an old biddy as they passed.

"I think Brooke is jealous of what my parents have."

"Definitely, because she doesn't. Now be quiet."

The song drew to a close. X-avier kissed Caressa's fingertips with their gold-painted nails and honored her by starting off the applause. A moment later, he let her be the center of attention as he moved away and came to sit at their table. Caressa launched into the incredible Etta James song, *At Last*.

"She gets better every time I sing with her. What a talent. She should have a recording contract by now. Because she's heavy, I guess, but that ain't right." X scanned their table for a drink. "I see the well has gone dry here. Be back in a second." He returned with a half a bottle of champagne and filled three glasses.

Mack pushed his away. "Got to stay sober for the grand finale."

The brows raised in X-avier's mocha-colored, sharp-featured face. "That's not your usual reputation."

"I'm working on a new one."

"Good, good. Rumor says Prince Dobbs is talking retirement to concentrate on his Church of the Dreadlocked Jesus and spend more time with his family. Truth is, he's slowing down and doesn't take the hits as well. Keep in mind the Sinners can always use another good wide receiver if the Cowboys don't want you back."

"Oh, they'll want me. Sarge is making sure of it."

"Sarge?"

"Sorry, I didn't introduce you. This is Sarge, my trainer."

"Prettiest Sarge I ever did see," X said with his usual charm. "Care to dance, Miss Sarge?"

"Well, I…"

"Go on. But, X, the last dance is mine."

Hard to believe, she would dance with three handsome men by the end of the night. That had not happened before, not in her entire life. Why not revel in it? She rose into the embrace of X-avier Hopkins who had the footwork of a wide receiver and the charisma of a crooner. He held her just close enough and gave her cues as to his next moves, a twirl or a change of direction. Not quite as tall as Mack or as heavy, he did have a light-footed grace Mack had not yet regained.

She noticed how Caressa eyed them as they went by the bandstand—with longing, Sarge thought. But the band and the singers rarely got to dance. As the song came to its end, X-avier again led the applause, and Caressa's dark, shining face lit from within. She wondered if he knew Caressa loved him. He'd be easy to fall for, but probably had lots of women available exactly like Mack.

"A pleasure, Miss Sarge." X bowed before her. "I have to stand by to give that lady her midnight kiss."

"Do that," Mack said. He positioned himself to take over, seeming steady enough, pulling her close.

Caressa leaned into the mic again. "Our last dance for the evening that will take us to midnight. Stay near your loved one for that first kiss of the New Year. I give you what we all hope for, *Stand by Me*."

Sarge watched the significant glance the singer sent toward X-avier, but he had engaged a few of his fans in conversation. Still, he'd said he'd be there for her at midnight. That counted for something.

"I guess this is our song."

Sarge shrugged. The song made no difference. That he had the confidence to dance did. "Very popular in military circles," she told him.

Mack embraced her tight against his chest, whether because he wanted to or simply needed the support of her solid body against his. Other couples crowded the floor for the final dance of the evening. They had very little room to practice their routine but still managed to move around the floor. Once when an opening occurred, he spun her out quickly and drew her back just as fast to rest against him. She fought the urge to lay her head against his heartbeat and close her eyes as Nell had and drew herself up straight. He moved them gradually toward the wide windows overlooking the bayou with the reflection of a full moon rippling in the water.

As the final words sounded with the plea to stand by me, he whispered in her ear, "Dip."

"What?" She found herself draped over one strong arm and heading toward the floor but did not reach it before he drew her up again and wrapped that arm hard around her waist. He turned her to the view beyond the glass. Fireworks exploded, sending out shooting stars of gold and silver, bursts of violet and green, and blazes of red, white, and blue against the dark sky, outshining that low hanging moon.

Mack tightened his grip. "You okay with fireworks? I forgot to ask. I know some soldiers aren't."

"They're beautiful and high up in the sky. I'm fine."

As the pop and sizzle of the skyrockets faded, the band struck up the traditional *Auld Lang Syne*. Out of the corner of her eye, Sarge saw X up on the bandstand and embracing Caressa. She tried to turn back to the table, but Mack still held her firmly as he lowered his head and pressed his lips against hers. He didn't go any farther than that, but held the embrace long enough to light a few fireworks of his own deep inside her. Suddenly weak-kneed, she wasn't sure now who held whom upright. Then, it ended as he slid his arm heavy about her shoulders and said, "You'd better get me back to my cane. Thanks for standing by me, Sarge."

New Year's Eve, a traditional kiss, or an act of appreciation, that's all it was or could be. So she told herself as they waded through people, drunk and sober, wearing funny hats like Hollis Duchamp next to his embarrassed wife, or blowing noisemakers, singing along off key, all to bring in the New Year. She expected to find Joe and Nell waiting for their return at the table where they'd left the cane but couldn't spot them.

"Sit down. I'll look for your folks."

Mack did sit, but he pointed to a dark corner near the bandstand. "No need. They're over there making out. Jeez, when will they get too old to do that?"

"Never, I hope. We can wait."

When the lights came up to full again, Joe and Nell unclenched and casually strolled back to meet them.

Nell beamed. "We saw most of your dance. What a wonderful surprise. Nicely done."

Sarge wondered if they'd seen the kiss and hoped they'd been too involved with each other to notice. She wouldn't want them to think she and Mack had

135

something going on. They paid her well for his rehab and supplied room and board, had been nothing but kind. It just wasn't professional—and not her idea. Yet, she'd sensed no devilment in the embrace, only sincerity.

"I'll be able to do better next time," Mack promised, sending a naughty smile her way, damn him.

Ah well, they had only to get back to the ranch in a dark limo. The night would end and a New Year begin.

Chapter Seventeen

Why did the ride home seem longer than the outward trip? Possibly because his leg throbbed or maybe because his parents cuddled together the whole time. Mack sat close enough to Sarge to put his arm around her and draw her close, but he didn't dare. The kiss had been taking a big enough chance. He hoped she understood he could do better, but in the end, he'd taken a slide and not said what he meant, that he cared for her, the bravest, most stalwart woman he knew.

Of course, late traffic impeded their way. Their driver skillfully swerved around drunk drivers and slower-moving party buses. At last, they attained the main street of Chapelle where teens who stayed out after their curfew engaged in a running battle across the road, shooting balls of fire from handheld Roman candles at each other. Good way to lose an eye, he thought like some middle-aged grouch. He'd done the same once until his dad chastised him saying one-eyed wonders did not play football.

The driver honked the horn to clear the way. When they'd nearly gotten through the mob, one of the last delinquents gave the limo a finger and lobbed a homemade cherry bomb into their path. It went off like thunder, but the limo plowed onward, no harm done to the vehicle. He wasn't so sure about Sarge. She trembled against him. He wrapped his arm around her, and she didn't pull away.

His parents broke their embrace. His dad pulled out his phone. "Jesus, Mary, and Joseph, someone could be hurt. Everyone okay? Weren't those things outlawed back in the Sixties? I'm calling the cops."

"You can still get books that tell you how to make them. I looked it up once until you pointed out that a one-handed wide receiver would have a hard time getting drafted into the NFL and thought better of it."

His mom peered through the darkness. "Sarge, anything wrong?"

Close as he was, Mack took in her wide-eyed stare. He shook her gently. "Everything is fine now. We'll soon be home. You can tuck me in tonight." She didn't respond, not to the comforting words or the attempt at humor. "Mom, I don't think so."

Out of town now, the driver turned onto the rutted road that led to the ranch and sped up as if sensing a need to hurry. At the gate to the ranch, his dad used his opener to get them inside as fast as possible. As soon as the car stopped, Nell darted out to open the door, not waiting for the niceties. Joe shoved a large cash tip at the driver. "Thanks, you were great. I'll tell your boss."

"Do you need help getting the lady inside? It won't be the first time I've had to do that after a party." Maybe he didn't want to clean vomit out of his vehicle.

Mack bristled. "She's not drunk. That cherry bomb might as well have been another IED. She was in the service."

"Sorry, I didn't mean…" the driver said as if his tip and recommendation might be snatched away.

"You didn't know. Dad, take her upstairs." He relinquished Sarge into his father's arms. Damn, double dammit, he should be able to do that instead of limping along behind on his cane, the elegant one Sarge had given him to boost his confidence.

His mom dashed ahead, turning on lights and summoning the elevator. All the while, his dad cradled Sarge against his chest like one of his own beloved children. They laid her on her bed. Mack sat beside her, pulled a blanket over her still shaking body.

"I'm going to get her a cup of herbal tea, then come back and help her undress and get to bed. Keep her warm, Mack." His mom left.

He chafed her cold hands. "Sarge, speak to me."

"I'm f-f-fine." Her teeth chattered as she struggled to get the words out.

"You aren't. You'd call me on that if I claimed the same." He stretched out full length beside her to lend his body warmth and kept talking to her though she didn't answer. "I know this is bad, but we had a great night, didn't we? Think about that. I almost had to beat men off of you with my cane. Great cane. Many uses." He knew he babbled. Didn't care. He sat up and shut up when he heard his mother approaching.

Mama Nell entered clasping a steaming mug. "Thank God for microwaves. I put honey and lemon in it."

"She doesn't have a cold, Mom. Mild PTSD she told me. If this is mild, I'd hate to witness bad."

"The heat will help, and honey is good for shock. I wish Xochi hadn't gone to New Orleans."

"We'll help her." He seized the mug and held it to her lips. Sarge took a sip or two before taking it in her own hands.

"Now, you get out of here. I'll help her get ready

for bed. I might stay with her tonight," Nell ordered.

"I'll stay. She's sat up often enough with me when my leg hurt. I'd like to return the favor."

His mother pondered for a moment. "All right. But don't upset her. Now, out for a minute."

Mack went to his room and stripped off his suit and tie, left them in a heap, as he drew on his hound dog pajama bottoms and a T-shirt. He unfastened the leather thong from his hair and raked his fingers through it. Then, he went out and paced the hallway like an expectant father.

Waiting, his dad simply leaned against a wall. "I know it's hard to stand still when someone you love is hurt. God, I remember the day your mother nearly died and almost lost Rex and Edie thanks to that mad woman."

"I wouldn't say love, but I do care no matter how hard she is on me."

His father answered with the same wicked grin he saw in his own mirror. "Oh, I think you are well on the way and will get there one of these days. If she'll have you."

Before he could deny that, his mom exited the bedroom carrying the white silk pajamas. "These could use washing, so I put the pink ones on her. Clean night clothes always feel so good against the body, especially silk. I didn't know what to do about her prosthesis. Leave it on or risk damaging it if I took it off wrong."

"It should come off for the night. I've seen her do it often enough in the gym. I'll take over now. Mom, Dad, thanks for the evening out. I know she enjoyed it a lot."

"And you?"

"Not as bad as I thought it would be. I'm used to less sedate parties."

His mother sighed. "The whole world knows that." She turned toward her husband and asked, "Ready for bed?"

"Always." The suggestive grin appeared again.

Mom enjoyed it as his parents walked off hand in hand. Sarge would sock him in the arm. He opened the bedroom door quietly, hoping she might have dozed off, not that he wouldn't stand by her all night long just in case bad dreams overcame her. But no, Sarge sat on the edge of the bed with her legs dangling. She did look wonderful in pink and a bit like an injured child with her light hair ruffled and all her makeup washed away by the damp cloth his mother left behind in a shallow basin.

"Hey, Pinkie, feeling better?"

As she glared at him, the pathetic child vanished and Sarge returned. "Don't call me that. Get me out of these pajamas."

"Oh, you want to sleep in the buff. I get you. Naked, my favorite night clothes. But I will warn you in advance I'll be staying right beside you all night and seeing you through this. Want help taking off your foot?"

"No, I don't need your help." She bent over to remove her stump from the prosthesis. Her hands still trembled, and she took longer than usual, but succeeded at last.

"Should I put it in the closet for you?"

"Yes, out of the way. I won't be wearing it again for a while."

"Don't let what happened with those kids ruin it for

141

you. It's a great foot, and it will dance again."

"Maybe." She swung her legs onto the bed and pulled up the covers. "You can go now."

"Nope. My mother was going to stay with you. I talked her out of it. I said I'd take care of you. But if you want her to come back…"

"No. We're used to each other. If you have to stay, turn out the light and lie down."

Used to each other, like her parents perhaps? He hoped not. They'd formed a bond during those long nights together. At least, he believed they had—and he'd ruined it by getting sexual with her. Not tonight. He stretched out beside her on top of the covers.

"Under," she ordered. "I'm still cold, and you give off heat like a blast furnace."

"Yes," he admitted with false modesty. "I've been told I'm hot fairly often."

"Shut up and hold me."

"Glad to oblige." He fluffed a pillow and slid in next to her, extended his arm, and drew her close. Her head dipped and rested on his chest, the way he'd imagined she might do when they danced, but hadn't. "Does your stump hurt? I could rub it for you?"

"It's a little sore, not much. But thanks. I'm surprised you'd touch it."

"Not a coward like your former fiancé." At least, he hoped not, not exactly sure how he'd manage. She'd tell him. Sarge excelled at giving orders.

"I—I need a distraction more. How's your leg?"

"Throbbing some, but I don't want you to worry about that tonight. What we do is up to you."

"Really? Then, I think I'll take you up on your previous offer. I'm not ready to be on top, and you shouldn't do that either. So, if you do me, I'll do you by hand."

"Hand jobs? The same suggestion that caused you to exile yourself from me? That can't be right."

"It's what I want now. My idea, not yours, but I won't beg you."

"No begging necessary." He moved his hands under the silky pajama top and up toward her breasts, her skin still cold and clammy, his warm and he hoped, distracting to her. He cupped both breasts, firm and not overflowing, but nice, very nice. His thumb massaged her nipples until they hardened under his touch and rose to greet him.

"You're going in the wrong direction. Get down to business."

"I believe in being thorough. I've wanted to do this since the first time I managed to get my hands on you. Patience."

She didn't protest again. Some of the rigidity disappeared from her body as he massaged the heat back into her flesh. Then, he let his hands wander down the length of her until he found the fluff between her legs and the clit hiding there. "Aha, you don't wax."

"If that turns you off, stop now." She tried to issue another order, but it came out soft and shaky with desire.

"No way. It's like baby chick feathers. I could call you Chickie."

When she didn't answer, he knew his thumb worked its magic. Her breath quickened. He could feel her pulse where he rubbed. She rocked her hips into his hand, her fingers digging into the sheets, and then a long shudder and a wordless cry. He allowed her to rest for a few moments, then began again, needing little buildup to make her lose control once more. After the third time, she begged him to stop.

"Enough. Enough." She squeezed her legs tight to force him out and rolled over onto her belly for relief. "Give me a few minutes, then I'll do you."

"No, not tonight."

"But I could feel you, hard as a rock along my thigh."

"Tonight is yours for all you've done for me. I'll just lie here and count our siblings until my hard on goes away."

"Don't be ridiculous. Let me help you…"

"You can help me by going to sleep. Here, cuddle with me, Chickie. Close your eyes and rest."

"Only if you never call me Chickie again."

He kissed the top of her head. "Deal."

Chapter Eighteen

A gentle tapping sounded on the door followed by a jiggle of the handle. Sarge woke at once, shoved Mack's sheltering arm aside, and called out, "I'm awake. I'll be downstairs soon." Thank heaven, he had locked them in last night because Mack lay beside her, one leg thrown over her thigh, still keeping her warm.

Nell's voice answered. "I wanted to be certain you'd recovered. Make your own omelets downstairs along with sweet rolls and fruit cups. It's nearly ten, so consider it brunch."

"Sounds great. See you soon." She waited for Nell's footsteps to fade away before removing his good left leg from her body and shaking him awake. "Get up, get up. Your parents have breakfast ready, and it's ten o'clock."

"So what? We have a holiday. And they know I'm in here."

"Regardless, we need to get dressed and have breakfast with them."

"You want to shower first, you, me, or both you and me?"

She gave him a mighty shove that sent him over the edge of the queen size bed and onto a thick, fluffy throw rug. He sat up easily.

"Strange to wake up on New Year's Day without a hangover. I could get used to it. Okay, I'll shower first—if you give me a hand up." He extended an arm which she grasped and rolled back to get leverage. The second he was on his feet, he pulled her toward him, nearly dumping her on the floor, a playful move rather than one of revenge. He leaned close and whispered, "Anything I can do for you this morning?" in his most suggestive voice.

"Yes, hand me my everyday foot and get out of my room."

He handed her the prosthesis sitting near the bed. "You know my parents understand these things. They won't mind."

"I will. I was weak last night, very weak."

"Maybe you don't have to be strong all the time. Think about it." He peeled off the snug T-shirt, giving her a good look at what she was missing by chasing him off, and sauntered toward the shower in his sagging hound dog pajama bottoms.

She wasted no time in finding a pair of wide-legged jeans and a casual deep blue top that turned the steel of her eyes to a milder shade of blue-gray, maybe not a good choice for what she had to do, but speed mattered. After attaching her leg and running a comb through her hair, she set out to do what must be done.

The elevator seemed especially fast this morning and the hallway to the kitchen shorter than usual. She entered to find only Nell and Joe, both indulging in large omelets. Pretty fruit cups holding chunks of various melons sat at the other two places. In the center of their end of the table, a platter of untouched Danish and cinnamon buns tempted. By the stove were two heated pans gleaming with butter, a bowl of raw scrambled eggs sat alongside with smaller dishes of chopped ham, green pepper, onions, mushrooms, broccoli florets, bacon bits, and grated cheese, fresh salsa also available. She headed right for the coffee pot, pleased to find it full strength and laced with the caffeine she dearly needed. Sarge turned to face Mack's parents, both dressed for a day of relaxation and college football games.

Before she could open her mouth, Nell said, "You're looking much better this morning. Make whatever omelet you want or just scrambled eggs. It's not as fancy as what Corazon would have prepared, but she and Knox went to New Orleans yesterday to babysit the grandchildren and give Xochi and Junior a carefree night out. Knox wasn't too happy about it, but didn't get much say."

"Thank God for that. With all that went on last night, I left the gate open for the limo to leave, got, uh, distracted, and forgot to close it. Knox gives a pretty harsh tongue lashing about sloppy security." Joe dug into his pile of eggs oozing cheese from the sides and topped with bacon.

"We had those two kidnapping attempts on Tom years ago, so his worry is warranted. Though I often think he doesn't need that arsenal he has in the guard house, but just likes to collect guns." Nell finished off the chunk of cantaloupe in her fruit cup.

"Those weapons have come in handy. Junior rescued Xo with some of those, and Trin did use the gun Knox gave him when Josee's ex threatened her." Joe continued eating as if such matters amounted to everyday happenings in the lives of the Billodeauxs.

For a moment, Sarge lost her train of thought. She remembered reading about some of those incidents in the tabloids, but the family rarely revealed the true details.

"If Mack is in the shower, go ahead and make yourself something. We know he can take forever," Nell insisted.

"It's that long hair. Washes and dries it every day." Joe raked his short do with his fingers and dislodged the trademark curl, now iron gray but still sexy, onto his forehead. "Dean and I keep it practical or else we'd have a head of thick curls like he does. A man shouldn't need that much time in the bathroom."

"You've probably noticed Mack is a little vain." Nell sent Sarge a small, almost pleading smile as if begging her to put up with her son's shortcomings.

"Most handsome athletic men are." Thrown for a moment, she recalled running her fingers through that mane as he pleasured her last night. Heat built in her cheeks.

"You seem flushed. Sure you are okay?" Nell asked with motherly concern.

Hating to destroy this interesting conversation, she had to get back on track and make her confession. "I wasn't at my best last night, but I'm fine now. Usually, I can control these episodes, especially if I know what is coming like the fireworks at the Hilton. The sudden explosion undid me. It resembled the way I lost my foot. I'm sorry. If you'd like someone more stable to work with Mack, I'll understand."

"Not at all, you are doing wonders with him in so many ways. He showed true caring toward you last night, and frankly, he's been rather self-centered in the past. I gather these episodes are rare?" Nell had only sympathy in her eyes.

148

"Yes, not often, though I do have nightmares at times, but I can handle those."

"Then think nothing of it." Joe dismissed the problem with a wave of his hand.

"There's more." Her hands went cold. She hugged them around the coffee mug, took a sip for courage. "We, ah, Mack and I engaged in a sexual act last night. My fault. I initiated it. Not intercourse, but bad enough. I wanted the release, and that was unprofessional of me. I don't engage in sex with my patients. I mean I haven't before. Again, if you want to get another trainer, perhaps a man, I won't object."

"I would. It's none of their business what we do in private." Mack loomed in the doorway, so handsome, so pissed off. "Which was nothing until last night. Not for my lack of trying."

"I could promise it won't happen again," Sarge offered tentatively. She didn't want to leave this place or Mack before she must, but certain they'd sack her now. They paid the bills for her services, not their son. She drank more coffee to brace herself.

"Nothing wrong with a little recreational sex as long as it doesn't get in the way of his recovery. That's only my opinion," Joe said, quite serious, with a glance toward his wife.

Nell had a different viewpoint. "I might have anticipated this when I asked you to take our son on for the start of his rehab. You are both adults. I know Mack can handle casual relationships because that is all he does. But what about you, Sarge? Can you keep it recreational? You are together all day with no others of the opposite sex around except for us. This might be only proximity. I don't want him to break your heart as

149

I am sure he has others."

Stunned by their understanding, she could only repeat what she'd said before. "It won't happen again."

"The hell with that. I make no promises." Mack stalked to the coffeepot and poured his brew. "What have we got for breakfast?"

"Make your own omelets. I do mean make your own. Your father and I were up very late, too, and we plan a leisurely day. We'll watch Rex play in LSU's bowl game and see if we can spot Edie in the crowd."

"What do you want in yours, Sarge? I'll take care of it." Mack ladled the egg mixture into both pans and waited for her response.

"Uh, all the veggies, lots of cheese, and some salsa on top."

"You got it." He threw everything available into his except the broccoli florets and folded the omelets over with a deft hand as they cooked. He plated them and delivered breakfast to order. Just like that, the crisis ended, the only thing unsettled being Sarge's conscience.

Chapter Nineteen

Sarge made sure her client engaged in two strenuous workouts a day, always holding the treadmill until the end. She gradually increased the speed and gravity and watched him respond to every demand she asked of him. She wasn't as cooperative to his desires. No, they weren't going to have sex on the mats or in the gym's showers or later in bed. Making sure she wore him out each day helped to keep him in check. Only one of his demands softened her heart a little.

"Can't we cool down by dancing again?" he insisted. "I need to get my moves back. I was clumsy on New Year's Eve."

"Not that I noticed, but not quite as smooth as your dad and X-avier. Are we talking about dance moves, football moves, or sexual moves?" Oh, she fell right into the trap.

With a roguish grin, he answered, "Any or all. Whatever you are up for. Don't you need to practice with your fancy foot some more?"

"My fancy foot, that's an interesting way to describe it. I should, but don't feel like it."

"Hey, I won't let those delinquents ruin something you wanted so badly. Tomorrow, bring it along. By the time we're finished with my rehab, we'll be ready for Dancing with the Stars: quick step, waltz, salsa, what do you call it, a Paso Doble."

"You watch DWTS?" She couldn't keep the disbelief from her voice.

"Oh, hell no. My sisters ate that stuff up. They'd put it on when a perfectly good football game ran on another channel. They were always after Dean and me to try out the dances with them. Like I said, Dean does a wicked salsa."

"What did you specialize in doing?"

"That Paso Doble. The bullfighter theme made it less sissy and more sexy. I'll teach it to you if you bring your fancy foot along tomorrow."

"We aren't ready for advanced ballroom dancing yet, but okay. I'll bring it. We can start with some line dancing. That should be good for your footwork."

"You wouldn't be trying to keep my hands off of you?"

She feigned an innocent expression. "Not at all. We need to start simple."

He didn't let her forget, prompting her to bring the fancy foot at breakfast and loading an iPod with country music. He added a dubious brag over pancakes and sausage. "I've danced in every honky-tonk in Texas, and once I get a few drinks in me, I can go all night and still have something left over for my date of the evening."

His mom shook her head over her cup of decaf. His dad said, "Maybe we could join you. Sounds like fun."

Nell shook her head harder. "I have clients today."

"I thought you had them yesterday?" Joe proved totally clueless to his wife's scheme to let them dance alone, but she'd been very transparent to Sarge.

Mack stood and grasped the cane he rarely needed anymore. "The sooner we get started, the sooner we dance. You sure you brought the right foot?"

"It's in my duffel." She nodded toward the bag slumped by the door.

"Finish your coffee. I'll put that in the golf cart. I'm driving." He cadged the keys from the peg board by the door and went out whistling.

"Well, that certainly boosted his optimism." Joe dumped the decaf in his cup. "The livestock is calling me. A rancher's work is never done."

Hearing a few impatient neighs from the barn, Sarge exited with him. Maybe she'd encourage his parents to drop in and participate. More fun for her and less for Mack. He'd probably forget about it anyway by the end of the day.

No such luck. As she released him from the treadmill late in the afternoon, he reminded her. "Better get your fancy foot on because I'm stoked to start dancing. You know the Electric Slide?"

"Yes, everyone in Texas knows the Slide. The nuns let us do it at school dances because we didn't get close to the guys. The grapevines in it should be a help to you." With no way to escape, she sat and replaced her blade foot, which she'd used to run beside him on an adjacent treadmill, with the normal-looking prosthesis. Both of them were hot and sweaty and probably wouldn't do more than one dance anyhow. She rose and moved into the open area of the gym.

He started the music, "I Like It, I Love It" sung by Tim McGraw. She glared at him. "You chose that song on purpose."

"Sure, I did. It's the best one for doing the Electric Slide, my favorite in fact. Come on, join in. I'll bet you're gonna want more of it. Grapevine right, touch, grapevine left, touch. Scuff and turn toward the wall."

She hadn't done the dance in years but managed to keep up until he threw in an extra turn at the end of a grapevine, and they almost collided. "If you're going to go advanced on me, give me a heads up," she said. "Unless you intended for us to bump together."

"My pleasure, but now you know my trick. Just add in a turn at the end of the grapevine."

She did. It made the dance more fun and said much about his increased agility. As the music petered to an end, she found she'd enjoyed the exercise, but wouldn't admit it.

"What next? The Cowboy Cha Cha, the Double D, Tango with the Sheriff, or best of all, the Tush Push."

"I'm all in for today. Maybe the tango tomorrow." She vaguely recalled that the tango consisted of box steps, slides, and stomps, pretty safe stuff. "Heaven forbid if we attempted the Tush Push at our school. We would have been put into detention."

A naughty smile appeared on his face. "You've got a great tush, firm and rounded. We'll have to give it a try."

"Yours is better than mine. You'll only show me up. I really need a shower before dinner—but you did great. Dancing is very therapeutic." Also sexy if done right in tight jeans instead of sweats or her trainer's uniform. She had to beware.

****

The idea was to get Sarge to drop her guard, lulling her along with safe line dances, then the contact they'd enjoyed before a few days prior to New Years. Eventually, they'd get to dirty dancing and end up on those mats together. Or so he thought.

His training had gotten more intense, requiring more energy. Mack slept deeply without waking—to his disgust. No creeping into Sarge's bed late at night for some extracurricular activities. She kept the adjoining doors shut now, saying she could hear him if he really needed help, but that didn't seem likely. Their time together drained away the more he improved. All he wanted was…well, to show her a good time, to demonstrate how giving he could be in bed when he wanted. That little episode, it amounted to nothing compared to what he knew how to do with a woman.

Eager, he waited until the end of the afternoon training session, tapping the toes of his good leg while she put on the fancy foot. As she stood up ready to go, he heard them approach, for sure his dad who tended to be loud, certainly talking to his mom, but someone else, too. He shot Sarge a glance.

"I thought it would be more fun with a group. While you were putting my duffle into the cart this morning, I invited your parents and Corazon to join us."

Corazon came first through the gym door. "*Si*, I am so excited to dance. I asked *mi esposo*, but Knox, he don't want to come." She still wore her housekeeper's uniform, the one Nell had told her years ago wasn't necessary, minus her usual bright apron.

His parents dressed for the occasion, both of them in jeans and boots and western style shirts, while he stood there in sweats and athletic shoes. They got into a line without being asked. Sarge took a place next to his father with his mom on his dad's other side, then Corazon, and presumably himself.

"Okay, if this is how it's going to be." Mack stood in front of his line dancers. "Y'all probably know the box step painfully learned in middle school. Back, over, down, and close that box." He demonstrated. "We add in a slide-slide, some crossover steps, and back to the box, that's Tango with the Sheriff done to music by the same name."

He cued the song and off they went. He had a fine view of Corazon's broad behind adding a distinct Latin rhythm to the simple dance. Meanwhile, Sarge received the treat of seeing his father's taut butt in worn jeans every time they turned. Nothing he could do about it but finish the song. She'd won this round.

Corazon clapped her hands at the end. "So much fun."

"I think we all enjoyed it," Nell piped up. "What are we going to do tomorrow?"

"Don't know. I guess the Cowboy Cha Cha."

"We'll be here. And, son, don't worry about a career after football. I can see it now, Mack Billodeaux's School of Western Dance." Chuckling, his dad led his little group back to the house.

"Not a bad idea," Sarge claimed as they rode the golf cart. "Women would buy videos of you teaching dance steps in a nice pair of snug jeans. You've got your dad's backside. You should consider it."

A low growl issued from deep in his throat as if he tried to intimidate a rival. "I'll teach them the rest of the dances I know, and then we're going back to the two of us. We need to practice the waltz and the two-step together for the ball."

"What ball, and who says I'm going?" She'd folded her arms across her chest, not a good sign as she did that when she thought he underperformed his exercises.

"I keep forgetting you're from Texas. It's Mardi Gras season here. Starts on January sixth when Epiphany ends. Hell, we're almost at the end of January and haven't been to a single parade or had a slice of King Cake yet. I'd like to take you to New Orleans, but we'll have to settle for the local affair here in town. It's pretty nice. I used to take girls to it before I moved to Dallas and went cowboy. The Community Center is brand new since it burned down the other year, and they couldn't salvage enough to do repairs. You don't have to belong to a krewe or anything as it's sponsored by the town civic organizations. No need for a limo as it isn't far or for my parents to chaperone."

"You'll have to excuse me. My ballgown is in mothballs back in Lubbock."

"Plenty of time to get it out and pressed, but I'd rather buy you a new one to show off your legs. The theme is The Roaring Twenties this year, and the date is the first Tuesday in March. Put it on your calendar because we're going."

"Such a gracious invitation. Maybe…"

"Maybe you'll go with me?" He parked the golf cart in the usual place but didn't get out.

Her gray eyes sought his. Did they seem a little sad? "Mack, by the first week in March, you'll be ready to return to Dallas and begin training with the team's men who specialize in sports rehab. You won't be in my care anymore. So maybe one last dance wouldn't break my promise to your parents or my own professional ethics."

Did she really mean a dance, or could he hope it to be a euphemism for sex? That's certainly what it meant to him. He wouldn't press her anymore on the topic.

"I'll get the tickets."

Chapter Twenty

As if Mack had conjured the holiday season simply by telling her about it, a large King Cake appeared on the breakfast table the next day. The pastry, twisted into a circle and robed in icing topped by garish purple, green, and gold, really yellow, sugar sprinkles screamed calories and a good time. Nell had already sliced it into pieces, several of them missing, to go with their coffee and milk.

"It occurred to me we weren't doing the season justice, so I asked Corazon to drive to Pommier's Bakery and buy a King Cake for us to have this morning. No cooking eggs for her today. She took pieces for herself and Knox back to their cottage. It's hard to believe we used to get three of these at one time to feed the family." Nell appeared to be having one of her wistful moments when she missed the crowded table and the noise and bustle of her children.

"Looks scrumptious." Sarge slid a wedge onto her plate and poured both coffee and milk for herself. Had to get some protein in there some way.

Joe arrived, sexiest rancher alive, freshly shaven, groomed, and ready to go for the day in his usual barn gear. "Good idea to get this. You see, Sarge, the colored sugars represent purple for justice, gold for power, and green for faith."

He helped himself to two portions as Mack stalked

in, obviously still miffed about having to teach group line dancing, but close to his dad's twin only with a dark scruff on his jaw and unkempt black hair barely contained by the leather thong. He wore snug jeans and a tight black tee that showed off his assets. His face brightened when he saw the cake. "You read my thoughts exactly, Mom." He shoveled up a couple of pieces and got his coffee.

"Don't forget your milk," Sarge prompted almost simultaneously with his mother, the difference being that Sarge's words ended with her spitting something into her palm and holding up a tiny plastic baby for all to see. "This was in my piece."

"Aren't you lucky? You got the Baby Jesus, and now you're queen for the day," Nell explained.

"It also means you have to buy the King Cake for next Tuesday," Mack informed her. "How lucky is that?"

So, he's still grumpy, Sarge concluded. "I don't mind at all, just as long as it isn't some kind of fertility charm." She went on to enjoy cake for breakfast, something that did not occur in the farmhouse outside Lubbock. In fact, she went for seconds.

As she finished, she admonished Mack, "Go change into your sweats. That tee and those jeans are too tight for your exercises. We'll have to work extra hard to burn off these calories."

"But they are right for line dancing."

"Bring them along then and change before class." This afternoon, she might situate herself next to him simply for the view.

While he changed, she put on the old Army jacket she'd taken to leaving on a peg by the door against the sunny but brisk day. When Mack appeared in his exercise clothes and reached for the golf cart keys, she batted his hand away. "Today, we start walking to the pool house. You can use the cane if you want."

"Don't need it."

She shouldered her duffle with her dancing and running feet inside and set off. He had a gym bag, presumably stuffed with western wear, but offered to take hers, too.

"No, thanks. I can carry my own gear." She inhaled the fresh morning, watched a flock of robins on the lawn stoking up on worms for their incipient journey north in a few weeks. They'd be gone from the ranch about the same time as herself. She felt a little tug inside to be leaving this haven and, if she were honest, Mack. She doubted if any other man would flirt with her so boldly again because she was brave, tough Sarge, not some fluffy sex kitten. Irritating as it could be, she'd miss it a little.

"Do your warmup exercises, then we'll stretch and go for a mile run. You don't need the antigravity machine anymore."

Mack stowed his bag in one of the cubbies. "I'm going to miss that thing. It made me believe I'd run again like I used to be able."

"You're well on the way, but not there yet."

Clearly eager to get outside again, he rushed through the warmups while she switched to her blade foot. They stretched for safety before she gave the word. "Okay, let's go."

They started out on the curving path through the palm grove. She lagged behind a bit because he'd taken off like a man with something to prove, but she caught up and kept pace with him in a short while. "Don't rush. We aren't racing."

"Not yet we aren't."

As they approached Teddy's house, she told him to veer right down the drive, back toward the house and then the gym. He objected. "How about we go left and take the path around the pastures and follow the bayou road back."

"That's more than twice as long, you shouldn't overdo"

But he was gone, running like an unbridled stallion with his black mane streaking out behind him. Behind the glass doors of Teddy's house, Lizzie and May waved at their passing. The white Charolais bull in the pasture kept pace with them when they went by as if they might be very fast predators after his cows and the first of the spring calves. Rounding the fence line and paralleling a small woods dominated by live oaks and southern magnolias, they soon came to the pony pen where the small horses, shaggy with winter fur grazed largely uninterested in their progress. They flushed a greater egret from the shallows of the water. In its hurry to spread its wide white wings, it dropped the now lucky frog it had in its beak. Sarge started to point that out to Mack, but he ran with a focused determination, not appreciating the beauty of their surroundings.

She sensed he was flagging, too much, too soon, and dropped her pace as if she needed to slow down, not him. They had about a half mile to go, threading through the summer cabins and then back to the path to the pool house at a slow jog to cool off she said. Once back in the gym, she sat to change into her regular shoe, not panting at all while Mack did. He downed a bottle of water as a cover, she suspected.

"You must have an advantage over me using that blade."

"Not much. You saw I was slow to start because I can't dig in with it as a runner can with a normal foot. Once I get going, I do have some advantage because I don't require as much energy to run on it. On the other hand, I need to take small steps in the curves and lose some time. I could have beaten you back here, but there is no need. As I said, we aren't racing, we are building your stamina. Besides, you need to save some energy for our Cowboy Cha Cha today." She added a slightly smug smile to nettle him a bit. Better that than having him depressed.

"Maybe I can do another few miles in the Anti-Gravity this afternoon."

"I'd rather you work on your vertical leap right now." She stacked the square blue cushioned boxes in one corner of the gym two high. "Let's see if you can do it."

"Piece of King Cake." He pushed off, landed on top of the boxes, and sprang down again.

She pulled out another one tier higher. "How about this?"

He did it, but she didn't like his slight wobble on top. "Enough for now. Let's move on to the kettlebell swings between your legs. Give me twenty, then grab the five-pound weights and the same number of lunges. While he sweated, she sat and recorded the new exercises on the laptop. Good progress, and she had enough variations to take up the rest of their training sessions until four o'clock rolled around, announced by the eager voice of Corazon.

"This time I come prepared for the Cowboy Cha Cha." She wore a flared skirt with a large ruffle on the bottom and a peasant blouse that showed a bit too much older woman cleavage, but Sarge would never mention it to her and squash her enthusiasm. No boots, though. She'd come in her thick-soled housekeeper's shoes. Nell and Joe were western perfect again of course.

Mack had gone into the men's locker room a half hour before with his bag and reappeared decked out in his snug jeans and tight tee again, but he'd added cowboy accessories, boots and a western hat worn at a cocky angle. He made her feel absolutely homely in her trainer's outfit, which didn't take much. When he passed close, she realized he'd rinsed off with his favorite bath gel, too.

"Change of plans. We're going to do the Tush Push today."

"No Cha Cha," Corazon said with some disappointment.

"Tomorrow, Cory," he promised, using the shortened form of her name he'd called her as a child to soften the blow. "You'll be great at this."

She smiled and slapped her bottom. "Because I got *mucho* tush to push.

Being Queen for a Day, Sarge took the place with the most advantageous view of Mack's rear. He ran through the heel taps and hops and then the quarter turn followed by two hip bumps right and left and a single rotation of his entire backside before turning back to the original confirmation. "Let's see y'all do it. Mom, you're great at this."

"She sure is," his dad agreed.

"Well, I might have sat in on Miss Starr's dance

class for the Camp Love Letter kids a time or two."

"Corazon, you're getting it—but Sarge, not so much."

"I told you the nuns wouldn't let us do this one, and now I know why."

"You need some help. Here." He clamped his nice wide hands, big enough to cup her hips, on her body. "Bump, bump, now rotate all you've got. Loosen up and let her go."

The others were watching, making her more tense. "I think I've got it now. You can let loose."

"We'll see."

He started the music, a song about everybody wanting it, needing it, and unable to do without it, supposedly love, but somehow, she kept thinking sex. Also, he'd maneuvered himself to be in back of her every time a hip roll came around. Twice, she felt his hands grip her again as he directed, "Give it little more sway." She heard a giggle, possibly from Corazon, as she couldn't imagine Nell doing that until they turned again, and she realized Joe had placed his hands in the same position on his wife's body. At last, the endless song ended.

"That's enough for today. I worked you hard. You'll be stiff, Mack."

"I am already, but I think I'm good for one more round. Everyone else?"

They all agreed as if engaging in a conspiracy to embarrass her. This time, she bumped and gyrated with the best of them and got an accolade from Mack. "Nice view from back here. I knew you had it in you, Sarge." He leaned close enough for her to feel his hot breath on her bare nape. "And don't try to tell me you weren't ogling me earlier." Caught, she knew a blush crept up her neck. Sweet revenge in the form of line dancing.

"That was wonderful," an exhilarated Nell stated. "Since Sarge is our queen today, let's all go over to On the Riverside for dinner tonight. Invite Knox along, too."

"Him, he will not come and leave the ranch unguarded. I will get him a takeout steak and stuffed potato," Corazon said.

"I have to agree line dancing can work up an appetite." Joe grinned like the devil but didn't state what kind of appetite.

"I'll say," his son agreed with the exact same smile.

"I have to shower and change. Why don't you go without me?" Sarge did her best not to extend the day.

"No, no, you are the queen. We cannot go without the queen." Corazon's statement sounded more like a plea for an evening out.

"Okay, y'all go ahead, and I'll be along as soon as I can."

Mack gave her a suspicious stare. "If you aren't there, I'm coming back for you."

"I'll be there."

At last, she got them to move toward the house and loaded into the SUV. No escape from this either. A brief shower with no more than soap and water, a change into wide-legged jeans and a flattering top since no one else was dressed up got her on her way. She put on athletic shoes again and left her dancing foot in the closet. One good thing about the delay, she could leave in her Jeep if the rest decided to linger.

At On the Riverside, their group had already

claimed a bayou view table in the rustic restaurant. With Lent still three weeks away, the air held the scent of sizzling steaks, but the chosen appetizer already ordered was a tray of a dozen roasted oysters swimming in their shells full of butter and topped with parsley and bacon bits. Each place offered glasses of water and iced tea to which Joe had added a beer. Sarge marveled that Mack hadn't done the same as he'd cut way back on his meds.

He checked his watch as she approached. "With five minutes to spare."

"I hope you didn't wait for me to order."

"We did, but have these beauties to tide us over." Joe pushed the oyster tray her way. Four were missing. "You as queen get the extras."

"Two will do. Corazon, Nell, I order you to eat the others." She tried for an imperial voice, but it drew a laugh.

"No, you need to do it the military way. Open those slack-jawed mouths and finish this appetizer or give me ten pushups," Mack mocked her. He did a fairly good Sarge imitation after all these months. More laughter, but she joined in this time.

Though Corazon ordered that steak for her husband, the rest got seafood, her own order being Junior's Best Crab Cakes touted as rich and creamy and full of lump crab meat. They were. With the huge stuffed potato mingled with cheese, bacon, chives, and sour cream, she had more than enough to eat before Joe ordered the To Die For White Chocolate Bread Pudding with five spoons.

As she ate her share, Junior Polk joined them. "That dessert is on me. Wish you'd called and told me you were coming, Mama." He kissed his mother's cheek.

"You are busy since football ends."

"Always got time for you."

Joe clapped his son-in-law on the back. "The Sinners were robbed in that last playoff game. They should be playing the Pats this weekend. Anyone could see Jock in the end zone reaching up for that last pass, and he gets hit in the side. That blind ref calls it an incomplete pass on fourth down, game over. Hell, that was pass interference big time." Joe's indignant voice had gotten louder and louder, but far from bothering the rest of the customers, cheers sounded along with "You tell 'em, Joe."

"I did. I was there."

"How about coffee," Junior offered. "That bread pudding can be a little sweet."

"But wonderful," Sarge admitted. Lulled by excellent food, she had little desire to leave. As she spoke, the February dusk lowered, and the railings and eaves of the restaurant suddenly glowed with Christmas lights of various colors and sizes. Across the road beside the river, an old pavilion glowed to life with the same scattered along the boughs of two ancient oaks that appeared to be holding the dilapidated structure together with their mighty branches creating a leafy canopy over the sagging wooden floor. Indeed, one had grown into a support pillar. "That's beautiful, too."

"I keep meaning to fix it up for our customers to enjoy but haven't gotten to it yet."

Mack, who hadn't joined into the conversation about the Sinners losing in the playoffs, probably pleased since the Cowboys hadn't won either, studied the site. "That's a place where we need to go dancing."

"I don't think it's large enough for line dancing," Sarge countered.

"Did I say line dancing?"

Oh, no, another challenge to be avoided.

"My mom tells me you are teaching them all some moves, Mack. She says you have snake hips." Junior offered them his wide, toothy grin.

"The snakiest, right, Sarge?"

"I have to agree. You can out snake most snakes." She feigned a huge yawn. "I need to get going. We have lots more work to get Mack up to playoff levels again."

She stood. They all stood, making her feel like a party-pooper.

"You're coming to the house for the Super Bowl on Sunday, right, Junior?" Joe said as they departed.

"I'm bringing the chili, both hot and mild for the kids."

Mack tailed her down the ramp to the parking area. Again, he got very close, whispering," I'm bringing the heat just for you."

Chapter Twenty-One

Mack kept his word, exhausting his store of line dances, though Sarge got closer and closer to electric sliding out of his life. He added the Duck Dynasty, Slap Leather, the Watermelon Crawl, and the Sleazy Slide to his repertoire. Some of them he had to look up on the computer and practice in secret, but he didn't let his small group of enthusiastic dancers down. They always wanted to end with the Tush Push, all except Sarge. Finally, he told them he was done and had to concentrate on his rehab.

As for Sarge, she pushed his vertical leap exercises and extended their runs. The short Louisiana winter ended. Redbuds bloomed at the edge of the woods on the far side of the cow pasture, a blur of purple as he ran past them. The robins left town for places farther north, abandoning the ranch as Sarge would soon do, leaving him on his own.

Recently, she'd strapped him into a parachute device and made him race as air filled the canopy causing drag. She timed his dashes, measured his leaps, recorded the growth of his calf muscles, and photographed his best efforts. Lent loomed two weeks off. After that he'd be without her like giving up a dessert he craved.

She also kept her word and practiced the waltz, both Cajun and Viennese, the Two Step, any others he could think of to hold her close. Hey, she didn't pull away. They'd be totally ready for the Mardi Gras Ball, Chapelle style. His dad had beaten him to the ticket counter and purchased a table for eight: his parents, again, Junior and Xochi, Teddy and Jessie, and of course, Sarge and himself. But they'd drive alone in his Jaguar.

At the Super Bowl party, another mass gathering of Billodeauxs, he'd laid further plans she wouldn't be able to refuse. Sidling up to the family fashionistas, Josee and Stacy, he announced he wanted to take Sarge to the Mardi Gras Ball as a reward for all her hard work. Josee immediately offered to get him last minute tickets to the lavish Rex affair in New Orleans.

"No, we want to keep it local. Dad already has a table for us homebodies." He noted their exchanged glances at calling himself a homebody. Maybe he'd overdone it. "But I don't think she has a ball gown. You know how catty women can be if a person shows up in the wrong thing."

Josee nodded, but Stacy said, "Not in Chapelle. You can wear any old dress, and no one will care."

"I want her to look great, so I'll pay for the gown, but I don't know where or how to go about it."

"We could take her to the city, or I could loan one from a designer," Josee suggested.

"Actually, we have a place in town that specializes in pageant dresses, wedding gowns, ball gowns. It's called Belles, Beaux, and Brides. Don't raise your eyebrows at me, Josee. The new owners, Regan and Rachel, were both local beauty queens who used to work there and bought out the shop. They also provide hair and makeup for whatever big day." From Stacy's expression, she'd already decided to root for the home team.

"That might be best," Mack conceded. "I think you'd have to hogtie Sarge and put her in the trunk of your car to get her to New Orleans. Every time I suggest we do something fun, not that dress shopping would be on my list, she says she's here to train me and nothing else."

The two Billodeaux blondes were doing that glance thing at each other again as if they knew something he couldn't figure out. "Well, your suggestions might not be to her taste, like drunk line dancing." Josee reminded him of their single disastrous date together.

"If we can get her for half a day, I think Regan and Rachel will turn her out splendidly. If I'm wrong, we'll take her or her measurements to the city. I'll stay over tomorrow and let Dean take the kids home if you'll give me a lift back to the Garden District when we're finished with Sarge."

"Done."

Mack half expected them to do a high five to settle the issue. "She's right over there talking to Jessie. See if you can get her to give me tomorrow afternoon off. If not, guess I can fake a muscle pull on the morning run. Have what's their names send me the bill for the works, hair, makeup, everything."

Again, those raised eyebrows, but the women moved toward where Sarge sat eating the hot chili with a topping of grated cheese and onions as if she wanted to ward him off. Ha! He'd eaten the same thing and wouldn't notice if he got a kiss out of her.

Xochi, where was she in the crowd? Of course, in the kitchen spooning the mild chili into KC and doling out more corn chips to Pilar. He took a seat by her side, moved away her own half-eaten bowl with no toppings and a glass of milk to give him some table room.

"Say, Xo, how's it going?"

"Very messy, I'd say. KC can't get enough of his daddy's chili even if he's wearing half of it."

KC now walked, ran, and tumbled, but wasn't very verbal yet, a great big kid for his age. Nothing Xochi liked more than a compliment about her children. "He'll be playing cornerback in no time—or maybe he'll be a chef or both like Junior.

His adopted sister gave him her glowing Mexican Madonna smile and took a sip of milk. "Did you want another treatment for your leg? I know you don't believe, but I am willing to help you any way I can."

"Maybe I believe a little, but no. Sarge has taken good care of me. Say, what do you think of Sarge?

"Very competent, very courageous."

"Sure, but what do you see when you stare at her the way you do."

"Her aura? My woo-woo stuff as you call it." KC opened his mouth like a baby condor and tried to steer the spoon his way.

"Yeah, what do you see. What color is she?"

Xochi laughed, so rich and full, people always wanted to laugh with her. "Why green, naturally. She's a healer like me."

"And me?"

"Still ambitious orange, but…" she cocked her head and studied him. "You've mellowed some, not so many flares and spikes. You've gentled."

"That's not good for a football player."

"It won't affect your playing. I believe this is a

good thing for you, Mack."

"Mom calls it growing up. So are green and orange auras compatible?"

"More chips, Mama, please," Pilar interrupted, making him wait for an answer.

"You've had enough chips. Try dunking your baby carrots and celery into your chili and see how delicious it makes them. Remember, no football cake if you don't eat your veggies."

The cake shaped like a football was rumored to be chocolate inside its carefully crafted brown icing with white lacings. Mack planned to get a hunk for himself as soon as his mom cut it. Afterall, he'd eaten his veggies along with his chili.

Pilar didn't look as if she was buying the suggestion, but she gave it a try.

"About compatible auras…"

"Oh, it's not like Zodiac signs. Any colors can attract, but I do think you are getting to her. I see little glints of orange in hers, and I'm not sure if that's good or bad. You have a sort of halo of green around yours."

"I hope that doesn't make me an angel. Also not good for playing football. Would you like me to keep stoking the little man here while you have a chance to eat?"

Gratefully, Xo turned over the spoon. "Maybe you *are* becoming angelic." She picked up her own bowl which had no toppings.

Pilar scattered a handful of corn chips on it. "You need chips. I need *more* chips."

"Thank you, honeybee. You may have a few more since you ate your vegetables." Xochi pressed two fingertips to her lips to suppress a burp.

"Yeah, Junior's hot chili does that to people." KC accepted another mouthful of the presumably mild version from the spoon Mack held.

"This is the mild." Xo drank more milk, reminding him of how his mom and Sarge were always plying him with that beverage. He'd have a beer today, just one, during the game. A thought occurred, one he wouldn't have made before his ego started shrinking as his injury healed. "Xo, are you pregnant again?"

"Hush, hush. Little pitchers, big ears." She canted her head toward Pilar who immediately asked, "What's per-gant?"

"A big word for a nice surprise you'll get this summer. It's a secret only we know."

"And Uncle Mack?"

"Yes." She turned back to her brother. "I haven't told anyone yet. KC was such a demanding feeder, I had to give up nursing and start him on solids. Stuff happens when a woman stops nursing."

"Yes, it does. Ask my parents who tried to practice rhythm." Sarge stood in the kitchen doorway with a bemused smile on her face. Her gray eyes seemed softer as she tracked the trajectory of another spoonful of chili from Mack's hand to KC's mouth. "I won't tell."

Thankful his trainer hadn't gotten there any sooner in the conversation, Mack said, "Ah, Sarge. Were you looking for me?"

"Yes. It appears if I don't give you tomorrow afternoon off in order for Stacy and Josee to take me shopping for a ball gown locally, they will kidnap me and drag me to New Orleans, and we'll lose more than a day of training. I was forced to agree, but I will get something practical that I can wear again and pay for it myself."

"If that's what you want. I'll do my vertical leap exercises on my own and get Dad to toss me a few balls. Gotta get my grip back." He hoped she'd swallow that exactly as she had Junior's chili.

Chapter Twenty-Two

Escorted by two tall blondes dressed in high-heeled boots and stylishly ripped jeans topped by silk blouses, each with a friendly arm entwined with one of hers—as if she'd try to make an escape—Sarge entered Belles, Beaux, and Brides. Even the name of the place made her cringe. Both Josee and Stacy had gym fit bodies, but she knew she could easily break their benign hold, take both of them down with a sweep kick, and march the five miles back to the ranch with no sweat as she carried only a credit card and her driver's license in the pocket of her wide-legged, untorn jeans. Why buy jeans that already had holes in them, anyhow?

Soft music and fragrant air wafted out when they opened the door as if they were entering an expensive spa, not that she ever had. Instantly, a woman who had former beauty queen written all over her from her blonde chignon and beautifully applied eye makeup to high heels that took practice to strut in appeared to offer her assistance. "Hello, I'm Regan, one of the owners. How may I help you?"

She let her companions take the lead on this. "We're seeking a gown for the Mardi Gras Ball here in Chapelle in a couple of weeks. I know it's rather short notice," Josee said. "We might have to go to New Orleans."

"Not at all. Here at Belles, we pride ourselves on

having exactly what everyone needs to meet their greatest potential as a bride, contest competitor, or Mardi Gras ball queen. I'll admit our stock is somewhat picked over for the dance right now, but I'm sure I can fit either of you. You have the bodies of models." Her perfectly manicured fingers tipped in pearl pink matching her lipstick gestured to the clothing racks.

"Oh, not for us. For Sarge." Stacy turned and gripped her arm before she made it out the door.

"Ah well, you are also very fit, Miss Sarge, compact, not an ounce of fat on you."

The owner might as well have said, small-busted and not much of a waistline, as compared to her own bountiful breasts and slim middle. Behind their group, an equally beautiful woman, her brunette opposite with black hair cascading down her back, bagged a red ruffled pageant dress for a proud mother. "I know Aimee will win Little Miss Pepper in this outfit. We'll be cheering her on from the audience." The happy customer left, and the brunette turned her attention to them.

"Did you say Sarge? When Brooke DeVille came in to pick up her Mardi Gras gown, she mentioned a Sarge, gorgeous Mack Billodeaux's trainer."

An unexpected competitive rush surged through Sarge. She stepped to the front as if on review, spine ramrod stiff, no smile on her face. "What is Mrs. DeVille wearing?"

"Oh, green satin, full-length, rather revealing bodice but not tacky. We don't do tasteless here at Belles. I'm sure she'll convince her husband to buy her emeralds to match. It won't do for you however."

"Of course not." She should have known better

than to think of challenging Mack's ex.

"Like everyone else, she wanted a traditional gown. No imagination and not much fun. She wouldn't have made it on the contest circuit where you have to smile, smile, smile. When we heard the theme was to be the Roaring Twenties, we ordered dozens of flapper style dresses. Some of the court who didn't want to sew their own costumes or have them made bought theirs here. We have a few left over that might be ideal for you. Regan, why don't you watch the front. I've got this."

"Terrific, let's get a dressing room, and you can try them on," Stacy said with great enthusiasm.

Terrific, wasn't its word origin terrifying? Sarge kept her shoulders back and head high as she did a sort of death march toward a curtained room bedecked with mirrors designed to show every angle of a person's body. At least, she possessed no flab, and Mack seemed to find her hips alluring, though heaven knew why.

"Up, up on the platform. Take off your clothes, all but the bra and panties." Seeing Sarge hesitate, she added, "We can give you some privacy. I'm Rachel, by the way, the co-owner of our boutique."

"No, it's okay. I've stripped down in front of women before." Her many sisters, her fellow female soldiers. If only she hadn't worn a sports bra and cotton granny panties.

"Yes, I can tell you're an athlete. Your body type is perfect for the Twenties, not big at the top, toned arms. Those flappers got rid of long sleeves and skirts. Your hair is exactly right, a boy cut, and such a beautiful pale blonde, natural, I'll bet." Dropping her voice, Rachel whispered, "Not dyed like Regan's. And your eyes, a true gray, most aren't. All you need is the proper makeup to bring them out. Don't you think so, ladies?"

"Absolutely," Josee agreed.

Sarge dropped her baggy jeans. She noticed the moment that Rachel spied her prosthesis. Her companions had insisted she wear her fancy foot and dancing shoes. As artificial limbs went, it looked real from a distance, but not this close.

She gave the woman credit for not ignoring the issue. "Yes, I'd heard you had only one leg."

"One foot," Josee corrected. "But she dances really well despite that, I'm told." Nice to have someone on her side.

"No problem. I enjoy a challenge. My sister's body is so out of proportion, yet I've done wonders with her. Those shoes won't do."

"Nothing too high, please." She hated to plead.

"We also stocked Cuban heels, all the rage back then, easy to dance in, and still stylish today. Your size?"

Sarge told her, wincing a little. She didn't have dainty feet because she'd hiked too many miles in them. Rachel made no comment, only swirled from the room and returned with a couple of shoe boxes tucked under one arm and several dresses draped over another.

"I brought the gold, but I think it's too bright for your hair. Now this pink outfit…"

She held up her hands to ward it off. "No pink."

"Oh, try it on. You never know," Stacy recommended.

And so, she allowed it. The dropped waist, sleeveless dress slid easily over her head. It ended in layers of flounces. Fine, the color flattered her pale skin, but all those ruffles, no. She shook her head. "Take it off."

"I think this is the one. Glamorous silver. I brought shoes to match."

Sarge closed her eyes as the gown fell into place. Another disaster for sure. But no, she could tell by looking at Josee and Stacy that this dress worked. Finally, she peered into the multiple mirrors. This one, also with a dropped waist, had narrow straps that held it up but also cut out sleeves that formed silver crescents on her upper arms and dripped argent fringe down to her elbows. The skirt ended above her knees but sent a of shower of long fringed layers well below her knees. As she moved her fancy foot, it peeked in and out of this camouflage. Now you see it, now you don't.

"Perfect." Josee, whose opinion really meant something, breathed.

Rachel beamed. "Thank you. That means a lot to me. I do know who you are, the famous model Josee Riley, but I didn't want to gush all over you. You probably get that a lot."

"More so in the city even though I've retired from modeling."

"Yes, now you're an entrepreneur like me and Regan. I so admire you."

"Ah, we need to try the shoes and decide on what to do with her hair," Stacy interrupted.

"Her hair is fine for this theme, but yes, hmmm, a tiara?" Sarge's shaking head cued her. "Not a tiara—a browband. Be back in a jiffy."

Sarge balanced against Josee as Stacy took a pair of sparkling slippers from a box and put them on her feet. They looked wonderful but felt tight and uncomfortable. "Wouldn't my black ones do just as well?"

"Sometimes, you have to suffer for beauty. If they aren't killing you, wear them when you practice dancing with Mack. Get them broken in well before the ball. Besides, they glitter when you walk."

Rachel reappeared with a brow band sporting a white plume. It also glittered with tiny rhinestones embedded in the silvery band. She brushed Sarge's sweep of pale hair aside and placed the band over her forehead. "Wonderful if I do say so myself."

"I'm not so sure about the feather"

"Then you can take it off. It fits here in this holder and slides out if you don't want to use it, but many of the women who bought their flapper dresses here will be wearing plumes. People will think you are part of the court."

"Is that good? I don't want to intrude on their party." She didn't want to stand out in any way and have people staring at her from the foot up trying to see where her prosthesis ended and her skin began even though the makers had gotten the colors very close.

"No one will mind, especially after a few drinks. You and Mack will be stunning together." A wistful sigh crossed her vermilion-painted lips. "I'm a few years older than he is and was out of high school before he started playing football at Ste. Jeanne's. Busy with my pageants, too. The blue-eyed blondes like Regan always seemed to win first place, but I did take my share of trophies. We had a friendly rivalry, and now we're successful business partners."

Did she need to know Rachel's regrets and successes when what the woman really wanted was—

"If you are going to the ball, I'll introduce you." Out of the corner of her eye, she caught Stacy subtly shaking her head, but no harm done, she believed. "What is all this going to cost, dress, shoes, browband…?" Perhaps an introduction to Mack might rate a discount.

"Add in makeup on the day of," Stacy added.

"Pedicure, manicure?"

Desperate, Sarge nixed that. "No one will see my foot, and I can do my own nails." Such as they were, always clipped short.

"Evening bag, earrings?"

"I can loan you those items," Josee offered. "What's the total?"

"Five-hundred-fifty." Sarge knew she must have blanched because Rachel hastily added, "The long gowns are much more expensive."

She had to repeat to herself that the Billodeauxs paid her well plus her room and board. She'd put away a nice amount despite the Christmas gifts. But her disability had expenses, and she wanted a nice cushion built up for replacement prostheses. Oh well, she nodded her assent.

Stacy said, "I'll take care of the billing while you get dressed. "See, it didn't take long and wasn't that painful."

Not as painful as having a foot blown off, but it did cost her. Getting back into her clothes took no time at all, but Stace had everything settled by the time she arrived at the checkout desk.

"They'll hold the dress and brow band here until you come in for your makeup. You can pay then."

Probably thought she didn't have the money and would have to shift funds around. Fine, a couple of weeks more to collect interest on her savings. Feeling like an insecure teen, she felt compelled to ask, "Will one of you be here for that?"

Josee gave her an understanding smile. "No, we'll be at the Rex Ball, but don't worry. I'm going to write down exactly what Rachel should do for you. Make certain you get pictures. I have to see the finished product."

"I know they will do as well as anyone in New Orleans," Stacy said with utmost confidence. "Here, take the shoes and start wearing them today."

She'd never been more glad to have something over with, not when hiking ten miles in the rain, not when doing painful rehab on the parallel bars, as she was to get out of that perfumed and pretty place.

Chapter Twenty-Three

Mack watched for the return of the shoppers as he and his dad tossed the football back and forth in an easy rhythm that recalled his happiest memories of having Joe all to himself after Dean and Tom left for college. Trin had no interest in playing the game, and T-Rex was still tee-tiny. Sometimes, they included Teddy in his chair, but Ted preferred reading and writing in his free time. His father accepted his decision to be a wide receiver, not a quarterback, with only the slightest regret, seeming more upset that he'd signed on with 'Bama rather than LSU, making the family choose which games to watch or attend. That hadn't squelched Joe's attention to his training.

Today, the balls came neither high nor low, no airy leaps or low-down dirty passes like Dean had thrown for Jock at his tryout, he'd heard. They did a series of one-handed passes, first to the right hand, then the left. He'd dropped a few of those which was to be expected, but his muscle memory returned stronger with every catch.

Beautiful day here on the grassy area by the barn, soaking in some early spring sunshine, and awaiting the return of his possibly furious date to the ball. A strange contentment filled him, springing up from who knew where like the clumps of his mother's early paper white narcissus planted near the house, gone all winter and now tall and full of scent. This place he'd pushed so hard to leave was home in the best sort of way, nothing like the bleak place Sarge sometimes described.

They ceased for a moment when Josee's white Lexus came down the drive, both of them waving. Sarge slumped in the backseat, and when she emerged, carried only a shoebox, not the fancy garment bag he'd expected. What had gone wrong? He glanced at Stacy who was supposed to take care of the bill. When Sarge stomped inside, Stace gave him an okay sign before following her.

"How about a water break?" he suggested to his dad. Not that they'd been working terribly hard, but he wanted to hear about the shopping spree in a most unmasculine sort of way.

"Sure. Maybe your mom has some good snacks around."

"Not likely, but I'm sure there is fruit." They shared a laugh knowing that to be all too true of something Nell would say.

Entering the kitchen, they found only Josee and Stacy, no Sarge. "Did it go that bad?" Mack asked.

"Not at all. Sarge knows what she does and doesn't like. I think I've seldom accomplished a shopping trip in such a short period of time." Josee sipped on a sugar-free Sprite, and Stacy a Coke Zero. "We'll be heading to New Orleans shortly. My beloved will forget to eat dinner if I'm not there to prompt him and drag him away from game development."

"No problem of that with Dean, but he'll order something like chicken wings with celery as a vegetable for the kids if I'm not around. Then, I'll have the mess to clean up. Let me get my bag, and we'll be on our way." Stacy rose to leave.

"But she did get a dress for the ball, and she will look great, right?" Mack took a bottle of water from the fridge and tossed it to his father.

"Oh, yes, but maybe not what you expected. We went along with the theme of the ball. She'll be the most spectacular flapper there. I almost wish I could be around to see her, rather than go to Rex. You need to stop by Belles and pay the bill. Watch out for Rachel and Regan. They are both on the prowl." Josee also prepared for the long journey to New Orleans by finishing her drink and fishing out her keys.

"How much?"

"Five-hundred-fifty, and it includes her makeup on the day of."

"I'll chip in," his dad offered.

"No, it's my gift to Sarge for all she's done for me. I can still afford it. My contract doesn't run out until August, and then I'll get a renewal or go free agent." He spoke with a confidence he didn't have quite yet. Once he trained with the team, he'd know for sure.

Sarge reappeared. "Are we dancing today or not?"

His eyes took in her footwear. "You're very sparkly today."

That didn't please her. "I have to break in these toe pinchers before the ball. Let's get to it." She preceded him out the door.

He turned back to say a quick thanks to the ladies for their help, then sprinted after his trainer, catching up easily. She wasn't walking as fast as usual in those new shoes. As they entered the gym, he said, "Maybe we should warm up with the Tush Push," simply to prick at her a bit. He'd done a good thing, and here she stood exuding irritation like a volcano about to spew red hot lava all over him.

"Let's just get on with it, the two step and the waltz, though the Charleston or the Lindy Hop might be more fitting for the theme of the ball."

"You'd be cute doing the Charleston."

"And you'd hurt yourself trying to lift me over your shoulders for a Lindy Hop."

"Would not. We'll have to see."

"I don't want to set your training back weeks. Let's do our usual stuff."

Since he liked the two step the best because he could hold her in the promenade and twirl her out and hard back against him, he cued up the music for that. They had it down pat, the waltz, too. Usually, she loosened up as they danced, but today she remained tense in his arms. When they took a break, he asked, "Do those shoes hurt that much? When we were walking here, I thought you looked like Dorothy in the *Wizard of Oz* with her ruby slippers, only yours are silver. Still, if they pinch, wear your black ones. I don't care."

"In the book, Dorothy's slippers are silver. Didn't you read it as a kid? Red showed up better on the big screen. Anyhow, these need breaking in. That's all."

"Ah, no, not my kind of reading. Interesting factoid though. Not happy with your dress? You still have time to get a different one, but Josee and Stacy said you looked gorgeous. That is high praise coming from them."

She didn't fall back on modesty. "I do look great. It's simply that I went to buy a reasonably priced gown that I could use again and ended up with an expensive costume I'll have no use for unless I go to a Halloween party, kind of like a wedding dress that hangs in the closet turning yellow year after year. It's a ridiculous purchase, and I hate being foolish."

"I don't think you've ever been foolish. Might do you some good. You're stiff as cardboard today. I've been foolish lots of times. You can survive it. Once, Lorena badgered me into dancing the Paso Doble with her at a DWTS fund raiser for the Day School. You should have seen me in my tight pants and patent leather shoes making like a matador or a flamenco dancer." He struck a pose, arms entwined above his head, and stamped his foot a few times.

"I had a red shirt open to my navel, hardly any chest hair at seventeen, and my sister who is supposed to be my cape throwing herself all over me and collapsing on the floor at my feet at the end. I thought I had the arrogant attitude done to perfection."

"You lost and were teased about it for years," she guessed.

"Hell, no. We won a big frickin' trophy and had to do it a second time. The trouble was my performance got back to the football team—and I was teased about it for the next two years. I told them dancing contributed to my great footwork so I could hold up my head in the locker room, but a few of the guys wanted me to teach them on the sly."

He had her smiling now. "Did you?"

"Nope, I told them it was my training secret, not to be shared."

"But you are sharing with me."

"I'm more mature now." He took his time unbuttoning the chambray shirt he'd worn with his jeans right down to the belt buckle and spread it open. "Got lots of chest hair now, which I'd wax for you and you only."

"Don't expect me to make the same offer."

His grin spread across his face with devilish glee. "I like your fluff." He stared at her crotch, then at her shoes. "I should call you Sparkly."

"Sarge, I will only ever be Sarge. That's part of the problem with all this. I feel as if I have to change in order to be seen with you, buy dresses I can't afford, slather on makeup, or people will wonder why you are going out with a one-footed woman."

"A one-footed wonder. You amaze and inspire me every day. I wanted to give you a special evening, but if getting dressed up bothers you, we can go in jeans as far as I'm concerned. I won't wear any makeup either."

"Oh, you are incorrigible." She pushed against his exposed, hairy chest.

That quick, he moved his arms around her and pressed her close, walked her backward toward those always handy gym mats, and lowered her down beside him—at last. His lips took hers. His tongue gained access. His hand roved between her legs. She answered him with the same moves, not resisting, participating, opening for him, fighting his buckle, and delving into his briefs with her competent hands, stroking. She wore only a soft sports bra under her top, easily raised for access to her perfect, Sarge-sized breasts that tasted as good as they felt. He pulled her hands away and up over her head, or he wouldn't be able to hold out. When had he waited so long for a woman? Not ever. They came to him, all but Sarge, trainer, friend, and soon to be lover.

She turned her head aside to get the words out.

"We can't go all the way now, Mack. I promised your parents. Two weeks, only wait the two weeks when my contract is up."

Damn a woman who kept her word. All the others lied to get what they wanted, at least the ones he'd dated. They loved football, weren't interested in his money, right, and were always on the pill, which he didn't believe considering what had happened to his dad and Dean. Why did he have to fall for a woman with integrity?

Taking a deep breath, he released her wrists and removed his body from hers. It hurt as much as ripping flesh. With his head in his hands, he felt her arm come around him. "Two more weeks. It won't be long," she whispered.

Maybe not for her because she didn't love him the way he did her. Yes, he finally admitted to it mentally, but did not say the words, fearful of rejection. He had two more weeks to postpone a declaration.

Chapter Twenty-Four

Mama Nell jollied Sarge out of her mood. "While I am sure Mack meant what he said about going in jeans, I for one want to see you in that fabulous dress. In fact, I called Belles, and Xo, Jessie, and I are going to have our makeup done in a group with you that afternoon. I'm looking forward to the fun."

While Sarge suspected a plot to make sure she kept her appointment, she'd do anything to please Nell who had been so kind during her stay. What was slapping on a little paint anyhow to make someone you loved happy, the opposite of what she'd told Mack. Perhaps because Nell didn't expect her to change because of one special occasion.

She treasured this quiet moment with a mother so unlike her own. Joe, as usual, had gone about his barn chores. Corazon cleaned up the kitchen and left for grocery shopping. Mack had not come downstairs yet, bringing along his energy and attitude to fill the kitchen. The two women shared a second cup of coffee and broke a cinnamon bun in half. She wished she could come clean about all she felt for Mack, trouble that he was, but buried that away somewhere deep in her soul.

Yet, Nell unearthed it. "When I asked you to be my son's trainer, I wanted to present him with a different kind of woman from those he pursued, one with strength and character. I know I hoped you might fall in love as Joe and I did. I wasn't exactly his tall, busty blonde type."

"Patients fall in love with their nurses, not their PT trainers. We dole out pain to make them well. Besides that, he hasn't had access to other women. He'll revert to his type when he's back in the world again." There was no fooling Nell, however.

"I believe you have come to care for our son, and he returns that emotion. I am sure you have only fuzzy memories of his reaction after that kid threw the cherry bomb, the concern on his face, his insistence on staying with you through the night."

"I remember." She did, all too well, the gesture that showed Mack could be a giver and not always a taker. Not something she wanted to share with Nell, and grateful the man they discussed entered the room and groused about the coffee pot being empty.

He eyed the platter empty of cinnamon rolls and the dish of scrambled eggs and bacon ready to nuke back into tastiness. "How's a guy supposed to carbo-load on this?"

While Corazon might have rushed to make him something else, these two women did not. "There's more cinnamon rolls in the freezer," his mom said.

"Whole wheat toast is better for you," Sarge added. "Why don't you make more coffee while you're up?"

"I must be fully healed. No one is waiting on me hand and foot anymore."

"As it should be. Only a couple of days, and I'll sign off on your training and turn you over to the sports rehab guys in Dallas." Sarge popped the last of her bun into her mouth.

He put his plate into the microwave and punched the buttons. "A lot can happen in two days."

She let that enigmatic statement pass.

"I'll be ready for our run fueled only by orange juice soon. Let's not overdo it. I want to spend some extra time on our Charleston today."

"Yes, I heard…" Nell began before she intercepted his sign for silence easily noticed by Sarge.

"What, you aren't going to tell me?"

"You need some surprises in your life, Sarge." Self-satisfied, he downed his juice and devoured his eggs and bacon.

"I told you no lindy hops."

He'd switched directions in their dance workouts again, showing up with music and instructions for the Charleston. An easy dance, they caught on fast and added speed to their steps. She had to admit, they looked great in the gym mirror and imagined herself in that silver dress, fringe flying, next to that darkly handsome man with an amazing grin on his face. Nope, they wouldn't be going in jeans.

"No lindy hops, I promise."

****

One day before the ball and at first nothing special about it. They went for their run, shorter than usual, and returned to the gym where Sarge took his measurements again and put them on her laptop. She ordered him to do his basic exercises while she tapped away on her keyboard. With a final flick of her finger, she sent her report to Mack's athletic trainers in Dallas, telling them she could do no more for him and to expect his return to that city for specific physical guidance. She'd included a note saying he was highly motivated to return to football and play for the team again. There, contract fulfilled.

Her gaze wandered to where he did his vertical leaps onto the padded boxes. Astounding. She knew she couldn't achieve that height and most likely shouldn't try. After a minute of covert admiration, all she allowed herself, she called him to her side. "We are finished training."

"Great, more time to dance."

"No, I mean I've cleared you for transfer to the sports facility. I've completed my contract." A small pang of sadness squeezed her heart, but his grin spread across his face like a flag of victory.

"Even better. Now I really feel like dancing."

"After the ball, I'll be leaving, maybe visit my family until I decide on another job."

As if recalling a former strategy, he glanced at the gym mats. She intercepted his play. "No, I am not having sex on the mats with you."

"But you aren't working for my parents anymore. The spell is broken, Sleeping Beauty."

"Do I look like I'm sleeping? Besides, she required a kiss to wake her, not a report on your athletic prowess."

"Is that all?" He didn't need encouragement or an invitation to wrap his arms around her and draw her in for a prolonged exchange of tongues and burning lips. She let herself respond with a passion usually kept tamped down, permitted herself the pleasure of raking her fingers through his long hair, and pressing against his ripped body as hard as she wanted. If only this could last forever and not fade as he went out into a world full of beautiful women.

"To the bedroom," he said.

"In the middle of the day with your parents and Knox roving around. I don't think so."

"Put your hand in my pants pocket."

"I'm not falling for that. I already know you want me."

"No, the rear hip pocket."

Still doubting what she'd find there, she drew out a key with a #2 tab on the ring. What had she expected, an engagement ring? "And this is for?"

"Our own private cabin right here on the grounds. My folks always keep one ready with fresh sheets in case someone needs to stay over for any reason. The Polks have the first cottage, but Corazon is usually at the big house, and Knox is outdoors most of the day."

He'd given this some thought, she could tell. Before she was able to conjure up an excuse, he put his hand at the small of her back and guided her out the door and down the path to where the Camp Love Letter cabins stood. After a quick glance around, he opened the door and flipped the light switch to illuminate a dark interior with all the shades drawn.

On the small kitchen table, a sprig of hot pink azalea blossoms poked out of the top of an amber beer bottle. Two glasses from the cupboard framed a bottle of champagne in a makeshift ice bucket made from a bowl holding mostly cold water by now. Through the open door to the bedroom, the blankets were turned down over a plaid spread on the queen-sized bed. Someone had been very busy before breakfast, and it hadn't been her.

"Sorry, best I could do with what I had to work with here. The ranch doesn't supply flutes or vases."

"Yet, you managed champagne?"

"Easy, I got it out of the wine closet last night."

"And the beer bottle?"

"I poured out one of my dad's brews. I have no idea where my mom keeps the vases. We have to celebrate. You have healed me." He coaxed the cork from the champagne and poured the contents into the tumblers, a great deal more than a flute would have held. "To us!"

He handed over her glass, clinked his against hers, and took a deep swallow. She allowed herself a few sips, not a cheap vintage, neither too sweet nor too sour. He topped off her tumbler and steered her again, this time toward the bedroom.

"All the cottages have a queen bed for the parents and two sets of bunks in the other bedroom for the kids. Sure beats Teddy's narrow bed or a gym mat. I've been waiting for this moment."

If she were honest with herself, so had she, but still he'd caught her off guard. She'd expected a nighttime visit when she planned to wear those silly pink PJs. Now, here she sat on the edge of a bed sipping champagne from a glass, dressed in her sexless khakis and knit shirt, without much makeup or lipstick, not exactly a special occasion scenario.

Mack took her champagne and set it aside on the night table. He opened the three buttons at her throat and kissed the skin exposed to his lips. The shirt came off and the sports bra beneath it. "Ah," he said as he palmed her breasts. "I get to see them in the light of day. Lie down, and I'll take off the rest."

That took little time, just the lowering of her slacks, taking her utilitarian panties with them, and dragging off her athletic shoes as well. She lay there exposed, prosthesis and all, glad she wore the dancing foot she'd been breaking in. Mack didn't appear to notice or care as he stripped off his exercise clothes and kicked them aside, bent and removed two condoms from the other hip pocket. "I came prepared."

He laid out his long body beside her, opened the packet, and handed it to her. "Would you do the honors, Sarge?"

She smoothed the condom over the length of his shaft, hot, throbbing, and responsive in her hands. She'd dreamed of this moment. Some dreams do come true. She closed her eyes to her modest surroundings, a setup he might have used in high school, as he applied his lips again and massaged her breasts, stopping to tweak her nipples until they peaked beneath his fingers. The world went away as he worked downward, parting her labia, licking her clit. All of her centered right there, grew and grew, until she burst with intense feeling, barely done before he entered her and started to pump, keeping a slow, steady rhythm. He accelerated. She came for him again before he let go himself with a long, low groan. Perfect.

Yet he said as he rolled to her side, "Next time will be better," as if this would happen again and again and again. Not likely. She wouldn't deal with that thought now. They had tonight and tomorrow. Let that be enough.

Chapter Twenty-Five

He'd come to her in the night, making what he called lazy love, lifting her above him and settling her down on his erection, letting her set the pace and dominate while he laid there savoring every moment. She closed her eyes and threw back her head. He watched and waited and held back until she came, glad she didn't take long because he had only so much forbearance and wanted to follow his father's dictate of always letting the lady go first, a great rule for making love. He might flit from woman to woman, but he did not leave them unsatisfied. This time meant more. He wanted to show her the unselfish lover he could be. He stayed the night by her side. They didn't achieve much rest, and he should have left her alone. After all, she had to go for hair and makeup with his mom, Jessie, and Xo in the afternoon while he could loll all day before taking a second shower, shaving close, and donning his tuxedo.

But first, he took her to downtown Chapelle for the Mardi Gras parade that started at ten a.m. and ran straight down Main Street the length of the town from a small shopping center on the outskirts with a local grocery store all the way to the park with several old Cajun houses on display at the other end. It wasn't New Orleans nor were the floats, all homemade products, but to watch Sarge's anticipation, they might have been standing on Canal Street watching the krewe of Rex throwing its wealth of beads and doubloons or Zulu handing out the coveted painted coconuts. Instead, they clumped together on a cracked sidewalk with Xo and Junior bearing his two children on his wide shoulders, and Teddy and Jessie trying to hold their excited children in their laps. Corazon, his mom, and dad provided backup for bead grabbing and spelling tired parents.

"You've never been to a Mardi Gras parade," he guessed.

She shot him an "are you kidding me" glance. "No, Mack. I come from Lubbock where we have rodeos, and the army didn't provide King Cakes either. It's beginning."

A firetruck cleared the way, siren blaring, with the children of the firemen throwing wrapped candies to the crowd. The VFW provided the color guard. The Furious Flames marching band of Ste. Jeanne d'Arc Parochial School in their red and gold uniforms played the music. They escorted the queen's float reigned over by a beautiful young blonde woman about eighteen attended by six of the local debs all dressed in white. With hands clad in long gloves, they did the Queen Elizabeth wave and threw no beads.

"How is the queen chosen?"

"Around here? Depends on whose daddy has the most money and a daughter the right age. I can tell you the Ste. Jeanne girls are more fun than the Day School snobs." The queen, though at least seven years younger than Mack, offered him a flirty smile. His reputation lived on in Chapelle.

"You'd know of course."

A dance school squad followed shaking their booties in some fairly skimpy outfits to a rap song booming from a pickup truck. Mack leaned in. "Now comes the good stuff. Get ready."

The first float hauled a cargo of men in white suits and fedoras, sporting fake sub-machine guns and guarding a stash of giant whiskey kegs most likely borrowed from the pepper sauce factory. Their flapper molls sat atop some of the barrels. The gangsters wore masks, some of political figures past and present, at least a couple of Richard Nixons in there, while the women favored feathered half-masks. All fished handfuls of plastic beads from an open barrel and pelted the crowd with cheap treasure.

The Billodeaux family, being well-known, came in for more than their share of tossed loot. Mack jumped up to catch whole handfuls, and what he missed, his dad collected. They draped their take around the necks of the children and the women. Mack adorned Sarge with the best of his, keeping only one of huge, round orbs in Mardi Gras colors for himself.

"Hey, don't you think I can catch my own beads?" Sarge challenged.

"I know you can. I just want to show off my amazing vertical leap and thank you for it."

Before she countered that, Starr's School of Dance arrived, doing modified line dances to loud country songs. With no scanty outfits, they shuffled and twirled in boots, jeans, country shirts, and western hats led by a spry woman who must have been beyond eighty.

Over the music, Nell shouted to Sarge, "That's Miss Starr, a hippie who showed up here in the Seventies and opened the first integrated dance school in town. She does a free class for Camp Love Letter every summer. I doubt I could keep up with her. Oh, look, the Tush Push. I wish we could join them."

Mack bumped against Sarge's hip. "Maybe tonight at the ball."

"So that's the big secret, we'll be line dancing in our Twenties clothes."

"He's joking. They don't do line dancing at the ball. Here comes another float." Nell thrust her arms up, jiggling the beads she already wore, as excited as her grandkids.

Mobsters in natty checkered suits played at craps and roulette tables, their girlfriends pulled the arms of slot machines. Besides beads, they lobbed pairs of fuzzy dice and handfuls of doubloons imprinted with the theme that gleamed in the sunshine as they showered through the air. A side banner thanked Mamie's Loose and Easy Casino, Hwy. 90, for the props. Some of the dice landed gently in the laps of Teddy and Jessie, thrilling their daughters. Mack caught a pair and bedecked Sarge again as well as shoving a fistful of doubloons into her hip pocket and lingering there for a quick squeeze.

"Tomorrow you are supposed to confess and wear ashes," Sarge said. "You'd better go early because you'll have lots to tell the priest."

"If I go at all."

Another dance group, another float, this one with a fake New York skyline and dapper men in dark suits living it up with their molls. A few did the Charleston to the tune of a live jazz combo on board while the rest threw necklaces and fake paper money with discount coupons on the back for various local businesses, gathered up by adults and scorned by the children.

The large Chapelle High band, the Swinging Saints, wearing older maroon and gold uniforms and playing some obviously long-used instruments marched along doing fancy footwork that made up for any lack. Their drum major bent back nearly to the ground as he strutted along the way. They preceded a float bearing numerous men hiding behind Al Capone masks under light fedoras worn with dark suits. Squabbles broke out over the choicest of their throws, plastic cigars. Mack scored two and offered them to Sarge.

"No, thanks, you know I don't smoke."

He gifted them to Junior's two children instead. "I swear my babies have gained ten pounds each in beads," Junior said. "About time they get off daddy's shoulders. He slid Pilar and KC gently to the ground. Xo grabbed their hands.

The tail end of the parade came into sight. The king's float bore a golden throne holding a prosperous local businessman poorly disguised by a fake black beard and royal crown weighed down by paste jewels and cutting into his forehead. His heavy cape of red velvet covered in gold embroidery couldn't have been comfortable as the March day turned warm. A trickle of black hair dye made its way from crown to chin, but wearing white gloves he didn't dare touch it. Instead, he smiled and waved to the crowd with imperial grace. Finally, one of his male attendants, the escorts for the debs, took a tissue from his suit pocket and swiped the streak away.

"Gene Matlock, he owns that big auto dealership out on the highway," Nell told Sarge. "Loves doing his own corny commercials. This is right up his alley, and he can afford the honor."

"Yeah, they're always after dad to be King Louis, but he gives them a polite hell, no," Mack added.

The local bookmobile escorted by motorcycle police brought up the very rear, not as exciting, but the librarians did toss beads and Fine Free cards. Nell gathered some. "You know somebody in our family needs these. I used to pay off all my kids' fines at the end of each month. I swear we built a wing of the new library."

The crowd began to disburse, going home or lining up for snow cones and cold beverages. The Billodeauxs made their way a few blocks to Xochi's old Victorian, dubbed the Mardi Gras house because of its bright colors, across the bridge on the other side of the bayou for lunch.

Mack and Sarge let the families go first and scuffed along in the parade debris of broken beads, beer cans, and paper detritus. He enjoyed seeing rosy cheeks on her pale face, her neck weighed down with false jewels like an Indian woman carrying all her wealth on her body. He'd like to replace some of the fakes with strands of real pearls and a diamond necklace or two, but knew she wouldn't accept them. She did accept his hand in hers. Let people stare. He didn't care.

"Junior's famous lasagna awaits with salad and garlic knots, your choice of beverage and mint chip ice cream for dessert according to Xo."

"Good thing we end with something minty. I wouldn't want to offend the owners of Belles with my breath while they torture me into beauty. Be glad you and the rest of the guys only have to babysit while we're gone, and Corazon will most likely do all the work."

"You are beautiful as you are." She didn't deflect the compliment. He swooped in for a quick kiss. She didn't break away. More progress.

Chapter Twenty-Six

Lord help her, Sarge sat in a comfortable chair under harsh lights being made beautiful for Mack. Despite what she'd said, she wanted to look Brooke DeVille straight into her outlined eyes as an equal in appearance tonight, and that went for any other of his old girlfriends who might turn up. She watched in the mirror as her brows became darker but not too dark, and her lids received liner and a gloss of silvery shadow. Rachel, her own lush, black curls pulled back, had prepped her skin with some kind of foundation that made her a little less pale and then brought out her cheekbones with a muted dash of pink, coating the rest of her face with a powder that also seemed to gleam. Her lips received their own liner, darker, then filled in with a deep shade of red, which made them seem plumper in the center, the bow-shaped lips of the Twenties, the kind of lips men liked to kiss.

She'd tussled with her makeup artist earlier about doing her eyes. Rachel presented a pair of light brown false eyelashes, her own not making the grade, to be glued on. Oh, no. She'd drawn the line at having the spidery things that might fall off affixed to her face. They compromised on an eyelash enhancer containing fibers that would increase the length of hers and darken them as well. The woman in the mirror was a new and improved Sarge for sure, one she'd never be able to reproduce by herself. She'd leave it on to say goodbye tomorrow, then disappear into the Texas dust leaving Mack with this face in his mind's eye rather than her stern, sweaty trainer's visage.

Rachel carefully groomed her light blonde hair and sprayed it into place. She lowered the browband as if it were a crown and handed over the feather to be placed later. "*Et voila*, we are *finis*," she said as if using French were mandatory after so much exertion.

Becoming aware of her surroundings for the first time in over an hour, Sarge watched Regan put the finishing touches on Jessie, a natural beauty with blonde-streaked light brown hair finger-waved down around her shoulders. Her gorgeous hazel eyes now leaned toward green with the help of her eye shadow. A former cheerleader, Teddy had revealed about his wife, but one of the nice ones. She hadn't known any of those in Texas, only the kind who mocked those wearing secondhand clothes and knew nothing about putting on makeup. Jessie trained patients newly wheelchair bound as well as raising two young daughters. She had her own flapper dress in green and gold, a short skirt being less likely to catch in her wheels. Her legs remained shapely with regular passive exercise. Sarge admired her.

With Rachel's help, Nell had gone total flapper, though because of her short stature, the hem of her skirt went below her knees. She'd chosen red again with lots of fringe. Her dark pixie haircut had been gelled into a sleek cap with spit curls on either cheek and one on her forehead.

She smiled at Sarge with red-painted lips. Nell held out a jewelry box containing a three-strand choker of garnets that matched the deep tone of her gown. "Could I have some help with this?"

As Sarge affixed the necklace, Nell said, "Isn't this fun? Oh, I almost forgot." She rummaged in her handbag and fished out a small package. "Josee sent these things to go with your outfit."

She found a silver evening bag on a long chain and a black and gold velvet box containing two clip-on diamond studs for her ears. The tiny note inside the box said, "I wish I could see you wearing these tonight. Enjoy."

"Oh, put them on," Nell urged.

"These better be cubic zirconias, or I'll owe her for life if I lose one. Ouch, they pinch."

Nell eyed the box. "Schifferman's, they will not be zirconias."

"You won't notice them once your ear lobes go numb," Jessie said.

"Glad my ears have been pierced since birth," Xochi added. Being curvaceous, she hadn't gone with the flapper style, but Regan made her large, brown eyes more dramatic and applied a blush that blended perfectly with her tan skin. Her hair with its long waves needed no help other than the addition of silk roses the color of her full-skirted coral gown with its flirty petticoats. The dress had stayed at Belles for alterations to the waist and bodice. Sarge wondered if she was the only one who knew why, but suspected the others merely waited for an announcement of another baby on the way.

They gathered up the garment bags after each gown had been inspected and admired a final time and went to pay their bill. Nell, despite her short legs, managed to get out in front, and thrown down a credit card. "My treat for all of us."

Sarge moved to the desk. "I never got the bill for my dress." She groped in her hip pocket for her own credit card. It wasn't platinum like Nell's but would have to do.

"Oh, it's been paid." Rachel returned her card.

"Paid?" She glanced from companion to companion. All shook their heads. Only Nell appeared to be harboring a secret she wouldn't tell. "I hope Josee or Stacy didn't do this. I already owe them for their help, not to mention the loan of earrings and a bag. Don't we need to give these ladies a big tip, too?"

Tossing her blonde hair, loose today, Regan rushed to say, "You don't tip the owners. Just tell everyone where you had your faces done when they rave about your makeup. We'll be seeing y'all at the ball this evening."

Rachel handed each a cosmetics bag, silver with the store's name emblazoned in hot pink. "These are the products we used for your makeup. You can buy refills here whenever you need them. Get some rest. You'll be out late."

They returned to the red handicapped van chauffeured by Jessie, packed everything and everybody inside including her wheelchair, and returned to Xo's house where they would dress before the big event.

The men sat on the back porch watching the children wear themselves out racing across the large, shady backyard that ran down to the bayou now rimmed with a low picket fence to keep babies from falling into its muddy waters. Lizzie led her playmates round and round the gazebo in a dizzying circle. The babysitters were sustained with lemonade and a tray of snickerdoodles with a great number missing. Their heads turned as the women arrived. They whistled and applauded as well-trained husbands should to acknowledge such effort when all they had to do for the night was shave, and blond Teddy barely needed to do so. Men were lucky that way, Sarge thought.

She cared only about her effect on one person, the man who greeted her with a salacious grin that indicated he'd like to mess up her lipstick right here and now. Success!

The children charged onto the porch. Pilar spoke. "My mommy is beautifulest. She got flowers in her hair."

"No, mine is beautifuler," Lizzie insisted.

"Now, now, Liz, all the women are beautiful," Teddy gently reprimanded.

May said, "Yeah, but Granny looks funny."

"Because I'm going to a costume ball as a person from another time, darling. Wait until you see me in my red flapper dress." Nell gave her a reassuring hug.

KC, already learning the ways of men, kept quiet, but not Mack. "I think Miss Sarge will be the belle of the ball."

She intended to give that a good try. Not daring to mar her lipstick, she passed on the cookies and announced she'd be going upstairs to rest a bit before the dance. Wisely, she'd worn her practical foot to the parade, but they'd stood a long time. She needed to rest her stump before putting on her fancy foot and silver shoes. As she entered the house, Corazon bustled past.

"I am feeding the little ones early. If you want to

eat something, come to the kitchen. They don't give you much at these balls, only the heavy hors d'oeuvres, whatever that means."

"Usually, chicken livers wrapped in bacon on a toothpick."

"Terrible."

"Thank you, but I've survived worse food."

She continued on her way to one of the six bedrooms assigned to guests, removed her prosthesis, and lay down on the mattress very carefully, face up. One pillow went under her legs, another under her head, and the other two on either side to keep her from rolling over if she slept. Frankly, she'd be more comfortable in combat gear sleeping on the cold, hard ground than lying here in a room papered with flowers and butterflies on a bed so soft she sank into the linens.

Butterflies on the walls, butterflies in her stomach, and yet she dozed.

Chapter Twenty-Seven

The men lined up, tuxedo clad, to claim their dates at the base of the stairs in Xo's spacious foyer. Pleased that his custom tux fit perfectly again, Mack carried his cane for effect since he no longer needed it. His dad had added a silk top hat and patent leather dancing shoes as a bow to the theme.

Teddy and Junior didn't go for add-ons, but Junior clutched a box with a wrist corsage to match Xochi's dress. Though the man looked like an overgrown high school prom date, Mack wished he'd thought of that, too. Teddy hadn't done anything special or so he thought until Jessie wheeled from Xo's first floor suite, and his brother beckoned his wife close to drape a triple strand of gold chains around her neck. He'd paid for Sarge's dress and the diamond earrings with Josee's help, but couldn't tell or risk ruining the evening. Flowers would have been easy. Xochi rustled behind Jessie and exclaimed over the corsage nearly as much as Jessie had about gold jewelry.

His mom made her grand entrance coming down the stairs with fringe swaying and greeting everyone with a twenty-three skidoo. Which means, she informed them, "Let's get out of here." She'd been doing research again.

"Wait, we're missing one." For a moment, he feared Sarge had climbed down the trellis on the side of

212

the house and made an escape, but no, she moved from the shadows at the top of the stairs with her shoulders thrown back, her posture so stiff the plume in her browband barely nodded as she took step after step from darkness into the full light that made every inch of her glitter. He moved forward to take her hand. "I'm dazzled." The right words because her smile emerged making her expression shine, too.

They stood there gazing into each other's eyes until his dad clapped his hands and said, "Let's twenty-three skiddoo, then, and pile into the van."

"I brought the Jag over here last night. We have late dinner reservations at On The Riverside. I didn't want to inconvenience anyone who wanted to go home early." His folks exchanged one of those glances that implied they could read each other's thoughts, but what thoughts?

Corazon insisted they line up on the staircase with Ted and Jessie at the bottom to commemorate the moment, again shades of prom nights long ago. He'd gone to every prom since ninth grade because older girls kept asking him out—and put out. That part wasn't the same at all. Sarge didn't put out. She participated with all her might, and she had quite a lot of it.

"The children will want to see."

And they did since all four had slipped out of bed and sat at the top of the stairs. "You are all beautiful," Lizzie proclaimed, arms held wide. Corazon turned the camera on them for a priceless snapshot.

"Okay, now you've seen us. Off to bed again." Xochi shooed them with her hands.

"I will settle them after you go," Corazon assured her. *"Vamanos."*

At last, they were underway. He helped Sarge into the low-slung Jaguar leaving its top up. One thing he did know about women, you did not muss their hair on the way out. That came later. Most of all, he hadn't wanted her to arrive in the handicapped van, because she wasn't, or rather he didn't see her that way anymore.

He knew very well that she wasn't impressed by expensive cars or his handsome face or, for that matter, what money could buy. The one thing he could give her tonight was a memorable evening, the kind of fun she'd never had growing up poor. He'd do his best to make it so—and wouldn't tell her about the earrings until tomorrow after they'd spent the night together.

Driving carefully through town to avoid the late revelers still on the streets, some of them drunk, he wished he could open the Jag up and show her what it could do. As they passed under streetlight after streetlight, he glanced at her face and recognized joy and anticipation in her gray eyes, softened and accentuated by the makeup she wore. He guessed he owed Rachel a dance for making them so.

The Community Center, not far, came up fast. They hadn't spoken a word the whole time. Now he told her, "I'll drop you off at the door. I don't want to park close and end up with dings on the Jag. You can go inside with the family if you want."

He jumped out to help her up as the red van entered the lot and took advantage of handicapped parking near the entry. She shook her head. "I'll wait for you."

Good, they'd make a grand entry on their own. Finding a secluded spot in the shadows of the large tulip poplar trees bordering the lot, he crunched through the fallen leaves that gave them their name and went straight to Sarge. She stood under the portico of the metal building that had been dressed up with two columns and a hanging lantern, waiting as if she would all night for him to arrive, him and no one else. They entered together.

The others had gone ahead but were still proceeding to the table. His dad, always a scene stealer because he couldn't help himself, stopped often to speak with friends who told them they were the bee's knees or the cat's pajamas. He held back until the central aisle between the tables cleared, then offered her his arm. A small tremor ran through her. Could the dauntless Sarge be nervous? "Big smile," he prompted. "Like this." He exposed his own rakish grin.

She bumped his side with her elbow. "No one smiles like you, but could you dial it down a notch. People will think we just had sex."

"Later," he said, and brought them out into the light. Her color had heightened, but a smile also lit her face. They gathered compliments like handfuls of Mardi Gras beads as they passed. He slowed as they approached Brooke DeVille's table, stopped, and told her she looked lovely. "You remember Sarge?" Sarge who outshone her tonight.

"Yes, but not like this."

Hollis DeVille leaned way forward and said, "I'd like to see you in your cat's pajamas, pretty lady." From his height, Mack noticed the bald spot on the back of the man's head. The alcohol on the banker's breath hit hard. He'd gotten an early start or maybe had been drinking all day.

It said much about Sarge's character that she

ignored the crass comment and told Brooke, "What beautiful emeralds. They match your gown perfectly."

"Yes, they're bought and paid for, not rented like some of the jewelry here tonight. Nice earrings." Brooke stared at the studs as if she'd never seen a diamond despite the rather large one on her ring finger.

"On loan from Josee Riley. She's really very nice, not full of herself at all. Our group is waiting. We should go." She tugged Mack's arm, and off they went.

"Well, that was awful and embarrassing," she said to him. "What made you stop?"

"Just wanted to get your worst fear out of the way. You were great, finer than her in every way. That her husband made a pass at you, oh so much better."

"You have a vindictive streak, don't you?"

"Only when people I love are involved." Her hand tightened on his arm. He added hastily, "Like when Jock Brown wanted to marry Lorena—and smashed up my leg."

"You need to put that aside. You can dance again and will play football in the fall. I am sure of it."

Glad one of them was entirely sure, he got them to the table without more stops, but found his family placed next to Rev Bullock's table populated by his light-skinned, green-eyed doctor wife, his very tall daughter and her taller husband, his bulky football playing son, Li'l Joe, and Mack's very own orthopedic surgeon who assessed, "I studied your gait as you came in, perfect. I'm really good at what I do."

"Modest, too," his sister, Riley, said. She favored her dark-skinned father and had embraced a natural hair style wearing it well as she did a long, slim column of a white dress that showed off her athletic, basketball playing figure. She'd married the NBA star sitting next to her, taken a year off from her own career to give birth to twin girls, and in Mack's opinion had never looked hotter. Older than him, she'd once had a crush on Dean that came to nothing.

He'd known them all from birth on, the last couple at the table less so, but he believed they were the town library director and her cattle rancher husband, around his parents' age. Curvaceous like Xo, the librarian wore a silver gown with a full skirt. An impressive necklace of garnets or maybe rubies filled in the space between her neck and cleavage. Her husband wore a tux, probably rented, though the tanned and lined face beneath his thick salt and pepper hair revealed the outdoorsman he was. Not being a bookworm like Trinity, he couldn't quite recall their names. Fortunately, the woman introduced herself to Sarge.

"We're Laura and Robert LeBlanc. I've heard from Nell that you're a wonderful trainer and made a big difference in Mack's recovery."

Before she could speak, Mack cut in. "Absolutely. Wait until you see us dance."

"It's going to be a special night then. Bob and I were married on Mardi Gras eve. Since the date shifts every year, we celebrate twice." The librarian gazed around the ballroom. "This place is nicer than the old one, but the costumes are less fancy, and protocol is more relaxed. I've worn the same dress every year since then—though it has been let out a few times. Having babies does that to a woman."

Behind him at their own table, Xochi coughed, but he hadn't given up her secret. Bob LeBlanc said, "Yes, we caused quite the scandal eloping to Broussard's

Barn and letting the old man out there marry us. There was alcohol involved, but as they say around here, Broussard's marriages last as long as any others."

Mack gave Sarge a sidelong glance. All decked out, she could easily pass for a bride, but he suspected she'd have to drink bucketsful to accept him tonight. Go easy, one step at a time, he prompted himself. Saved from further chitchat as a local radio personality, hair parted in the middle and slicked down, wearing a conservative suit unbuttoned in order to expose an empty shoulder holster, mounted the stage and asked the crowd to take their places so the presentation of the courts could begin. Mack guided Sarge to her seat before Riley told any childhood tales about him.

The emcee took care of a few details first. "I'm your host, Elliot Ness, here tonight because I've heard some big names in crime will be appearing any time now. However, I've relented on my crusade against liquor for one night only. All tables have a complimentary bottle of wine. Should you want anything harder, the gin joint on the side of the hall will be open all night, cash bar." He gestured toward two long tables covered in white cloths and staffed by mixologists in red jackets.

"Following the procession and introduction of our special guests, some of whom might be arrested, the buffet will open on the other side of the hall. After that, dancing begins with the introduction of our debutants and a Charleston contest. We have a great evening ahead. Let the procession begin."

At the words Charleston contest, Sarge shot him a sharp glance which Mack refused to intercept. If she'd caught on, too late to back out now.

King Louis entered wearing a tux under his ponderous regalia, the red cape held up by two little boys in mini-tuxedos. Queen Marie Antoinette followed, assisted by two of her maids. A cadre of other girls and the escorts trailed her. The royals took their places on the carved and heavily gilded thrones from the floats with the attendants fanning out behind them after a careful placement of the capes to show off the stunning detail of the garments. Behind them hung a geometric art deco backdrop.

"Aren't those names a little dated for the Twenties?" Sarge asked.

Mack shrugged. "They use the same names every year, same capes, crowns, and the queen's gown. The stuff is expensive for a small-town Mardi Gras Association like this."

Personally, he could have done without the pageantry. Watching Sarge's rapt attention made up for his own boredom. Still, he couldn't resist a remark. "I've been asked to be an escort, but those girls are only months away from being jailbait. I prefer a real woman."

"My guess is you aren't supposed to sleep with them as part of your duties. Hush up." She punched his arm lightly.

Eliot Ness stepped to the mic again. "Our first guests of the evening from the city of Memphis, Jack Kelly, also known as Machine Gun Kelly and Pop Gun Kelly, his moll, Kathryn Thorne, and his gang members." The men in white suits from the float marched down the aisle threatening the audience with their submachine guns.

"See here, Kelly. This is neutral ground tonight.

You'll pile those weapons at the base of the stage."

"Don't forget I supplied the hooch for this bash." After the pause for laughter, they disarmed with a clatter of plastic hitting the tile floor and mounted the stage to pay their respects to the royalty before exiting down the other side.

"What's so funny?" Sarge asked

"He's the local beer, wine, and liquor distributor," Nell answered.

"Next, we welcome Benjamin "Bugsy" Siegal from Las Vegas and his mob queen, Virginia Hill. The G-men are keeping an eye on your gambling operations, Siegal," Ness warned.

"We're legit, completely legit." The lobber of fuzzy dice threw a few more to the folks at the tables and moved on with his mobsters and molls.

"I see we have Jack "Legs" Diamond, alias Gentleman Jack, from New York City with his mistress, Kiki Roberts, lurking in the rear."

This time the woman made the comeback. "Listen here, I'm a dancer and Legs is pretty good, too. We might just take that contest you're touting." Kiki looked her part with endlessly long legs, turned down hose, and rouged kneecaps. A very short flapper dress patterned with red sequins shimmered as she moved up to curtsy before the queen.

"She's one of Miss Starr's dance instructors. That will be some stiff competition," Nell said.

"Whose competition?" Sarge asked and received no answer before the next group moved down the aisle. His mom had almost blown it.

"Last but far from least, the gangster's gangster, Alphonse Gabriel Capone, alias Scarface, boss of the

Chicago Outfit, Public Enemy No. 1, and his moll, Mae Coughlin."

Al, sporting a realistic scar on his cheek, entered with a woman on his arm. She issued the retort. Dressed in a long black gown with a fox stole around her shoulders, the animal's head biting its tail, Mae spoke up. "I'm no moll, I'm his wife. He doesn't like being called Scarface, and he's the best dresser in this room. Show some respect."

"I'll show him to a cell in Alcatraz. Capone, you are under arrest for tax evasion." Ness signaled to two of the attendants to take Scarface away.

"Tax evasion, who says?"

"Mabel Walker Willebrandt, Assistant Attorney General of the USA. We couldn't nail you for the St. Valentine's Day Massacre, but we got you on this."

"Some broad?"

"That's right. Cuff him."

The little skit drew applause. "He's a prominent lawyer here in town, Pete Lamperez," Nell said as she joined in the clapping.

"Someone did a lot of research," Sarge remarked.

"Yes, the town librarians always help. The Little Theater does makeup and helps with the costumes. We sponsored one of the floats. It's a community affair. You don't need to be rich, and no one goes broke." Nell held out her glass for the last of the wine.

While the ceremony progressed, the caterers had quietly filled the buffet table with the hors d'oeuvres. The scent of seafood and fried delicacies filled the air. Before a stampede began, the emcee spoke up again. "Please allow the court to eat first, then the tables in front and so on. Plenty for everyone. *Bon appetit*." He managed to get in line just behind the king and queen who had been relieved of their heavy capes left behind on the stage to be dry-cleaned and stored away for next year.

As the crowd gorged on tiny crab cakes, oysters wrapped in bacon, boudin balls, and the humble but popular pigs in a blanket, the stage shifted to a bandstand as the orchestra set up. Sarge placed a small skewer of fruit chunks, another of grilled vegetables, a mini-quiche, and a crab cake on her plate.

"Not hungry, not feeling well?" Mack asked, concerned. He'd piled his rather small plate high with crab cakes and pigs in a blanket.

"I have a terrible premonition that I should eat light."

Junior popped a crab cake into his mouth, chewed, and considered. "Not nearly as good as mine. You aren't missing anything."

"True," Xochi said. She'd accepted a half glass of wine but hadn't sipped a drop. Sarge took a large gulp of the rose wine, good for fish or meat, as if she needed courage for what was to come.

"Okay, okay, don't get drunk. I did enter us in the Charleston contest. Really, it's no big deal. We probably won't win against Legs Diamond and his moll," Mack confessed.

"How could you without asking me?

"Because you'd say no. You always do."

"Not nearly enough," she muttered, and she still didn't know about the earrings.

Joe and Nell had walked alongside Teddy and Jessie in case they wanted help with their plates and also managed to make up some for the table. "Smallest plates I've ever seen," Joe remarked as he placed a medley of the offerings in the center of the tablecloth for all to share. He'd scored a mound of chocolate-covered strawberries and small pastries from the dessert trays.

Nell put down her contribution of extra fruit and vegetable skewers. She placed one of each on the side of Mack's plate and gifted Sarge with a strawberry. "Eat your fruit and veggies."

"We're going to On The Riverside after this. I'm sure our meal comes with a salad."

"It certainly does," Junior affirmed. "I'll see you there. We're booked solid until two a.m. They'll need me."

Xochi touched his arm. "No, they don't. You have a good manager and plenty of waitstaff since the tips are high on Mardi Gras. You just want to be there."

"Come with me."

Xo shook her head. "I'm already tired." All eyes stared at her still untouched wine glass to her selection of bland foods to her well disguised belly. "Okay, okay, I'm pregnant again. I don't want to hear how we should have been more careful."

With the minor spat going on, the dance contest had been pushed to the side to Mack's relief. In fact, he was the first to say, "I'm happy for you. You're a great mother."

The others joined in with congratulations no matter what they truly thought. Jessie claimed she wanted a third child, just not right now. Sarge said pragmatically, "You can handle it."

His dad declared they needed to toast the good news and went off to purchase champagne from the bar.

Mack counted the minutes until the contest, now simply wanting it over and done.

Chapter Twenty-Eight

Though some people still browsed the leftovers, the emcee called for a drum roll and began reading the names of the debs who would dance with their fathers. "Our Queen Marie Antoinette, Petra Lamperez, daughter of Mr. and Mrs. Peter Lamperez." The lawyer, still in his Al Capone guise, led her out. "First maid, Lissa Matlock, daughter of Mr. and Mrs. Gene Matlock." The car salesman had shed his fake beard and crown which left red marks on his face.

As the list rolled on, the knot in Sarge's stomach pulled tighter. What if she fell? What if she made a complete fool of herself? Worst of all, what if folks voted for her out of pity? She wanted sorely to kick Mack in his good leg so hard he'd have to drop out. Until she'd uncovered his deceit, she'd been having the best time with a family she loved and respected. Damn him.

The debs swirled by, their full white skirts floating like water lilies on the surface of a pond. Their daddies had been practicing, not one out of step. The emcee urged the audience members to join in now. Joe and Nell flowed into the current. Junior asked if his wife felt well enough to dance. Her answer came back, "Always, with you." Teddy moved his wheelchair close to Jessie's and transferred her onto his lap. They claimed a small corner of the dance floor and twirled round and round, Jessie with her cheek pressed closed to his, an elated smile on her face.

Mack cleared his throat. "Shall we?"

"Don't you think we should save our energy for the contest?"

"If that's what you want." He moved his chair out of kicking distance. "Say, I added something to our routine that works better for me than the jazz hands. I thought I'd do a few side-to-sides and taps with the cane."

"Sure, let's improvise at the last minute. Why not?"

He chose to ignore the sarcasm in her voice. "Exactly. We'll be great."

When the waltz of the debs ended, their tablemates returned flushed and happy. "I guess you two are resting before the contest. You already have our vote," Nell assured them.

"I'd rather you voted for the best dancers. I don't like to win unfairly in anything." Sarge polished off the wine in Xochi's glass for courage plus the champagne toast.

Eliot Ness returned to call out the names of the Charleston contest competitors and requested they line up by the stage. Never had Sarge been so slow to answer an order. She and Mack stood third in line behind a group of Miss Starr's students and an elderly couple who vowed they'd danced it in the Twenties but couldn't possibly be that old. The fourth was Legs Diamond and Kiki, and the last a pair of middle-aged women who claimed they'd been blackmailed into doing it by Al Capone.

The teen girls were charming and the old couple

gave it their all, drawing a few laughs from the audience. The announcer introduced couple number three as Chapelle's very own Valentino, Mack Billodeaux, and his "It" girl, Susan Kozac.

"Who wrote that?" she questioned as they climbed onto the stage.

"Maybe me when I signed us up."

"I'm surprised you didn't say Mack Billodeaux is back with his one-footed wonder."

He ignored her remark and stayed in character, throwing a smoky-eyed glance at the audience before the music started. A few women pretended to swoon. He followed that up with his lethal grin as they started their routine. Nothing hard about the Charleston: step forward on the left foot, tap the toe, back on the right foot, tap. Balance on the balls of the feet and move the heels in and out to add a twist. Speed counted.

Sarge's silver fringe flew in time to her hands going side to side while Mack used his cane in the same movement with an occasional tap to the floor. As their dance ended, he threw his cane into the crowd, neatly caught by his dad who seemed to be cued for the move. Had they all conspired against her? Before she could answer herself, Mack pulled her into a face-to-face dance position for a few beats, then twirled her out to face the audience for a bow. Engulfed in waves of applause, she guessed they'd done well, hell, she knew they had. She edged toward forgiving Mack for this stunt and went to sit by his side to enjoy Kiki's dance, a sure winner.

Or it should have been. Miss Starr's instructor danced rings around Legs Diamond who mostly stood there swaying on his cane like the contestants on

DWTS who had no rhythm. Kiki would have been stunning paired with Mack, Sarge couldn't help thinking. The last of the competitors provided the comic relief. Wearing red cloche hats and long strands of fake pearls, the two women appeared to be having the time of their lives, but couldn't do a Charleston to save their souls. They ended doubled over with laughter, and just might win the trophy for sheer exuberance.

The tables offered one score card for each person and little golf pencils to mark their choices. The debs circulated with baskets to retrieve the votes. Assuring the contestants they were all fabulous in their own way, the emcee motioned to the band to play another slow song while the ballots were counted.

Mack leaned close. "Do you forgive me for entering us in the contest?"

"Yes, I suppose."

"Will you waltz with me, Sarge?"

Though her stump throbbed from the effort she'd put into the Charleston, she accepted his hand. They glided around the outskirts of the floor as if they'd danced together for a lifetime like his parents, not only a few months. He spun her out and brought her back to the warmth of his embrace time and again. If watchers gawked, she didn't care. Any pain dissolved in the magic of the moment. Too soon, they were back at the table waiting for the contest results.

"And the winner is—Mack "Valentino" Billodeaux and Susan, his "It" girl, Kozac."

Summoned to the stage to receive an enormous three-tiered trophy topped by a golden orb that had obviously been a basketball in a former trophy case,

Mack held it high, then offered it to Sarge. They heaved it off the stage together. Their tablemates stood to applaud along with several others. The music started again and emptied their group onto the dance floor, but Sarge indicated she needed a break. Kiki came over to add her congratulations.

"You would have won if Mack had been your partner," Sarge demurred.

"Girl, you held your own with him, and I know that isn't easy."

She gazed into Kiki's kohl-lined eyes and knew they'd done more than dance together in the past. After she left, Sarge whispered in his ear. "Another old girlfriend, right?"

"We parted on good terms. I think she mostly wanted a partner. Hard to believe she married that stiff playing Legs Diamond, but they do have fun at Mardi Gras. How about you?"

"The best."

"So, you're in a really, really good mood." He studied her face closely.

"I'd say so." Her mood went far beyond that, on the verge of ecstatic.

"Great. I paid for your dress and the earrings." He watched her expression change.

"I'll reimburse you for the gown, but you'll have to return these. I can't afford them." She raised a hand to remove the diamonds.

He took that hand in his. "They are gifts. I know you have a hard time with the concept, but you deserve nice things for all you've done for me, and that goes way beyond rehab and dancing. Sarge, I don't want this to be our last night together."

"I don't see how…"

Their table overflowed with Billodeauxs again as the song ended. Joe refilled the champagne glasses and offered a toast, "To Sarge and Mack, the best partners in the room."

Mack's dad made it seem almost like congratulations for an engagement. She shoved that thought aside. The company, the crowd around them, the music, and more people coming to laud their performance, including Brooke who said, "Not bad for a one-footed woman," made personal conversion impossible. Even Brooke's comment didn't bring her down. She erased it with Kiki's compliment. But Mack did not get another chance to tell her how they could remain together.

Chapter Twenty-Nine

He put the top down on the Jag and propped the ridiculous trophy in the back. Bringing the car around, he handed Sarge into her seat. She removed the feather from her headband for safekeeping as they roared from the parking lot onto a short stretch of four-lane road that allowed him to pass the Mardi Gras traffic and screech to a halt at the first traffic light in town.

"If you're trying to scare me, remember I've been to war," she said.

"Speed is supposed to be exhilarating, not scary."

"That was more like a quarter mile drag race. The restaurant isn't very far. Do you want to end the evening early?" Her eyes had gone steely again. Despite the new makeup, she stared him down.

"No, ma'am. I'd like to have dinner with you without my parents hanging around."

"We can do that at a slower pace."

"Your wish is my command." He pulled out sedately but still managed to get in front of the car in the other lane. Shortly, the turn for the restaurant came up and again he left her at the door to park his car. He had to keep reminding himself that what impressed other women did not impress Sarge. Not jewelry, not fast cars. What would bring her joy?

On The Riverside rocked on Mardi Gras eve, the bar filled to capacity, all but a few reserved tables in use, the sound level nearly illegal. They passed the Bullock contingent again, minus the LeBlancs, pausing only for a moment to accept more congratulations on their trophy. "Someday, the Super Bowl," he said, only half joking.

Tonight, all possibilities seemed attainable, even a life with Sarge by his side. They took their place at a two-top with a bayou view. The quaint pavilion held in the arms of the oaks across the road glowed, its colored lights reflecting in the water, a perfect place tell her what he wanted to say. Too loud, too crowded in here. Later.

Sarge ordered the crab cakes again. He decided on the salmon. Might as well try to stay on a healthy diet if he left for Dallas this week for more training. The salads came with the hot, homemade rolls and honey butter, then the entrées. They split a white chocolate bread pudding, sweet and rich all the way down like this evening.

At one point, she asked what he'd started to tell her at the ball about staying together, and he'd shaken his head. Too noisy for much conversation. Junior, his tux covered with a huge black apron, stopped by the table to ask if they were satisfied with the meal and went on to schmooze other customers. As they left the restaurant, they passed the Bullocks again, their larger party just finishing up.

He went to retrieve the Jag, surprised no one had stolen the trophy, not such a big loss, but he did want Sarge to have it as a reminder of a perfect evening. She stood leaning against the railing at the top of the ramp, a vision in silver, her eyes gone dreamy in a way he'd not seen any other time, not even during sex when they darkened with passion. Across the river, someone played old vinyl records, soft and scratchy and well-loved, Nat King Cole singing "Unforgettable" solo that segued into Sinatra crooning "I've Got you Under my Skin".

The words drifted over the water like moonlight on this mild early spring night as he waited in the Jag, not wanting to disturb her obvious pleasure in the unexpected serenade.

Unconcerned about getting dings in his car doors, he parked, went up the ramp, and escorted her down and across the narrow street to the little pavilion by the water between songs. "Let's dance one more time."

She shook her head. "Mack, there's a big No Trespassing sign."

"How about breaking the rules for a change?"

"You always break the rules. Not me." Yet, he could tell she wanted to by the softening of her voice. He stepped up on the wooden platform and offered her a hand. She took it as the music changed to "Unchained Melody." He needed her love as much as the song implied. They swept around the perimeter boxed in by old wooden railings deep in the shadows of the oaks and out into the patches of colored light. Slowly, they moved inward as the last strands played.

Mack stopped and put his arms into the air. "Come on, do the Dirty Dancing pose."

"Don't be ridiculous. You can't lift me."

He gave her no choice, seizing her around the waist and raising her up into the leaves and the lights. She didn't fight him but planked her body, legs out behind, arms spread wide, and head thrown back, eyes closed, as if she flew there for one perfect moment.

He heard the crack as the rotted planks beneath his feet give way, his sole thought to protect Sarge from harm. He took the fall and held her close to his body, didn't let go when pain seared along his good leg.

People who witnessed the fall, perhaps envying the dancers, surged from the restaurant. Someone tried to raise Sarge from his chest, his sheltering arms, but he still clung to her.

"Mack, you have to let me up. I'm fine, really, I am."

He relinquished his hold and found Junior's bulk looming above him much as he had on the football field the day of the accident. He watched Dr. Connor Bullock gather his legs while Junior gripped his shoulders and on the count of three lifted him out of the splintered wood.

"Get some ice and clean towels, Junior. Mom, do you have the keys to the clinic handy?"

Dr. Arminta Green Bullock answered her orthopedist son, "Always. Do we need an ambulance?"

"I don't think so. We need to sterilize this wound and sew him up."

"Take him in my Escalade," Junior said, back with the requested supplies. "Mack, you idiot, didn't you see the sign?"

"You know I can't resist a challenge. Sarge, where's Sarge?"

"Here. I'll be right behind you in the Jag."

"You're going to drive my Jag? No one…"

"If I can drive a Jeep and a Humvee, I can drive a Jaguar. Let's get going." Her eyes appeared more silver than steel as she bent over him, maybe a reflection from her dress or his vision going blurry from the pain.

While the doc wrapped his leg in clean dish towels and applied ice, Junior brought his large vehicle around. They laid him out on one of the back seats. He turned his keys over to Connor. "No rush getting it back. I'll be here for hours and can always walk home."

Another big man loomed behind him, Rev Bullock. "We'll be praying for you, son."

"Can't hurt, thanks."

Both doctors got into the front seats, and off they went, but not very far. Most places in Chapelle were within blocks of each other, but the trip seemed endless as pain raced up and down his leg, his once good leg. Connor's mother raced to the clinic's door surprisingly fast in her Cuban heels, opened the place, and brought up the lights. Leaning heavily on both, he limped to a handy wheelchair and got a ride to an examination room. There lying on his stomach, he winced as Connor cut away the leg of the expensive bespoke tux. They began washing the wound with antiseptic before the painkiller they'd administered quite kicked in. He hissed as they washed the wound over and over, the orthopedist pausing to search for splinters of rotten wood which he deposited into a pan his mother held, her festive gown covered by a white lab coat. What an end to all their evenings. When finally satisfied, Connor sewed up the gash that seemed as long as a ten-yard line.

"Sarge, are you there?"

"Right here." She moved forward and grasped his hand.

"I guess I screwed up everyone's fun."

"Doctors are used to that," a consoling Dr. Arminta Bullock uttered. "Don't worry about it.

"It was wonderful until the fall. I will never forget tonight," Sarge assured him.

"There was supposed to be more." He couldn't say what in front of an audience. "Will you stay while I recover from this? You won't leave in the morning?"

"I promise."

He was sure she'd keep her word, but something else nagged at him while the doctors applied a dressing over the wound and transferred him into the wheelchair for the ride out. Sarge put the passenger's seat back as far as it could go on the Jaguar to give him comfortable leg room. She drove back to the ranch at such a sedate pace it seemed an insult to the vehicle.

"Can't you go a little faster?" he complained.

"I'm trying to avoid the potholes. You'll feel every one as that local wears off." She kept her eyes on the road, not sparing a glance his way.

"Half the excitement is hitting a pothole, and all the more reason to hurry. We can still make love. You're great on top."

"That won't happen. It appears I've just been rehired."

Damn it all to hell.

Chapter Thirty

She'd signed on for another eight weeks as Mack's trainer. Not that she had expected the time to pass easily. It did not. When she suggested he could move back to his own room in the mansion, the one with the king-sized bed and full bath and shower, he declined. What if he needed her in the night—or she needed him. She denied the first. He had a few stitches in the calf muscle, not any broken bones, and she assured him she hadn't had any flashbacks since New Year's Eve.

Her major concern, though she didn't tell him, was the possibility of an infection in the wound, at worst one caused by flesh-eating bacteria. Daily, she checked the long incision for any signs of suppuration, no oozing, no pus, so far so good, and placed a fresh dressing over it. When he wanted to shower, she taped plastic over the wound and fended off propositions that they bathe together.

She made sure he took his antibiotics and doled out a pain pill if he needed one to sleep. He hinted he wouldn't need a pill if she'd come under the covers with him and play the recite the siblings game again. The one night she gave in on this, his hands were everywhere like a bad prom date, but if she admitted the truth to herself, he possessed skills no high school guy could duplicate. For a man educated by nuns, he had more reasons that touching each other intimately

237

didn't amount to sex than St. Augustine had arguments.

However, she'd finally figured out what Mack saw in her—a challenge like dancing in a prohibited pavilion or hitting potholes at high speed—not simply proximity. As he mended, he could have sought out other women, easy women, but didn't bother because he hadn't succeeded with her. Clearly, he wanted to replicate their night together, only better. He'd said as much. In her mind, she couldn't imagine any man being a better lover. He'd probably ruined her for others. If a one-footed woman did find another man, she'd have to pack away the memory of that night and be content with what she got.

He'd placed their dancing trophy in her room as a constant reminder of what they'd accomplished together, how good they'd been and could be again. She claimed her stump had hurt badly the next day as she'd worn her fancy foot too long. Well, it had been a bit sore, but she didn't want him to propose they go dancing again. She tried to wear him down with upper body exercises and stints in the anti-gravity machine once she got the okay from Dr. Bullock. Anything to avoid the closeness of a dance.

Once Dr. Bullock removed the stitches at her clinic after four weeks, he became even more of a handful, daring her to race him around the property, hinting he knew private spots where Knox Polk had no security cameras to observe them, nagging her to try the Dirty Dancing pose again.

"I swear I can hold you up if I'm not standing on rotten wood. Better if you took a running start this time." He held out his hands for the lift.

Damn if she wasn't tempted. That priceless

moment of soaring among the leaves and the fairy lights, the prosthesis on her leg weightless for a few brief seconds, how she would love to experience that again.

"Don't be ridiculous. I won't be responsible for messing up Dr. Bullock's work. Now give me twenty more pushups." She fell back hard on her military training to ward off her deep desire to give into anything he wanted. He was gorgeous and daring and didn't give a damn what others thought. All that she wasn't. Yet, she'd watched him evolve from sullen and self-centered to teasing and caring about her, lethal as a love potion some Cajun *traiteur* had mixed up to her specifications. She had to end this closeness soon or suffer for the rest of life.

He wanted to add dancing into his training again, a trap for sure. She called in the reinforcements, his parents and Corazon, who were happy to resume line dancing. Better for his footwork with all the side and backward steps than say a waltz which was mostly gliding. Okay if he constantly bumped into her doing the Tush Push. She could handle that.

He tried a new play as the clock ran down. "Did you enjoy Mardi Gras?"

"I had a ball," she said and laughed at her own pun. She could have lied but suspected he would know.

"Babe, stick with me, and I can get us a place to ride on one of the floats next year here or in New Orleans."

She let herself imagine that for a moment before reverting to form. "What did you call me?"

"Sergeant, ma'am, would you like to ride on a float with me next year?"

"That's a long way off. But sure, if there is no one else you want to invite by then." She made him miss the count on the exercise he did with her lack of resistance. By March of next year, he'd have moved on to another woman, most likely several. She'd place a sure bet on Mack Billodeaux to find other female companionship by then.

"Fine. It's a date. Don't go with anyone else."

"I promise."

Exercises, dancing, making hollow promises, all of it came to an end after eight weeks. Again, she took his measurements and sent her assessment to the trainers in Dallas. This time, she didn't catch him off guard.

"I know what you're doing, dumping me in Dallas."

"I am not dumping you in Dallas. I'm doing it right here in front of you. I've done all I can for you. Time for us to move on. Tomorrow, I'll be on my way home for a break, and you'll be sailing along in your Jaguar returning to your penthouse."

He flashed that charming smile, a sure sign he had something else in mind. She could read him so well. "I want to keep you as my…my personal trainer. They let Tom Brady have one. Why not me? Come along to Dallas. Stay at my place. Order room service whenever you want. Live in luxury. I'll keep paying you—but I want consensual sex whenever we both feel like it."

"That's quite an offer, but being a mistress won't look good on my resume."

"I knew you'd take it the wrong way."

"Then why did you say it?" She assumed a cross-armed stance and the steely gaze that usually served her well.

"Because I need you, Sarge. I need you to keep me on track and rock steady. I don't want to lose my career, and I don't trust myself not to go back to old habits. As for the sex, that would be a little *lagniappe*, something extra, for both of us to enjoy. I don't want you to shut me out anymore."

Why did she even consider this strange proposition? Because she wanted to stay with him—and yes, sleep with him as much as she could before it all ended. Call it a crush or call it lust, anything but love because that would undo her.

"They'll give you a few days to settle in before your advanced training starts. Give me some time to think about the idea."

His smile broke out again, but not in the usual devilish or naughty way. This smile shone like the kid who got a pony for Christmas or the guy who had his date accepted for the prom by the girl of his dreams. Mack put his arms around her waist and twirled her in circles, her feet off the ground, weightless and floating once more.

When she came to earth again, he asked, "You won't run off early tomorrow morning, promise?"

"I swear." She braced herself for a sleepless night ahead.

****

Knowing Mack would sleep in since he'd finished training, Sarge did get up early. She had a very pleasant breakfast with Nell, Joe, and Corazon before Joe took off for the barn and Corazon to the grocery store before it became crowded. Fortified by a second cup of strong coffee and a piece of raisin toast, she opened the subject with Nell, laying it all out, the penthouse, the personal trainer, the optional sex. By now her own mother would have proclaimed her daughter on the way to hell even for considering the idea.

Nell mulled it over, took the time to get more coffee herself. "I'd like you to do it because I trust you with my son. He does need guidance, a strong hand to keep him steady. I also believe he looks on you as far more than a personal trainer, maybe as a life partner."

Sarge shook her head in denial. "We'd be such a mismatched couple."

Nell smiled as if Sarge weren't in the kitchen with her, a dreamy smile of long ago. "You know I once tamed my own bad boy, that man out in the barn tending to his horses and all those ponies he buys for the grandchildren. I thought the way you do, great sex but…"

"I never said that!" She choked on the sip of coffee she'd just inhaled. Heat climbed into her pale cheeks, and she had the greatest urge to say they'd only had an afternoon and night.

"I know Joe told his boys how to please a woman. No need to discuss it. Great sex but not a chance of a great marriage. Joe made it clear he wanted children, lots of children. I believed I couldn't give him any at all and sent him away. If he hadn't had Dean with another woman and needed a mother for the boy, I might have thrown away the love of my life. Keep an open mind, Sarge. Don't think about what others say. How do you feel about Mack, not his looks because he is a handsome dog like his daddy, but what you see inside of the man? I know he's changed since the accident." Nell studied her as if she were one of her patients.

"Yes, I've seen growth. He's shared his fears of not

playing again and of going back to his old habits, but I can't be his crutch for life. He'd have to curb those impulses himself because if I caught him with another woman, I'd be out the door in a minute. Same with the drinking, wine or beer now and then okay, but sloppy drunk on alcohol, no. I won't enable him."

"Set the rules and stick to them. Have you discussed children?"

"Hardly. He knows I don't approve of bringing more into the world than a couple can afford."

"Also good, though he could afford a lot of kids if he makes a comeback, and I am sure he will." Nell couldn't hold back a laugh. "Adoption is an option. Lots of children need a good home."

"I think we are way ahead of ourselves right now."

Mack sauntered in wearing those sagging hound dog pajama bottoms again and nothing else. Still, he made pouring the last of the coffee into his mug an erotic act as he lounged, broad chest bared, against the counter, long, dark hair not yet tamed for the day. He came to the table and greeted his mother with a quick kiss on the cheek, but he stared at Sarge as if trying to read her mind.

"Have you thought about my offer—about being my personal trainer," he added because his mother sat right there.

Sarge inhaled so deeply her chest expanded. "Yes, I'll accept the position."

"Yeehaw! Dallas here we come."

Nell patted her hand. "God bless you both."

Chapter Thirty-One

Mack kept checking his rearview mirror to make sure Sarge still trailed him in her beat-up Jeep, that she didn't veer off on some exit because she'd changed her mind about taking a chance on him. Oh, he knew he wasn't a good bet, at least on the surface, but he would change that perception in the next few months. The day he signed his new contract, he'd reveal what he felt for her and call it what it was—love. He'd change her title from personal trainer to Mrs. Mack Billodeaux no matter what anyone else said about them.

He tooled along in his F-Type convertible, top down on a perfect blue sky May day, getting a little hot toward noon, but making his own breeze. Hard not to accelerate from sixty-five to seventy mph on I-95 where seventy was legal in the wide-open stretches past swampy land and piney woods, but he didn't want to lose Sarge. Rednecks in pickup trucks hooted and hit their horns as they passed doing eighty. "You know how to drive that thang, rich boy?" one of them shouted.

"That your basketball trophy, sonny?" mocked another. He really shouldn't have propped their dance trophy up in the back of his car, but he surely wasn't ashamed of it. Sarge hauled most of their gear in the Jeep. So, he shot them the bird, but didn't speed up to catch and leave them in his dust as he might have at one time on this oft traveled road. He could handle trash talk better than he had before the accident. No one would call him Slide again.

They'd agreed on stopping in Natchitoches for lunch. Turning on his signal as they approached the exit, Sarge followed him down the off ramp. He knew a place he wanted to share with her, Lasyone's, noted for its famous meat pies. They found street parking near the aqua and white building with faded red awnings on the outside and ordinary two and four top tables inside. Lasyone's offered cafeteria service only. He recommended the meat pie, stuffed with beef and pork and spices, that came with dirty rice and a small vat of gravy for dipping or pouring over the rice.

"Not exactly training food," she remarked, as she dipped an edge of the meat pie into the sauce.

"Hey, you said I had a few days off. Wait until you try the Cane River Cream Pie for dessert."

"Sounds fattening."

"Like Boston Cream pie only with a ginger cake bottom. Half the calories if we share."

"I'll bet you tell all the girls you bring here that. I think I'll have the hot spiced tea to go with it."

He shook his head. "I've never brought a woman here. I don't take them to the ranch. Besides, those Dallas girls are champagne and caviar types."

Sarge raised her pale brows at him. "I guess I'm a cheap date, then."

"No, you are a person I want to share my li…favorite places with, and the folks at the ranch already approve of you. I think I'll order our dessert and get another meat pie." He shoved back his chair in a hurry, almost toppling it, got in line, and grabbed a paper napkin to wipe the sweat from his brow. While he loved this place for lunch, it wasn't where he wanted to propose. They needed to establish a life together in Dallas, and when he signed his new and more lavish contract, he'd find some romantic spot, crank up his courage, and ask her to be his wife.

They ended the meal suitably stuffed and hit the road again. Usually, he made the six and a half hours in five, doing eighty or more on the lightly patrolled areas of the interstate. A few times his foot seemed to hit the accelerator of its own accord, but he always let up, keeping Sarge in view.

Tapping his horn lightly, he pointed out a tree, not especially large or beautiful, in the median. What made it special were branches entirely covered with Mardi Gras beads and all types of ornaments. She responded with an equally short honk to say she saw. He often wondered who came out here in the middle of nowhere to decorate that tree, but it had become a landmark on his journey, one Sarge had probably noted before, but now they shared the sight. Maybe one day, they'd stop and add a decoration. Almost to Shreveport now with its maze of highways converging on that city as the tree sat about seventeen miles out.

They found the lane to Dallas and kept going right into the tangle of roads around it. Deftly, he maneuvered the Jag through the traffic to the high-rise hotel where he kept his penthouse, had paid its rental all during his recuperation, and had called ahead to make sure the place had been cleaned and fresh sheets put on the beds. He wanted Sarge to be impressed, not that she would be. Didn't matter as long as she stayed with him. The doorman, as deferential as ever, remembered him and summoned a bellboy with a cart to move his belongings. Both eyed the trophy but said nothing about it. He handed over his keys and Sarge's and two twenties with an admonition to take good care of both vehicles.

"Certainly, sir. We'll move them to the garage immediately."

Sarge leaned in as they entered a lobby of marble and gold accented with deep red loveseats, comfortable armchairs, and immense floral arrangements. "I think he wanted the Jeep out of sight as soon as possible."

"His problem, not ours." At the desk, he introduced Sarge as a trainer who would be sharing his suite.

"If you say so, sir." A younger man, he wasn't as good at his job as the doorman when it came to choosing his words, but he did issue two passkeys for the private elevator and the penthouse suit. No tip for him.

As they rode up, he couldn't help himself from saying, "Cool, huh?"

"Yes." A person of few words was Sarge when she wasn't impressed.

He explained the key and code to her in the foyer before a glossy black door with a peephole like an eye in its center. Beside the door sat a delicate table bearing a bouquet of pink roses. He should have told them no pink flowers. Throwing it open, they entered a space with as much room as a small house: living area, kitchen and bar, a dining table set before a large window beyond which the city came alight as dusk settled over it.

"My suite and bath are down this way. The other hall has two bedrooms and baths. You can choose where you want to sleep."

The bellhop arrived at just that moment. "First bedroom on the left," she said, hefted her own duffle from the heap of belongings, and carried it into the place she'd chosen without giving it a glance.

No surprise, he guessed, but the disappointment did pinch a little. Not that the guest rooms were shabby. Both had queen beds and attached baths with deep tubs and a shower. Still, he couldn't wait to show her his domain. When she returned, she stared out at the view and remarked, "Though I'm still full from that lunch, we should have something light to eat and get to bed early."

"My thoughts also," he said, despite being sure they differed on what light meant as well as an early bedtime. "Room service menu is on the kitchen counter. Order what you want."

"Pick something for me. You know what's good here." She continued to study the skyline. "I've been through here dozens of times, but never saw Dallas from this height. I'm always down below fighting traffic. I guess we'll be doing that tomorrow morning to get out to the training center in Frisco."

"No way. They'll send a car, but not tomorrow. We need a day of rest after that drive. Room service, please. Send up a medium rare eight-ounce New York strip steak, baked potato, house salad, and a filet mignon with the same sides. Thanks." He turned to Sarge. "Give them thirty minutes. Want something to drink?"

"Sure." She ignored the wine offerings in a rack behind the bar as well as a selection of hard liquors sitting on top and went to the refrigerator for a bottle of sparkling water. A fruit and cheese plate appeared to be waiting for hungry travelers. She took it out, stripped off the plastic wrap, and set the platter on the bar. Snagging a bar stool, she sat and ate a cube of aged cheddar along with a few red grapes. "Want some?"

He sat beside her. "I thought you weren't hungry?"

"Seemed a shame someone went to all this trouble for us not to eat some of it."

He took a cracker from a basket left on the bar, removed its wrapping, and spread a small wedge of perfectly ripe Brie on it with one of the cheese knives, and ate. "There's always something like this in the fridge, especially after a game."

"In case you want to entertain?"

"No, in case I'm hungry." Of course, he'd shared the riches of his suite with other women, but he felt a little hurt she'd mentioned that on the eve of their new relationship. He got a beer and cracked it open.

"One more thing about our arrangement. As long as I am here, you won't sleep with anyone else. We'll be exclusive. If either of us breaks this deal, we're done." She said it in a way that assumed he'd be the one to cheat.

"I understand. I can do that. Try the Havarti." He speared a piece of the cheese and held it up to her lips.

She accepted his offering. "Good," she said, leaving him unsure whether she meant the cheese or his promise.

The steaks arrived along with massive baked potatoes and toppings to put on them. The salads were freshly made and large, everything bigger in Texas where they also knew their beef and how to cook it. She declined his offer to order a dessert when they finished and got up from the table.

"Well," she said.

"Well," he echoed, standing front of her.

"Time to get to bed."

"My bed, both of us, if you're willing."

"I thought you'd never ask." Her arms came up around his neck. Her lips neared his.

Impatient, he simply scooped her up like a loose ball and rushed down the short hall to score.

Chapter Thirty-Two

One thing she had to admit. Mack kept his promise that their next time together would be better than the first, a pretty hard act to follow, but he had. As if he'd memorized a playbook of her favorite moves, he started between her legs with his tongue and moved his way up with the taste of her lingering on his lips when he arrived at her mouth. He encouraged her to assume the dominant position any time she wanted and ride him like a high field goal perfectly centered between the uprights. If he massaged her back until she became pliable and turned over, welcoming him to enter and do what he desired, fast or slow, even better. With Mack, there was no bad sex. He'd practiced his skills so well she lost herself in pleasure, forgetting the other women that came before her. Her obvious enjoyment of each act seemed to spur him on to greater effort. When morning came, they awoke sated but exhausted.

Naked, black hair in his eyes, dark scruff on his chin, he rolled over in the bed and ordered a room service brunch of stuffed French toast with fresh strawberries, a meal as tempting as he was. Hanging up, he carried her into his shower which happened to have a convenient seat strong enough to hold both of them as she faced him, arms braced against the tiles, moving over him like the water that sluiced down on their backs. By the time they got out and dressed in thick terry robes provided by the hotel, their food had arrived and sat under silver domes on the cart, the traditional *pain perdu* but filled with a cream cheese mixture and topped with the berries, dessert for the first food of their day. She could get used to living like this. Perhaps his previous ladies simply expected to be treated this way. She took nothing for granted and vowed to herself to enjoy each minute that it lasted.

As if he read her thoughts in the steam rising from a truly superior cup of coffee, he said, "I didn't let them stay for breakfast, just put them in a cab and sent them on their way after we finished."

"I'll bet that ended many an affair."

"Because that's the way I wanted it. Hey, I gave them a Victoria's Secret gift card, too, to buy something nice for next time. A surprising number returned."

"Lured by silk pajamas, no doubt. So when you give me money for gas and a gift card in the middle of the night, we're through."

"That won't happen. I respect you too much."

"Which probably means I'll have to pay for my own gas."

"Don't talk that way." He changed the subject. "What do you want to do this afternoon? Once I'm in training we won't have much time alone together."

She assessed the blue sky beyond the window. "Looks like another beautiful day. What do you usually do on an afternoon as fine as this one?"

"Sleep till three, shake off whatever I did the night before, and go out and do it again."

She did appreciate his honesty, but said, "Not today."

"No, not today. How about a run in my favorite place uptown?"

That meant wearing her blade rather than her usual prosthetic. She'd stand out wherever they went, but nodded to agree. People often stared, then swiftly turned their gaze elsewhere. As it turned out, no one followed their progress through Greenwood Cemetery as few people visited on this day.

They jogged along the paths shaded by mature trees and massive crepe myrtles not yet in bloom. Founded in 1874, the grounds had a plethora of elaborate Victorian graves ornamented with statues of full-sized angels, weeping women, and one Confederate soldier overlooking rows of simple military headstones. The headstones tempted her to stop and read which they had no time to do if they truly wanted exercise, but Mack paused long enough to show her his favorite when they stopped for a water break—Mayor Benjamin Long "killed in a saloon when two men and a woman attempted to leave the beer hall without paying."

As they took their breather, she asked, "Do you really come here often?"

"When I've screwed up on the field or done something I know is wrong but did it anyhow. I put my hoodie up and run. No one bothers me, including the paparazzi. I'm a favorite of theirs."

"Yes, I know. I read plenty about you before I signed on as your trainer. Nice to know you do have a sense of shame after all."

"Instilled from birth, but I try hard to ignore it. Come on, we've been dogging it. Race you back to the gate."

He had the decency to give her a small head start.

In his current condition, no way could she beat him, but he didn't rub it in by outdistancing her so badly she could have gotten lost among the tombs. He stayed just slightly ahead as if guiding her more than trying to outdo her—but he did have to win. Back at the Jag, he suggested they return to the penthouse and clean up for dinner out at his favorite barbecue joint. Sounded good to her.

As they weaved through traffic, he asked, "What do you think of my place and Dallas in general? Think you could like living here?"

She yearned to say if she could stay with him always, anywhere would do, words never to be spoken. "I haven't been in the city long enough to know, but I have to say while the penthouse is gorgeous, I don't see much of you in it. It's still like living in a hotel, although a grand one."

"Oh, the hotel owns most of the furniture. Only the recliner and big screen TV are mine."

"You could display any trophies you have."

"Ha! I was always told not to make extra work for Corazon. That included picking up after myself and dusting any personal belongings. I hate dusting. You know dust always comes back."

"Good habits to have. Yeah, I do know about dust. With the winds we have out west, it creeps into every crack and cranny. I was glad when some of my sisters grew old enough to help me out with that."

"Well, the maids will take care of it here."

True enough. By the time they returned to the hotel, someone had changed their damp towels in the bathroom and replaced the remnants of the cheese tray with a fresh one. Sarge started to unwrap it, but Mack stopped her hand. "Save room for dinner. Shower?"

"I'll use the one in my room, or we won't get to eat."

"You got that right." There it was, the devilish grin she almost missed at times.

"I'm locking the door for practicality. It's not personal. Go, go get ready for dinner." She shooed him away with both hands, but it took most of her willpower.

In the privacy of her room, she took off her blade and hopped into the shower, gave her hair a good wash with some fragrant shampoo from a tiny bottle, made her way back to the bed again. She contemplated her three prostheses lined up in a row. Not the blade of course, metal rod or the fancy foot. Barbecue joints didn't call for fancy, but she selected that one anyhow along with jeans wide enough to get her foot into easily and a checkered shirt she tied at the waist. If she added a bandana, she could go entirely Texan, but decided against it. They only headed out to eat barbecue, but she felt compelled to add a tiny bit of the makeup from Belles and Beaux, plus a tad of light lipstick. Her hair, blown dry, never gave her any trouble.

Evidently, she'd primped too long because he paced the living area impatient to get on the road—Mack Billodeaux, the man who looked great in anything: jeans needlessly ripped at the knees, a tight black T-shirt minus any indication that he played for the Cowboys, both accented with snakeskin boots and a belt with a buckle studded with turquoise worthy of a bull rider. He stopped in mid-stride. "You look cute."

"And you seem to have forgotten your Stetson. Give me a minute to wipe this stuff off my face and change into something less—adorable."

"Oh, come on. There's nothing wrong with how you look, and I've built up an appetite. The Pecan Lodge is calling to me.

They drove to a venerable place with bare lightbulbs overhead, lots of small tables, a framed American flag on the wall, and a very long cafeteria line. Mack ordered two combo plates with ribs, brisket, sausage, a heap of slaw, a mound of pickles with onions, and enough mac and cheese for two, but he said wasn't sharing his.

"I can't possibly eat all this," she told him.

He only laughed and answered, "If you haven't noticed, I have a refrigerator. We'll work it off afterward. I noticed you have your fancy foot on. How about some line dancing later?

"Maybe for an hour or two. You have to be at the training center by eight."

"Deal. Dig in. Good as the food is in Louisiana, they don't have barbecue like this."

He demolished the mac and cheese, the brisket and ribs, and when prompted ate some of his slaw. She also concentrated on the brisket and ribs, but saved her mac and cheese for a later lunch along with half the slaw. Didn't pay to be too logy if they were going to dance.

With the leftovers boxed and taken along, they drove a ways to a large building under the sign of a neon boot, Cowboys Red River, live music all but Mondays and Tuesdays, and line dancing lessons at seven. They entered the cave-like building with the expected mechanical bull riding machine off to one side of a vast dance floor and stood for a few minutes waiting for their eyes to adjust to the dim light. The band pounded out a country/western tune. Customers bellied up to a long, narrow bar doing brisk business for a weeknight.

"Good, we missed the dance lessons—because we don't need them." Mack took her elbow and guided her to an unoccupied four-top between the dance floor and the bar, but they hadn't taken possession before a shrill voice cried out, "Mack is back in town."

In a moment, they were corralled by two examples of bodacious Texas womanhood who wore their hair big and had breasts even larger. Sarge figured if the brunette breathed deeply, she'd pop another button on her western shirt already open enough to expose lots of cleavage. Her jeans rode so low they exposed a bejeweled navel ring that glittered in the scant light with every sway of her hips.

The bleached blonde flattened herself against Mack's chest and showed off a tramp stamp that read honky-tonk gal while she smeared his lips with fire engine red lipstick. Her hands went round his neck and freed his hair from its leather thong. Her vermilion nails raked through his dark locks while she gave him some tongue. When she came up for air, the ho, slut, floozie, Sarge couldn't decide which word fit best, said, "Welcome home, cowboy." Full frontal, she wore only a black bra covered by a fringed leather vest.

"Let's see, Delilah and Harmony, right?" Mack identified them after a moment of thought.

"Delia and Harmoni with an I," the brunette corrected. "You save any sugar for me?" Without waiting for an answer, Delia helped herself to his mouth trying to outdo her friend. Sarge stood in their shadows observing. Mack didn't embrace either one, but didn't shove them away either. She folded her arms and cleared her throat loud enough to be heard over the music.

He removed Delia from his chest and turned her in Sarge's direction. "This is Sarge, my…date."

"Oh, honey, aren't you the lucky one tonight. He doesn't keep anyone very long, but makes it worth your while short term. Harmoni got that bra with her gift card. She calls it her get lucky bra. You don't mind sharing, do you?" Delia still had her nails caught in his hair.

Sarge narrowed her eyes to the steely slits that had kept many a PFC in line and said, "I've killed grown men." She let the words hang in the beer-scented air though she didn't know if she spoke the truth. When her convoy was fired on, she returned fire. Maybe she had killed someone, maybe not, but her words came from some deep well of jealousy she had no right to own.

"So Sarge isn't some cute li'l nickname," Harmoni assumed.

"Ex-military," Mack hurried to explain. "Notice, she didn't say she'd killed any women."

"I could make an exception." The flat tone of her voice appeared to unnerve his admirers.

Harmoni emitted a nervous giggle.

Delia said, "We know she's joking, but we do need to move along." She made the "call me" sign, slung an arm around her companion, and said, "Let's dance."

Mack had this amazed expression on his lipstick smeared face. "I don't think I've ever been so owned before."

"We have a deal."

"I wasn't having sex with those women, didn't plan to."

"If you'd been lying down, you would have come pretty close. Here, wipe your face. You look like a battle casualty." She handed him a wad of paper napkins left on the table.

He obeyed. "We came here to dance, and they're playing our song."

Not bothering to order drinks, they got into line for the Tush Push. If other women came between them, she bumped them aside with her hip. When the band played a two-step and they promenaded and twirled across the floor, anyone trying to cut in, male or female, they got a nope in response. After a couple of hours, Sarge declared the evening at an end.

"We need to get to bed."

"I'm good with that." The rakish smile blossomed again.

"We need to sleep, and you need to be fresh to start training tomorrow. No sex tonight."

"A little wouldn't hurt."

"No, it would feel really good, but you and I both know once we start it won't be a little. We'll see how tired you are tomorrow night."

"I won't be that tired," he insisted, but when they returned to the penthouse, Sarge went directly to her room and locked the door without bestowing so much as a goodnight kiss, one of the hardest things she'd ever done.

Chapter Thirty-Three

After a light breakfast, they arrived at the Star training center right on time. Two trainers waited to work with Mack. They eyed him and circled round him as if he were being judged for the best beef contest at the county fair. He knew because he'd once showed some of his dad's white Charolais cattle. He waited for them to pin the blue ribbon on him, knowing his weight was where it should be, his eyes were clear, and his hands steady. Gripping her laptop, Sarge hung back.

"Welcome, Mack. We expected you here eight weeks ago, but your orthopedist confirmed you'd sustained another, lesser injury that needed to heal. Something involving a woman and dirty dancing. But you look good. We'll see," Arnie, the head trainer said with some skepticism. He knew Arnie, still fit even if going bald, didn't favor him in any way since he'd rarely followed directions well.

"Glad to be back."

"This is Butch, one of our new trainers. He'll put you through your paces today."

Butch, young and muscular, nodded and offered a shake a little firmer than it had to be.

So, they'd relegated him to a newbie which didn't bode well.

Arnie nodded toward Sarge. "And this is…" as if he expected Mack to say, "one of my women." Not that

Sarge exuded that vibe. Without makeup, she'd come in her khakis, knit shirt, and athletic shoes. A steady, married guy, Arnie didn't approve of his personal life either because it impacted his training.

"This is Sarge Kozac, my personal trainer, and I guess you could say my life coach. She brought me along this far, and I want her to sit in on my sessions. Everything you need to know about me is on her laptop. She won't get in the way, and I'm paying her."

He'd decided in the night not to try to get the team to take her on because he wasn't Tom Brady no matter how much he wanted to be, just a guy with a bad reputation and a rehabbed leg whose contract ran out in August. Besides, if they paid her, she could be assigned to work with anyone.

Sarge didn't blink either light-lashed eye at his statement. She held out a hand to Arnie and shook solemnly. "Pleased to meet you."

Arnie assessed the way she stood, stiff and shoulders back. "Ex-military, I'm guessing."

"Yes, U.S. Army, medical retirement. Don't let him slack off."

"Oh, we won't. Butch will take over now. Make yourself at home."

Sarge climbed into the bleachers and flipped open her laptop. Butch started taking his measurements, ankle, calf, thigh, all of which she had at her fingertips, but he guessed they wanted to do their own. After that, he showed off his vertical leap, his speed in wind sprints and longer distances, his agility in jumping over cones. They went on to weight training and leg exercises. Ended up by putting him on a wobble board and heaving footballs at him. He didn't drop a single one.

"Lookin' good," Butch said, adding more to his chart. "We'll put you in the ice bath to cool down. Then, you're free to go for the day."

The ice bath, a small shudder ran down his spine, and he hoped it didn't show. A quick dip in a freezing tub of cold water and cubes supposedly improved healing and rid the body of metabolic waste rapidly. Not his favorite treatment, and Sarge hadn't used it, but he couldn't wuss out on his first day back.

He climbed into the tub already partly filled with water and Butch piled on the ice. He swore he felt the frigid temperature in every rod and screw Connor Bullock had put into his leg. He closed his eyes and thought of dancing with Sarge, making love to Sarge. No chance he'd embarrass himself by getting hard, but a nice mental diversion until the fifteen-minute timer went off. Climbing out, he sat for a while before warming in a hot shower and getting dressed.

Still fingering her computer, Sarge waited outside the locker room door. To have her there dispensed the rest of the chill. "What did you do while I froze my balls off in the ice bath?"

"Contacted some of my old patients to see how they are doing. A few live in this area. I'll have to do a ball check this evening to make sure yours are still intact and functioning." She said it deadpan, not raising her eyes from the screen.

"Actually, my balls weren't the problem. They retreated into my body to stay warm. The cold reminded me of all the metal I have in my leg. Now, that hurt."

"I'll speak to Arnie about switching to cold packs

instead."

"We can go now. Any idea what you want for dinner?" They'd both had a training lunch at noon and a short break for him, neither very satisfactory.

"Leftover barbecue. Are you up for more dancing?" She betrayed her joke by glancing at him with a smile on her lips.

"Hell, no, but the barbecue is fine."

She allotted him a beer with their supper. They watched some summer league football and opted for an early bedtime. He groaned when he heaved out of the recliner, making a sound as pitiful as possible.

"Are you sore? I could give you a massage," she offered.

What he really wanted was her in his bed. "That would be great. Why don't you put on your PJs and get comfortable?"

"Oh, I thought I'd cheer you up with a naked massage, but if you'd rather I be clothed…"

"You're the trainer. I should do what you say."

"Then, let's get to it."

Both stripped down and climbed onto a king-sized bed so much larger than Teddy's back at the ranch. She removed her prosthesis, and he took that to mean she'd stay a while, the hop back to her bedroom being so much farther. He lay on his stomach, and she mounted him, straddling the small of his back. Her strong hands dug into his sore shoulders and torso undoing the knots Butch had tied, but that bit of fluff between her thighs rubbing lightly against his skin distracted him from any pain. He missed that small joy when she moved down to knead both calves.

"Ah, Sarge. I think I'm ready for that ball check

now." He flipped over.

"I can see that, but I'd better make certain by rolling them in my hands. I don't want to miss any hernias."

He moaned as she worked him over with her warm hands, and his erection became more and more urgent. "You'd better stop playing and mount up. I won't last much longer."

"Neither will I," she said and proved it.

Chapter Thirty-Four

Their weeks fell into a pattern of training during the day and sleeping together most nights. Not every night ended with sex, and he slept like a bear in hibernation regardless, but every morning he woke to the comforting warmth of Sarge curled against him despite the bed being large enough for her to turn away.

In June, more of the team members returned for voluntary practices. Others joined in rehab, stretching out old injuries, getting in shape for the season. Some greeted him with a back slap and a glad to see you made it. Others, who recalled that his on-field antics sometimes cost them yardage, withheld their opinion of the new Mack Billodeaux and his largely silent assistant.

His primary rival, Levon Young, brought in to take his place, came back from Utah with his family in tow.

He greeted his competition with what he meant to be a joke. "You any relation to Brigham?"

"Yes, a direct descendant from one of his fifty-five wives." The man had obviously been asked this before and prepared an answer.

Despite the rough start and the rivalry, he liked the guy and invited him and his wife to go line dancing with him and Sarge on a Saturday night.

"Jenny would enjoy that. With four small children, we don't step out much."

They agreed to meet Mack and Sarge at Cowboys and were right on time at eight. He was struck with how much the couple resembled each other, both blond and light-eyed with healthy, fair complexions on faces with similar noses and chins, though her features were scaled down to the size to suit a pretty woman. They could have been cousins, but he wasn't about to go there.

This date turned out to be a good idea/bad idea as the couple clearly wasn't comfortable at Cowboys where Mack received a warm welcome from Harmoni and Delia dancing on one of the narrow bars. "Got my get lucky bra on," Harmoni shouted, exposing it to view. But at a glare from Sarge, neither climbed down to smother him with kisses. Their party claimed a table and got their drinks, two beers and two ginger ales with a twist. About then, it dawned on him that the place wasn't the best to take two Mormons with four kids already in the nursery, and Levon and his spouse being two years older than himself, already an old married couple.

"No Cokes, huh?" He stated the obvious.

"Actually, we can have caffeinated cold drinks, just aren't supposed to indulge in tea and coffee," Jenny informed them with a pleasant white smile free of coffee stains. "We happen to like ginger ale better."

"I'd be lost without my coffee," Sarge admitted. "Good thing I'm Catholic."

"The other good thing about being Catholic is you can sin one week, confess it the next, and have the slate wiped clean," Mack chimed in to keep the awkward conversation going.

Sarge gave him a side eye. "When was the last time you went to confession?"

"Um, Christmas maybe."

"I don't think so."

He sighed into the neck of his beer bottle, making a whistling noise. She didn't let him get away with anything. A heavy swat on the back saved them from further religious comparisons. "Hey, Mack. Long time, no see. You gonna ride the bull tonight, pal?"

"I already broke my leg once this year so I wasn't planning on it. This is Sonny Bridger, former pro bull rider. Levon and Jenny Young, and my friend, Sarge."

Short, squat, slightly bow-legged, and bedecked in a belt buckle the size of a Texas county, Sonny offered a big hand around the table in a series of manly shakes, a little lighter for the ladies. "Levon, I been watching your games. You're a big, strong guy. How about you and me taking on that mechanical bull for a small wager."

Sarge opened her mouth, but Mack surprised himself by saying it first. "Sorry, we have a clause in our contracts not to engage in dangerous activities off the field."

"That so? Never stopped you before from climbing on when you'd had a few. Maybe later in the evening." The bull rider's bushy brows raised in a challenge.

"Yeah, I'd have to be drunk. He always wins. It's that low center of gravity and the big mitts."

"You the one who talked some sense into him, little lady?" Sonny jerked his scruffy chin in Sarge's direction. "Because that's too bad."

Mack's hand shot out to cover hers. Sonny might have aroused her inner bull with the little lady title and the implication that she'd ruined him. She didn't shake him off, but looked at the man with that hard, scary stare that must have quailed new recruits. Then, her lips pulled back in what might have been a smile or a snarl. "Sonny, I think Harmoni and Delia are trying to get your attention over there by the bar. Harmoni is wearing her get lucky bra."

"You don't say. Great meeting all of you. Maybe some other time on the mechanical bull." He sauntered off, his gait rolling as if he sat on top of one of the ferocious animals.

"Thank you, Sarge. Levon did do a little bull riding in high school, and I was afraid he'd be tempted. When he decided on football instead of rodeo, oh, the relief." Jenny offered her that lovely, white smile again, and she collected another most like it from her husband.

"You knew each other in high school?"

"Oh, before that, in middle school. We did our missions when we graduated, then started college at BYU after we both returned, the longest we'd been apart since we were twelve. A year later we realized we couldn't live without marriage and had our first child nine months after we were sealed in the Temple. Oh, the children." Jenny whipped out her phone and displayed a series of photos of stairstep blond offspring, the last about a year-old clinging to his oldest sister's leg.

"Beautiful family," Sarge said without too much enthusiasm, which went unnoticed by all except Mack who knew her thoughts on large families well. Perhaps, she saw herself years ago having to take care of younger siblings.

"Levon went high in the draft and came up for free agency last year. Mack's injury got him into the action with a better team. Bad for you, but good for us, especially since we had number four on the way. I'm glad their competition is friendly." Jenny squeezed her husband's hand.

At last, the band returned from its break and struck up a country tune. Glad to talk less and move more, Mack led Sarge out on the dance floor. Mostly they stayed out there for a few hours, sometimes switching partners. Occasionally, they returned to the table for a breather and soft drinks. The Youngs called it an evening at eleven, and he and Sarge followed them out into a sticky June night.

"That was so nice," Jenny declared. "Let's do it again sometime."

Sarge agreed as she got into the Jag, its top down to take advantage of a light breeze. "We will." Their companions moved on to a large SUV.

As they returned to the hotel, Mack's curiosity ramped up. "How come it didn't bother you if I danced with Jenny, but Delia and Harmoni are off limits?"

She didn't mince her words, she sliced and diced them. "Because those women are sluts, and if Jenny and Levon had their marriage sealed they aren't looking for anyone else. That's harder to get out of than a union in the Catholic church. It's for all eternity."

"You're an authority on Mormons?

"I served with some. Good people."

"Ever think about converting?"

"Jesus, no. I might not get along with my parents, but I don't want to kill them. I'll probably be a lapsed Catholic for the rest of my life."

"Must be hard to find someone you want to be with for all eternity, but sometimes you just know." He glanced at her sitting right by his side, the fingers of the air ruffling her short hair.

"Yeah, sometimes." She held her face up toward the night sky and closed her eyes.

Chapter Thirty-Five

Finally, he felt sure enough of himself to tell Sarge she could take time off and visit her former clients if she wished or swim in the rooftop pool at the hotel. Of course, she rarely lounged. She trotted off to check on wounded vets, two of them women, one who'd lost a leg and another an arm, because she cared more about them than a perfect tan. He'd never find Sarge paddling in shallow water.

Summer training camp loomed with its two-a-day exercises designed to get a team into top shape and cull the weak from the herd. In fact, he had a plane to catch. He had few worries, knowing he'd excel thanks to all the PT and Sarge to keep him steady. At the end of the month, he'd tell his agent to start negotiating the new contract. Maybe, he'd try to take a couple of days off to consult with the peerless Leslie at Schifferman's Jewelry about a ring for Sarge, though he thought she might rather choose her own. By then, he'd have a multi-million-dollar contract to offer her. They'd tour houses and find a place to suit them both.

The camp to everyone's relief would be held in Oxnard, California which offered cooler temps and a Marriott Residence Inn situated between two football fields. Ordinarily, he'd be thrilled to leave the heat of a Texas summer for a short while, but of course, he couldn't take Sarge. That concerned him.

"I'll be gone six weeks. Maybe you could go home for a visit or better yet, stay with my parents at the ranch. Camp Love Letter is in full swing, and they could use someone like you to encourage the handicapped kids. I can't think of anyone better. The important part is that you'll be here when I return, right?"

She considered her answer far longer than he liked. "You've been paying me right along for my very minimal services. It seems to me we should end our agreement now."

"If it's about the money, no problem. I'm in line for a nice, fat contract renewal."

"I know you can afford to keep me on indefinitely, but that's not good for either of us. I need real meaningful work, and you should be able to stand on your own two legs alone."

He had to keep her near until he'd secured a future for them, a grand career, a beautiful home, children if she wanted them. "How about this. While I'm gone, stay with my parents and help with Camp Love Letter. You can't get more meaningful than that. I won't pay you a cent. But, when I get back from camp, meet me here and listen to what I have to say."

"Why not say it now?"

"I want both of us to be certain of the future."

Sarge shifted her gaze from his eyes to the place where her foot should have been. "If there's one thing I've learned, no future is secure. A severe injury ended my army career and another for you could do the same in football. My fiancé called off the wedding. In six weeks, you might find the woman of your dreams who would wonder what in hell I'm doing in your penthouse."

"Yes, I could get injured at camp, but I sure won't be finding the woman of my dreams there." Because she stood before him, steady, beautiful, and brave, but he held that back. "They work us so hard and keep an eye on all we do, the players have no time to fool around."

Her lips formed into a wry little smile. "Well, thank heaven for that."

He wiped that smirk off her face with a kiss, long and lingering and so hot it would have led to the bedroom if the phone hadn't rung with a message that his ride to the airport awaited. He listened but continued to hold Sarge against him, letting her feel his need.

"No one is sorrier that I have to go than me. Just promise you'll be here the day I return."

"I might end up being the one who is sorry, but yes, I'll be here."

She always kept her word. He grabbed his bag and headed toward six weeks of hard work.

****

When the call came, Sarge had been sitting in the penthouse for several hours, but Mack didn't need to know that. He'd returned to town, though a few details would keep him at the Star for a while. She should think about ordering something special for dinner that didn't resemble a training meal.

"You still have to eat your vegetables. How did it go? Find the woman of your dreams?"

"Some bumps and bruises, but I really showed them what I can do. No women at all, but I think I might have a crush on Levon. He and Jenny want to go dancing with us on Saturday."

"I'd like that. See you soon."

"It can't be soon enough."

That's how their call ended. It occurred to her she'd just agreed to stay the night if they were going to go out dancing tomorrow. How easy to slip up to extend her time with him and have one or more really great bouts of sex before their time together ended.

Her stint at Camp Love Letter had been fulfilling. Treated like family by Joe and Nell, she'd stayed in the big house since all the cabins were full. A parade of celebrities helping out kept life interesting. She assisted Miss Starr in the line dancing classes and helped the older children run in the anti-gravity machine. She allowed Josee to use her as a model in the makeup class. A team of football legends made watching basic drills an experience. But the young ones got to her— some in wheelchairs, some bald from chemo, some who knew they were dying and still lived life to the best of their ability. She shared their kid friendly meals of hamburgers, pizza, and spaghetti, and set an example by letting them examine her prosthesis and showing how losing a foot didn't stop her from swimming in the deep end of the pool. Her time had not been wasted. She offered to come back next summer from no matter where she might be.

Now, time slowed to a crawl. Waiting, waiting, waiting. The six o'clock news reported no Jaguars in spectacular wrecks. She gave in and rang him, using the pretext of asking if he wanted lobster for dinner. Her message went to voice mail. By eight, she'd polished off the cheese tray and at nine took a shower and put on the silly pink pajamas. At ten, she retired to the guest bedroom knowing they were over, but too proud to cry.

Chapter Thirty-Six

During camp, Mack made a point of being the first on the field and one of the last to leave, emulating Levon Young. Today, he wanted to be on his way so badly his stomach ached more than his bruises, but Levon lingered making a call to his family, speaking to each child in turn. Not paying much attention, his mind on Sarge, he failed to notice an intern in shorts and athletic shoes approaching him from the rear until the guy tapped on his shoulder and jumped back when he turned, fear all over the fellow's face. What the hell?

"The GM wants to see you. Here." He thrust a pink slip into Mack's hand and fled as if being timed for a wind sprint. Over his spindly shoulder, the intern shouted. "Don't forget to bring your playbook."

For a moment, Mack stared at the piece of paper not comprehending at first. He'd seen these and the stunned faces that stared at them before moving toward the office of the general manager. He'd been cut from the team.

Levon walked by him. "See you later. We're on for dancing tomorrow night, right?"

"No, I don't think so." He exposed the pink paper in his hand. "I've been cut."

"No way. You were great in camp, really gave me a run for my money. Is that it? They can't keep the both of us because of the salary cap. Look, I've been offered way more than we need on a three-year-contract. Why don't you come down a million, and so will I. Then, we can both play. A team can't have too many great wide receivers." Levon meant that, an incredibly generous offer.

"I haven't heard from my agent. I don't think that's it. I guess I'd better see what it is."

Levon slapped his should in encouragement. "Call me when you do know. Maybe we can do something about it."

"Not likely, but thanks." He took a deep breath, found his playbook, and went to see what he'd done to end his career.

The coach sat beside the GM, a large table between him and them in case he took the news poorly and became physical. They explained the why with incredible calmness.

"We can't be sure your leg will hold up for an entire season. You cost us a bundle this past year, and you played in only two games. We can't take the chance you'll break down."

"Didn't I prove myself at camp? I matched Levon in every way, and I've got better hands. You know it."

"Yes, you did, but Levon is steady, reliable, a family man. He won't go out drinking one night and injure himself pulling off some dumb stunt like you did months ago with that dirty dancing move. We were surprised Sarge let you get away with it. We all have a lot of respect for her. She's pointed out some flaws in others' training and suggested improvements in that quiet way of hers."

He wouldn't let Sarge take the blame. "She said no. I grabbed her and lifted her up because I wanted…" He could not say to give her pleasure. "I wanted to show her I was strong enough to do it. Didn't know I stood on a rotten board."

"Exactly our point. We checked out your personal trainer. She's as solid as they come."

The coach interrupted. "Yeah, no yakity-yak all the time like most women—and some of the team members."

The GM, dressed in a power suit fine for firing, frowned. "Yet you defied her for a pointless act. You had three years to straighten up, and you didn't."

"But I did. Ask Sarge."

"It's not her problem. Sorry. Here's a checklist for you to complete. Good luck with some other team."

He could have continued to argue, might have cried as some rookie recruits did, or charged the desk, all of which would have confirmed his lack of control. Instead, he slid his playbook across the table, nodded, and left the room, numbly looked at the list in his hand, went to sign his exit papers, and strip himself of special access to the locker room and training areas. He made his way to the equipment manager to pick up a garbage bag and clean out his locker, discarding his to-do list. No need for that anymore. He'd done everything right, even hung out with wholesome friends, and yet still he'd been cut.

How he arrived safely at the hotel he wondered as he had no memory of getting in the Jag and driving to where Sarge waited. He'd failed her big time and ended their future together. No other Billodeaux had been cut from a team. They'd retire when they were good and ready: Dean, Tom, and even Alix. Same went for his in-laws, Junior and Matt. He'd let his family down, at the same time knowing they would support and help him in every way. Right now, giving up the penthouse and crawling home held little appeal. If the team who'd spent big money on him didn't want him, who would?

Mack crossed the lush lobby and turned toward the elevator, but the glow of the bar off to the left caught his attention. Largely unoccupied at this early hour, he veered off course, took a seat and ordered a double bourbon on the rocks, bolstering his courage before he faced Sarge with the news that he'd failed. That took more than one drink. His phone buzzed. He turned it off, ordered another round, lost track of time.

A redhead wearing a snug black dress that accented the creamy breasts practically falling out of it sat down beside him. "You look like you had a bad day, tall, dark, and handsome."

"The worst."

"I'm Phaedra." She leaned in close. A strong perfume wafted off the heat of her body and coiled around him.

"Mack."

"I can make you feel better, Mack. Where are you staying?"

"Upstairs."

"I'd like to see your room."

"Got lots of rooms, the penthouse."

Her green eyes opened wider and glittered brightly surrounded by thick dark lashes and a wide ring of eyeliner. This close he could tell she wore contacts which somehow suppressed the allure. She pushed a lock of her auburn hair away from her cleavage in a gesture that almost seemed like a self-caress. His type, once upon a time, his type. No longer, but he couldn't seem to stand up and walk away.

She placed her lavish lips close to his ear and whispered in a breath so minty it made his eardrum tingle, "I'm great in bed because I'm a love goddess."

"So is Sha-Sha." His tongue tripped over Sarge's name.

"Did she dump you, big boy? I can take care of that. You won't remember Shasha once you've been with me. Let's go."

Mack slid off the barstool, knocked his last drink over, and steadied himself on the counter. The bartender came and quickly mopped up the mess as he stood there swaying. "Haven't seen you in here since you returned, pal. Charge the drinks to your room and send up a bottle of champagne same as always, right?"

"Oooh, I do love champagne. That would be fabulous," Phaedra cooed. "Let's do it," she told the bartender more like an order and less like a request. Stronger than she seemed, the redhead attached an arm around his waist and walked him to the elevator.

"Not that one, the private."

"Better and better."

When he couldn't get his key card in the slot, she very kindly did it for him and punched in the code he slurred. In the foyer, he narrowly avoided smashing a vase of white peonies balanced on the spindly table to the marble floor. With Phaedra's eager assistance, they got the door open and tumbled inside—where Sarge stood in her pink pajamas braced in the entry to the guestrooms. She wore her everyday prosthesis, the rod connecting her leg to her false foot clearly visible, the expression on her face saying she'd like to take it off and hit him with it, but she said nothing.

"I didn't know you had a live-in, but I'm up for it."

"I'm not his live-in. I'm his trainer."

"Oooh, kinky. Whips and handcuffs, huh."

"Not that kind of trainer."

"You're still welcome to join us. I've never had a threesome that included a one-legged woman before." Phaedra kept a firm grip on his waist though he tried to pull away from her intrenched claws. "You must be Shasha, the one who broke his heart. I can help you mend it. I'm Phaedra, the love goddess."

"*I* broke *his* heart? And I'm one-footed, not one-legged, Phaedra, the love goddess."

Phaedra shrugged, heaving her large breasts up and down. "Doesn't matter. You in—because that will be extra."

"Thanks, but I'll be out of here shortly."

"No, no," he tried to explain. "The GM broke my heart. I been cut from the team. I f-failed you."

"No, you failed yourself. Who should you have called the second this happened?"

"You."

"Wrong again. Your agent to tell him you are free and available. Then, who?"

"You."

"Your father. He has lots of connections."

"You," he answered again without being questioned.

"That would have been nice since I've been waiting for hours, but unnecessary now. If you can remember what I told you, you know we are done. I won't be here in the morning."

A knock on the door interrupted what he vaguely felt might be a very important conversation, bigger than the one with the GM. Phaedra draped him over the back of the sofa, answered, and claimed the bottle of champagne nestled in a silver bucket. She rifled his pants pocket for his wallet and handed over a nice tip, one for the bellhop, one for her, quickly hidden in her cleavage, and left the champagne on the bar.

With narrowed eyes, Sarge said, "Put the money back."

"Oh, honey, I'll get it sooner or later."

"Don't make me come over there and dig it out. I might leave bruises."

"Okay, okay." Phaedra fished out a couple of bills and shoved them into his pocket, giving his ass a little squeeze on the way. "Come on, handsome, we don't need this party pooper."

She gave him a shove in the direction of his bedroom, and he might have done a face plant if she hadn't caught him by the collar, pulled him upright, and marched both of them down the short hall. Her slam of the door went off like a gunshot. Another slam answered it in the guest wing.

If he'd been more sober, he'd have given her credit for being a real pro. Phaedra had his shirt unbuttoned and his pants down around his ankles in seconds. She did her best to make him hard with her hands, then her mouth from which issued a curse word, "Shit! You're too drunk to get it up."

"No, just don't want you. Here." He fumbled in his night table drawer, an automatic gesture he'd done dozens of times before, and withdrew a hundred-dollar Victoria's Secret gift card. "For your trouble."

"Better than nothing, I guess. I'm taking the champagne, too."

"Help your-shelf. Go, leave, adios." Though he couldn't feel his fingers, he shooed her away.

Phaedra didn't waste more time on him. He had to follow her down the hallway by hanging onto the walls. Sarge hadn't wasted the time either. She'd dressed and packed her duffle with military efficiency as if she needed to catch a helicopter to the front.

"He's all yours, babe. Couldn't get it up to save his soul. Gave me this." Phaedra waved the gift card in the air. "He said I could keep the champagne."

"Fine. Make sure you leave his wallet and key card behind," Sarge prompted.

The hooker emptied her tiny but stuffed purse on the bar, left the two items requested, and refilled it with a lipstick, a little cash, and a pack of topnotch Trojans. She huffed out the door. The vase of peonies crashed to the foyer floor just before the elevator arrived going down.

"I could so to get it up. Didn't want her." He'd made it as far as the sofa on his own, tumbled over the top and landed on the cushioned seat. The last thing he did was hold out his arms and say, "Come mere, Shasha. Can I call you that?"

Chapter Thirty-Seven

Sarge answered with an emphatic, "No," not that Mack heard her. He laid there out cold, that superb body exposed by his open shirt and gaping slacks, the handsome face slack and drooling from the side of his lips. Ignoring her silver gown in its garment bag and the sparkling shoes on the floor, she retrieved a blanket from her bedroom closet, went and covered him. Let him set his own clothes to rights in the morning. Right now, all she felt was fury. In a while, that would turn to pain. She'd better keep moving.

Taking a sheet of elegant hotel stationary and a complimentary pen with gold advertising on the side from a desk, she wrote out instructions:

Call your agent.

Call your dad.

Add some of this to tomato juice (no hair of the dog!) and take aspirin.

Don't call me.

Anchoring the message with a bottle of Joe's Hot and Spicy Sauce, she left it on the bar. Fetching her duffle, she shouldered it and marched out the door. Expensive white peonies littered the foyer. She took the time to gather them. If they'd been pink, she would have let them die. After all, she was leaving without a gift card or gas money. Nothing so beautiful should be wasted like her unrequited and ridiculous love for Mack

Billodeaux. Her mom might like them along with the privilege to say, "I told you so."

In the lobby, she asked the night doorman to summon her Jeep and pressed a twenty into his hand. "So long, Geraldo. I won't be back."

"If you will excuse my saying so, that's a pity. You lasted much longer than any of the others."

"I guess setting a record should count for something." But it didn't.

Stowing her bag, she climbed into her dilapidated vehicle, stopped at a well-lit gas station to fill it up, and pointed it toward I-20. The time didn't matter. In five hours give or take, she'd be home having learned her lesson not to fall in love again. Soldier on.

****

Mack woke to the Saturday sun in his eyes because no one had thought to draw the drapes. It pierced to the back of his skull. Cotton-mouthed and needing to pee, he kicked off the blanket and stumbled to the nearest bathroom, the one in Sarge's room where the bed had been made so tightly, he could have bounced the proverbial quarter on it. Maybe she'd slept on the king in his suite and had put him out on the sofa for getting sloshed. One glance in the mirror told him he deserved it—but she must have understood his devastation over being cut from the team and would give him some slack this one time. The small box on the dresser containing the diamond earrings should have told him different.

Huh, he didn't have to unzip his slacks. Someone had done that for him. He peed for what seemed like half an hour before washing his hands, taking down a bottle of aspirin, and consuming a handful that wanted to come up on him. He washed his face in cold water trying to clear his head before walking out in the living area and spotting the letter on the bar. Squinting his eyes against the light, he skimmed down the list. No, couldn't be. Sarge had to be in his bed waiting for a heartfelt apology. He moved to pound on the bedroom door, but it stood open, the bedspread only slightly mussed, his belt strung out on the floor like a waiting sidewinder.

Returning to the bar, he tackled her list in reverse order. Wherever she'd gone, she wasn't answering. No tomato juice in the fridge, but V-8 would do. Mixed with his dad's hot sauce, it burned all the way down but sure cleared his sinuses. He was in no shape to call his agent and didn't want to call his dad, but forced himself to follow Sarge's last commands. His agent didn't answer, probably already out on the golf course. He left a message explaining the situation and telling him to get on the stick and see what else was out there for him. Someone would be culled or injured during the exhibition games, and he'd get another shot.

He took the time to shower and shave, put on clothes that didn't smell of spilled whiskey and strong perfume because dialing the ranch came harder. His mother's cheerful voice answered. "So glad you phoned. Did Sarge make it back to Dallas okay?"

"Yes, I guess. We had a falling out. My fault. So she's not there?"

"She left when we shut down Camp Love Letter for the summer. We enjoyed having her. She really connected with some of the children who were harder to reach. What did you do, Mack?"

"Is Dad around? I need to speak to him." The only thing worse than confessing he'd been cut from the team would be owning up to his mom that he'd gotten drunk and lost Sarge. Uh-oh, she repeated in her strict mom voice, "What—did—you—do?"

"Look, Mom. I was cut from the team, so I went out got drunk and…there might have been another woman involved, but I don't think I did anything with her. Dad will understand."

"Glad you handled your disappointment so maturely. Here's your father."

He repeated his sad story to his dad who did understand. "That's how I fathered Dean, crazy drunk after a Super Bowl victory—but at least I won. If that agent of yours doesn't call you back today, leave another message saying you're getting a new one. Mine will take you on if you swear not to act out."

"Do you think I have any chance of getting picked up as a free agent this late?"

"Maybe not at the pay you want, but yes. I know of an opening, one X-avier mentioned. Prince Dobbs decided he'd rather retire than go through another training camp, though he said he's been neglecting his Church of the Dreadlocked Jesus, and that's why he can't conceive a son. I know you don't want to play for the Sinners but…"

"I'd be honored to play for the Sinners."

"Then, come home, son."

He heard his mother's voice still in strict mode. "Give me that phone. You didn't get Sarge pregnant, did you?"

"No, I don't think so. I always follow dad's rubber raincoat rule, and I was gone six weeks. She spent her time with you. I'm fairly sure we didn't do it last night. She left a note not to call her."

"Are you going to do that?"

"I already tried once. She didn't answer. I lost my job, probably my agent, and Sarge. Funny thing, losing Sarge is the worst of the three."

"Nothing funny about it. You go after her, apologize from the bottom of your heart, and don't come here until you do."

"Yes, ma'am." Strong women, he'd been raised by one and wanted to marry another—if she'd have him now.

Chapter Thirty-Eight

Six a.m. The sun rose bearing streamers of pink and pale blue filling her rearview mirror as Sarge parked in the mowed weeds of her parents' front yard. A light burned in the kitchen, her mother frying an egg for her father's breakfast, no doubt. Saturday, he'd be out early to mow and lime the high school's football field, one of his many side jobs. No other signs of life such as it was in the farmhouse.

Toting her duffle and a super-sized go-cup she'd filled with water and the peonies at a convenience store rest stop, she entered through the back door directly into the kitchen. "Hi, Mom. These are for you." She plunked the flowers down on the counter next to the stove and by her mother who barely glanced up from the eggs she scrambled in a skillet.

"Expensive posies this time of year. When they're in bloom, everyone has them in their yards. Did your— client, boyfriend, lover, I don't know what to call him—give them to you?"

"No, not exactly. I'm beat. I'll just go up to bed."

"Do you want some eggs? Seems you must have been driving all night if you came from Dallas."

"I had breakfast on the road." She didn't feel the need to add that she'd eaten a burrito at the convenience store. Soldiers ate what food they had when they needed it. They didn't pine, cry, whine, or lose their appetite because something non-lethal had gone sideways.

"He dumped you, didn't he? Kicked you out in the middle of the night. I told you so when you called to say you were moving to Dallas with that man."

"No, I dumped him, but you were absolutely right about whatever it was not working out. Let me get some rest, and you can hit me over the head with it after I wake." She stalked from the kitchen and passed her dad in the hall.

He immediately embraced her. "Hey, Suzy Q, nice to have you home any time of the day or night."

"Glad *you* feel that way. I need some sleep."

She shook herself free and took the stairs to the girls' dormitory, woefully empty now with Claire in basic training, Mary settling into an apartment in Houston where she'd found a teaching job, and Maggie still shacked up with Sam.

Theresa and Bernadette slept snug in their beds and, no doubt, visions of men like Mack danced in their heads. She'd have to warn them and encourage both to go to college. She'd help with tuition if they put in the effort, especially Terry, who would graduate next year. If she'd failed to teach moral strength and courage as well as physical to Mack, perhaps she could instill it in her siblings. Meanwhile, her baby sisters made the most of the last few days before school started to sleep in. Otherwise, they'd be up and groggy at six eating their grits and getting ready to catch the bus.

She couldn't save Claire who had sent a proud picture of herself with a buzz cut, all that straight brown hair down to her waist gone. Claire grinned wide in her square-jawed face. She'd labeled it "Free at Last!" Her cockiness might serve her well in the military or bring her down. She'd keep better in touch with her in the future, lend a little guidance.

Having no more energy to spend on her sisters, she took off her prosthesis, shed her outer wear, and pulled the blanket and spread up over her underwear-clad body. She'd have days and days ahead to work on forgetting Mack. Now that she was safely home in charge of no one and nothing, she might as well let go and cry herself to sleep.

****

Mack wanted to act on impulse and leave at once for Lubbock because where else would Sarge go to ground. However, he'd made his own checklist of items he needed to take care of before he left Dallas for good. No sense in paying his costly rent anymore. Picking his way past a broken vase that he'd probably smashed in his entrance, he sought out another office to settle up what was owed and winced at his final bar bill.

Nearly everything in the penthouse belonged to the hotel except his clothes, personal items, the TV, and the recliner. He packed two large suitcases and an overnight bag that included one of his custom suits and shirts and a tasteful tie in case he needed to impress Sarge's family by going to church with them tomorrow. Taking his luggage to the desk, he arranged for them, the TV, and the recliner to be shipped to the ranch, his home until he knew where he ended up.

Checking her room, he found the silver gown and shoes which he placed carefully in the bottom of the garment bag along with the diamond earrings. Strange how such a simple act could cause so much pain. Didn't she want to recall the good times they'd had together? It hadn't been all hard work between them. As he sat on the edge of the bed, weighing that in his mind, his phone rang. *Sarge.*

No. Only Levon with concern in his voice wanting to know how he was coping, and with the best of intentions saying, "At least, you have Sarge by your side."

In lieu of a priest, he confessed to Levon who agreed he'd been a stupid ass. "If I'd done that, Jenny would be halfway back to Utah by now."

"I thought you were sealed forever."

"If I kept acting like you did, she'd unseal me. It wouldn't be easy but can be done. I think though, she'd forgive me if I kept to the straight path."

"That's what I'm hoping. I'll be on my way to Lubbock shortly."

"I'm here for you, man. Keep in touch."

Nice to have someone say that. He'd spent so much time being obnoxious to his brothers, especially Trinity, he couldn't count on their support. No, he could. Because that's what Billodeauxs did, totally unappreciated until now. Hooking the garment bag over his shoulder, tucking the also abandoned dance trophy under an arm, and grabbing his leather overnight bag, he bid farewell to Dallas and hello to Lubbock which he reached in four hours, fifteen minutes doing eighty, sometimes ninety, in the Jag.

Using Google, he managed to find the house that belonged to a rural route address he'd once copied off a letter from her mother left lying on her bedside table in case he needed it someday. Paid to think ahead. The directions took him beyond the city through the summer dry landscape to a small town and beyond. "Turn left here."

He slowed the Jag to minimize the jolts caused by potholes in the long dirt farm lane running arrow straight toward a dreary farmhouse needing paint and landscaping. No sign of Sarge's Jeep. This is where she'd grown up—without horses to ride or a pool to enjoy or so many leftover foods always filling the fridge. From the outside, the place exuded no charm, no welcome, no warmth. No wonder she'd preferred Lorena Ranch to here. If only she preferred him after what he'd done.

He took courage and let it walk him to the door, ring the bell, and hopefully get him inside when it opened on the goggling faces of two teenage girls with long, brown hair and wide brown eyes, one with more delicate features than the other, but neither resembling Sarge. Had Google Maps led him astray? It could happen.

"Ah, I'm looking for Sarge Kozac. Is this her house?"

Though their mouths opened, no sound came out. An asylum for the deaf and dumb perhaps?

"Who's at the door?" a heavy, masculine voice asked.

Then, the girls both spoke at once. "It's him! The Cowboy."

Not anymore, but he didn't correct them. He could still be at the wrong house. A large, shambling man moved down the hallway behind them. Still no welcome. "What do *you* want here?"

"I'm Mack Billodeaux. Sarge left some things that belonged to her. May I see her?" He still stood on the other side of the door vulnerable to having it slammed in his face.

"She's not here right now."

One of the brown-eyed girls squealed. "Look at his car. May we go sit in it?"

No harm since he had the keys in his pocket. "Sure." They raced by him in a blur of baggy jeans and no-name athletic shoes, leaving him to the mercies of the man with bad teeth. "Could I step inside and speak privately?"

"I don't know if I want to hear from the man who made my baby girl cry. At least, that's what Bernie and Terry said. Her eyes were red and her pillow wet when she got up this afternoon, they claim. I didn't see the signs, but her mother started right in on her about making bad choices and suffering the consequences when she came downstairs. Suzy drove off. I don't know where."

And neither did he. A haggard woman, nothing like Sarge except for the stern, gray eyes, stepped up beside her father. "Probably to the den of iniquity for some similar company."

"Where might that be?" He expected to be given the name of a bar or honky-tonk

"She means her sister Maggie's apartment in Lubbock," Mr. Kozac said.

"Yeah, she's cohabiting with Sam, her fiancé. It bugs Mom. What is this thing, anyhow?" the elder girl asked. Between them, the two had dragged the dance trophy to the porch.

"Don't touch this man's things," their grim mother, hair screwed into a white bun, reprimanded as if it had been his genitals.

"No, it belongs to Sarge, ah, Suzy. We won it in a

dance contest. I brought it to her."

"A dance contest? Oh." Mrs. Kozac put a hand to her mouth and turned away.

"Another sore point. You'd better come in. Girls, take that trophy and…put it somewhere."

Mr. Kozac led the way to a shabby living room with an old sofa, a small TV, and a writer's nook with an out-of-date desktop computer filling most of the space on a tiny desk sloppy with printed pages. The only bright spot in the room was a cut glass vase of white peonies on a well-made coffee table. Mack seemed to remember those flowers from somewhere but identifying them was the least of his problems. He received an invitation to sit and sank deeply into the worn cushions of the divan as Mr. Kozac lowered himself into a beat-up recliner.

"Now, what do you want with my daughter?"

Why bother with pleasantries—how was your drive, nice weather, etc.? "I want to marry her if she'll have me after last night."

"When you threw her out and let her drive all the way here alone in the darkness."

"I'm fairly sure I didn't throw her out. She left me because I was sodden drunk after getting some bad news. If you know your daughter, distance and darkness wouldn't stop her. There might have been another woman involved, but nothing happened, I don't think."

"Did you hit her?" The man was serious.

"Hell, no. She'd kill me."

"From what I'm hearing, you aren't the kind of man I want for my daughter."

"I'd agree with you there, but you see, Sarge, uh, Suzy was my personal trainer for the past nine months.

I've been living a clean life with her guidance. I slipped because…" He could barely say the words. "I was cut from the team. I'd appreciate if you'd keep that to yourself."

"So now you're an unemployed alcoholic. What would she want with you?"

"We grew close during this time. I wanted to secure my new contract before I proposed. That didn't happen, but I'm not a pauper. From the first, my dad made me invest and save a part of my salary, and I'll get another position. She won't go hungry." Oops, he noticed a brief wash of shame cover Mr. Kozac's face.

"I couldn't give my family much, but none of them starved and all know how to work hard for their own living."

"I'm certain that's true, but I still want to ask permission to marry your daughter. That bender was the first time I've had hard liquor in a year. I swear I'm not an alcoholic." Maybe the old-fashioned route would work.

"That's what they all say, but I'll think about it." However, he walked to the small desk, found a scrap of paper, and wrote down a phone number and address. "Maggie's place. You can call ahead and see if she's there."

"If I do that, she'll leave before I arrive. Thank you, sir. I plan to earn your blessing."

"Good luck. She's the daughter of a hard woman."

Speaking of women, all three lurked outside the door. Mr. Kozac announced heartily, "Susan, he wants to marry our girl and make an honest woman of her."

"Like you did for me?" Those gray eyes held anger and regret. "I hope he does better by her. I'm sorry. We have a roof over our head, and we have been blessed with a fine family."

Mack looked from one to the other. "I want to add that Sarge is the most honest person I know and doesn't need to marry me to prove it."

"We eat at six if you want to come. Nothing fancy on Saturday nights. We watch a family movie and have popcorn afterward. Church tomorrow, and I do a nice Sunday dinner. Plenty of beds upstairs in the boys' room if you want to stay over with us."

"Thank you. I'll keep that in mind. First, I have to find her."

Glad to escape, he climbed into the Jag and programmed in another address, one that might take him to Sarge.

Chapter Thirty-Nine

"I cleaned myself up and went downstairs to see if Mom wanted help getting supper ready, and she started right in on me. I made my bed and now I had to lie in it. I let my morals slip, and this was the sorry result. Sometimes, I think she's really talking about herself."

Sarge finished the last bite of a ham sandwich that Maggie made for her and sipped on the Coke with lots of ice the way she liked it. The apartment was cozy or small depending on how you looked at it. She noticed the touches her sister had added, new curtains and a family afghan thrown over a possibly stained sofa. One bedroom and a bath, a kitchen/dining area beside the compact living room, Maggie had moved into Sam's bachelor pad and turned it into a home with a little vase of flowers on the coffee table and the aroma of baking in the air.

"Yeah, I've thought that myself. You're welcome to stay here, but you'll have to sleep on the sofa. I know it's not much compared to a penthouse." Mags offered her a plate of homemade chocolate chip cookies to ease her pain.

"Nothing is much compared to the penthouse or the ranch, but it's the people inside that count. The Billodeauxs are great, and Mack has that potential inside him. I thought I'd brought some of it out, but what I'd built all came tumbling down last night. I knew it would someday."

Maggie tossed her streaked hair over her shoulders. "I don't see why. You're by far the prettiest of the girls, but you've never done anything with your looks. You're tough and played hard to get. A lot of men enjoy the pursuit."

"I didn't mean to play games of any kind, but he saw my resistance as a challenge, flirting with me all the time, trying to embarrass me. We didn't really commit to anything until I went to Dallas, my big mistake. I wanted more time with him before it ended."

"You're not pregnant, are you?"

"No, on the pill. I took one look at that handsome face and knew I should be prepared in case I slipped."

"Just don't mention that to Mom. It sets her off. Sam and I are always expected at Sunday dinner after church. We go but leave early before she starts asking when we are getting married."

Maggie held up a very ordinary and small diamond engagement ring on a beautifully manicured finger. "I didn't want a big one. We're saving for a house, and when we buy one, we'll get married. But you know Mom, living in sin is her mantra. I'm thinking of making a sampler of that and hanging it on the wall." That elicited a smile from Sarge, amazed she could laugh at anything right now.

"I've promised we'll marry in The Church, but won't be bullied into rushing." Maggie shoved another cookie into her hand. "Go ahead, spoil your dinner. You know all you'll get at home is a casserole from the freezer on Saturday night."

"But there will be popcorn later." She eked out another smile. "I'm glad you're old enough to talk to now. It's very consoling."

"Exactly what did he do to end it?"

"We were supposed to have a fancy dinner sent up to celebrate his return from camp and in anticipation of a big new contract. He didn't come back to the penthouse and turned off his phone."

"Always a bad sign," Maggie agreed.

"Maybe around eleven he comes in falling down drunk with his arm around a woman so obviously a hooker you could pick her out in the darkest of bars. She offered us a threesome, but I'd cost extra. I declined. They went back to the bedroom. I packed my bag. Not in there too long when Phaedra, the love goddess, comes out waving a $100 gift card and saying he can't get it up. I made her leave his wallet behind."

"Good for you. That's really what she called herself? What kind of gift card?" Maggie's taste for the tabloids showed itself.

"Yes, that's what she called herself. Victoria's Secret, he gives them out to women he's finished seeing."

"Did you get one, because if you aren't going to use it…"

"No, he passed out on the couch. I covered him up and drove home."

"Maybe it isn't over if you didn't get a card."

"I should have helped myself to one—and given it to you."

"Because I would have made better use of it."

A car door slammed outside the first-floor apartment. Maggie checked her watch. "Must be Sam. I hate that he has to work Saturdays, but a lot of people want their computers repaired on the weekends. Even I get one a month off. I hope he brought pizza. You can stay for dinner."

Someone rang the bell. "Not Sam. Probably the Seventh Day Adventists dropping pamphlets again. Or maybe Sam sent pizza ahead." With that optimistic statement, Maggie got up to answer her door.

"Dear Lord Jesus, it's him and even more handsome in person. Sorry, Suze." She changed her tone from amazed to a snarl and addressed the man. "What, did you forget her gift card?"

"No, she forgot me."

"If it's Jesus, let him in, otherwise slam the door," Sarge directed.

Too late, he'd gotten his broad shoulders inside and being far too big and strong, Maggie gave way before him. In a few paces, Mack strode to the sofa and sat down beside her. He didn't start with words, but surrounded her shoulders with his arms and brought her face close to his for a passionate kiss using all he had, lips, tongue, teeth. She tried to stifle any response, but her hands betrayed her, rising up to cup his face. When he finally pulled back, she managed to say, "That only proves you're a good kisser."

"No, it proves I love you and haven't kissed anyone else like that in the past nine months, not that woman who picked me up in the bar, not anyone. Notice, I said she picked me up. Let's say I was too drunk to resist the way I should have. As soon as I saw your face, I wanted her to leave but couldn't get it out. I wished you'd tossed her."

"Why? You broke your promise not to be with anyone else while we had our agreement." She stashed her hands in her lap again and should have sat on them to keep them out of his hair where they wanted to go.

"Technically, our agreement had ended, but I don't want to get into that we were on a break business, because we weren't. I love you, Sarge. I should have told you sooner, but I had this crazy idea I'd score a huge contract and propose to you that night. We'd go ring shopping, then look at houses in the Dallas area. Get married as soon as you wanted and however you wanted. Pipe dreams. That woman…"

"Phaedra, the love goddess?" Her memory of every detail remained sharp as a pair of cleats.

"I tried to tell her you were my love goddess but couldn't find the words last night. She brought me upstairs, not the other way around, and shoved me into the bedroom."

"Yeah, a big guy like you couldn't push her away."

"Not drunk as I was. Once she got her hooks in me, I couldn't shake loose."

"You told me you didn't have to pay for hookers. Women offered themselves to you."

"True, but that's all in the past. Maybe that's why they're called hookers—because you can't get away from them."

Sarge shook her head. "No, they are named after the camp followers of General Hooker's army during the Civil War, a little military history." What was she doing getting so off track?—because she didn't want to end it?

"That so. I'm fairly sure we didn't do anything back in the bedroom because I didn't want to."

"I believe you. Phaedra critiqued your performance, one star. She accepted the gift card and stole your wallet which I made her return. I think she broke that vase of flowers in the foyer out of sheer spite."

"Oh, that explains it, why my wallet was on the bar, and I stepped on glass as I left. I remember I ended up on the sofa and little else."

"You asked if you could call me Shasha. Who is Shasha?"

"You, I made a mess of your name, of everything." He tried out a contrite smile which didn't come easy.

"Don't call me that again."

"Never. But you were wrong about one thing, too."

"How's that?"

"I should have called you first when I got the news I'd been cut. You would have buoyed me up, given me directions on what to do, which you did anyhow before you left. I've followed all your orders, only called you once, but you didn't say anything about not coming after you. If I'd asked Dean what to do, he'd say grovel with a honking big ring in your hand. My mom told me not to return without you when I said you were more important than my career. I can't lose both." He slipped onto his knees in the narrow space between the coffee table and the sofa and grasped her hands.

"I don't have a big ring. I don't have a job, but there is money in the bank to tide us over. I'm groveling as best I can. Sarge, will you marry me?"

A gasp made her turn her head away from his beseeching, gorgeous face. Maggie stood there with her phone held to her face. "I'm recording this for prosperity. Give him your answer."

"Stop that." Perhaps, she should grab the phone and erase all that had gone before, but nothing could move her from the spot as long as Mack stayed on his knees, gazing at her that way. "Okay, we'll get married, but on my terms. No huge wedding, no rings that outshine the sun, no wedding gown that costs enough to feed a small country. Something simple and quick and inexpensive."

Maggie stored the proposal and offered her phone with the information for Chapel Dulcinea. "My friend got married here. It's free, but they require a two-hundred-dollar deposit to hold the place. It's really beautiful, see, down by Austin. I'd get married there any day if I hadn't committed to a Catholic wedding."

While Sarge was tempted to erase all that had gone on, she became absorbed in scenes of the open-air church that resembled an old Spanish mission but raised to soaring heights. It sat on a hill amid a typical south Texas landscape, secluded, lovely.

Mack hiked up on the sofa and found the same site. "They're full up tomorrow, but I'm booking four o'clock Monday. That gives us time to get a license and some rings."

"Oh, Jared is open until eleven. Go, go get those rings," Maggie insisted.

She found herself standing, nodding as if she were drunk this time, drunk on love. Before she knew it, Mack was in the Jag and heading for the jewelry store while she followed behind in the Jeep.

Chapter Forty

Two simple gold rings, one narrow, one broad, in a velvet box, made a lump in the pocket of his slacks that he hoped the Kozacs would mistake for a wallet. Sarge fretted as they walked to the front door of the farmhouse.

"I should have looked for a dress after we got the rings."

"I brought your silver slippers and Mardi Gras gown. You looked sensational in that. I have a Sunday suit with me. We're good to go."

"I wish we could, just sneak out tonight, maybe get a license in Austin Monday morning." She showed signs of wedding jitters, his tough Sarge.

"Well, I sort of promised I'd have dinner with your family tonight and go to church tomorrow. I asked for your father's blessing and want to stay on his good side."

"Now who's the moral one?"

"We'll get through this together." This time the front door opened as if by magic to let them inside. Mrs. Kozac stood there, a rebuke on her face.

"We're sitting down to dinner. I didn't think you'd be back, Mr. Billodeaux."

"I found what I went looking for, and here she is." He gave Sarge a small bump forward.

"We're having tuna-noodle casserole if that's good

enough for you."

"If you made it, Mrs. Kozac, I'm sure it is." He might not have exerted it often, but he knew how to be polite and charming. Sarge's mother didn't appear to be susceptible.

As her mother led the way to the kitchen, she fired off another shot. "I'll bet you've never had tuna-noodle casserole."

"I don't believe so, ma'am. Our housekeeper tends toward Tex-Mex."

"Must be nice to have someone to cook for you."

"It is. Corazon is a part of our family."

Mr. Kozac and the two girls were already seated with a huge casserole emitting steam in the center of the table and individual green salads set at each place. The remaining spaces on the benches sat on either side of her father, no holding hands or playing footsie permitted, he guessed. They took their places and bowed their heads for a lengthy prayer extolling how grateful the family was for the food placed before them. When given the go ahead to start first, Mack scooped out a huge portion and swore to himself he'd eat it all and ask for seconds since Mrs. Kozac still cooked for thirteen. Hmm, not bad.

"We only have ice cream for dessert," Mr. Kozac said as if apologizing.

"We eat lots of ice cream at the ranch."

"What's your favorite flavor?" asked Bernie, trying so hard to make polite table conversation.

"Mint chip, but any kind will do. I like them all." He would not be trapped into being picky.

"How is Maggie? She skipped Sunday dinner last week. Said she had to work, but maybe she has morning sickness and doesn't want me to know." Mrs. Kozac took a scoop of the main dish and still plenty remained for leftovers.

"She's not pregnant, Mom. She's on the pill." There, Sarge put it out there on the table, honest like he said. Terry covered her face with her hands as if protecting herself from an explosion.

"I suppose you are, too."

"I'm over twenty-one, and I've fought in a war. I don't have to answer that question."

"This casserole is terrific. I hope Suze knows how to make it," Mack intervened, flashing his most intriguing smile. Her mother blinked and shut her mouth.

With dinner finished, he earned further points by offering to wash the dishes with Sarge's help and received the reward of chocolate syrup on his dessert. Afterward, they settled in the living room debating which movie borrowed from the library to watch, finally settling on an old black and white Fred Astaire/Ginger Rogers film, *Swing Time*. The choice seemed to be a tribute to the huge dance trophy now resting on the coffee table with the vase of peonies placed before it like an offering at a shrine.

From her rocking chair, Mrs. Kozac said, "Suzy always wanted dance lessons. I told her when she had a job she could pay for them herself. We couldn't afford it. Then she left for the army and came back without a foot. I knew she wouldn't dance again." Her glance strayed to Sarge's utilitarian foot.

"You underestimate your daughter. She's strong and works hard on her goals. I wish you could have seen her do the Charleston at the Mardi Gras Ball." He hoped to stave off tears.

"Maybe someone put it on Hulu or YouTube. If we could use the computer…" Bernie suggested, very hopeful it might be so.

"Tonight is family time. I'll go make the popcorn." Their mother had the final word.

They waited for her to slip the DVD into the player beneath the TV. When she returned, she still held a wrinkled tissue in one hand used to blot her eyes and the huge popcorn bowl in the other. "Go on, start the movie."

The old black and white film progressed with glamour and romance and lots of dancing. The strands of "The Way You Look Tonight" began another encounter between Astaire and Rogers. Mack jumped up and pulled Sarge off the sofa with his butter greasy hands. "Let's show them how we do it."

He spun her around the room, kicking up his heels at each step like Astaire and prompting her to hold up the skirt of an imaginary ball gown. When he completed one circuit, Bernie waited for a turn with her hands held out, then Terry. He didn't stop there. No matter their steps no longer matched the ones on screen. He drew Mrs. Kozac from the rocker and gave her a whirl, but instead of returning her to her place, he dropped her into her husband's lap. "Your turn."

The girls, all of them including his Sarge, giggled as their parents shook the rust off their dancing skills and kept going, one, two, three times around the circuit. "Why, Sarge, I think they've outdone us," he vowed.

"Oh, nonsense. But once upon a time we loved to dance. Not in ages now," Mrs. Kozac said, no longer weepy but nostalgic.

"We should go out again. The girls are old enough to stay alone, and the cover charges aren't that high. Yes, let's," Mr. Kozac insisted.

"I don't know," his wife said.

"You should, you must. None of us knew you could dance. I guess I came by it naturally," Sarge added.

"What matters is *you* can dance again. Thank you for that, Mr. Billodeaux."

"Mack." His smile blazed in her direction.

They watched the end of the movie, cleaned up fallen popcorn, and were ordered to bed. "You had a very long drive today, and I am sure Suzy is still tired, too. Terry, Bernie, go up with them. Mack, take any bed in the boys' room. Sleep well."

Ah, Mrs. Kozac sicced the adolescent chaperones on them. The three young women started up the stairs as Susan Kozac took the empty bowl into the kitchen to be washed, but her spouse put a staying arm on Mack.

"You have my blessing. Give my little girl joy like that any time you can. She's had so very little of it."

"That is my intention. Good night, sir."

He mounted the stairs and nothing else that night, even though Terry promised she wouldn't tell if he wanted to sleep with Suzy. "Great offer, but house rules. Let me say goodnight."

He took his Sarge into his arms again. This time she freed his hair from its thong and dragged her fingers through it as he pressed her hard against the wall, started with her ear lobes and worked his way down to the tops of her breasts barely showing in a modest top. How he wanted to go farther, but she could feel his desire, knew it was there but would wait until their wedding day.

****

He went to church, knelt beside his bride to be, and followed a service he knew very well from being carted to church by his dad and Mawmaw Nadine every Sunday for years. Neither a liar nor a hypocrite, he did not take the communion, but still managed to impress his future in-laws. Maggie and Sam sat with them, more interested in meeting him than in the sermon.

As promised, a pork roast appeared on the table for dinner along with mashed potatoes made from scratch, a rich gravy, and fresh green beans broiled in a wrap of bacon. Somehow, Mrs. Kozac made a thawed Sara Lee cheesecake stretch to eight people, her special talent. Mack remembered to thank his hostess for the meal and added in the peck on the cheek he would have given Corazon. She blushed.

The men settled in front of the TV for the first of the Cowboys' exhibition games. The commentators mentioned his absence from the roster which both stung and embarrassed, but he held up with a smile and a cheery, "It's all good. Now I'm a free agent and can do better." He hoped.

Mr. Kozac started to offer him a beer but hesitated. "Maybe not with your drinking problem."

Sarge, who had squeezed in between her sister and Sam said, "It's okay. He can have a beer. I'll get them and one for myself. Anyone else?" Sam put up a hand and so did Terry, but hers was shoved back down by her father.

Mack got up. "Let me help you with that."

They brought four beers from the kitchen where Mrs. Kozac and Bernie washed dishes. In the hallway,

Sarge stopped him. "I want to leave right after the game for Austin. I'm packed."

"I thought things were going well."

"They are, but I won't spend another night in the dorm without you."

Now, she'd made him smile. They distributed the drinks, watched and critiqued the game before announcing they'd be leaving to return to the ranch where Mack would meet with his father about prospects for a position on another team.

"So soon. I hoped you'd stay longer," Mrs. Kozac said. "You know my husband once had a smile just like yours, hard to believe now, but he wasn't as handsome. I do understand the temptation. You be good to Suzy. Make her happy. She deserves it. And give some thought to a nice Catholic wedding."

"We will."

With that they were on their way to Austin. They gave a Catholic wedding some thought—and rejected it. Maybe later, but not right now.

Chapter Forty-One

He couldn't give her the mansion he wanted, at least not now, but he could give her joy. They didn't hold out for the wedding night. He dubbed it a pre-game practice, and employed all the moves she liked best from bottom to top and back again, ending with a massage that led to a repeat. He figured those moans and a sharp cry or two translated into joy. Sarge fell asleep in his arms, but he reluctantly put her aside to complete a few more wedding details that would make her happy when she knew about them.

They rose early, snatched a hotel breakfast, and were first in line at the courthouse for a marriage license. At a conveniently placed flower shop near that building, they waited for the florist to create a bouquet of white roses, sprays of silver beads, and an accent of trailing ivy, not too large or overwhelming. The boutonniere was thrown in free along with best wishes.

They had barbecue for lunch, though Sarge ate only a small sandwich and a little slaw, an indication of her nerves. He ate heartily. Somehow, finally admitting his love for her and taking charge of her happiness had freed him from doubt that he could succeed at marriage.

Returning to their hotel room, they prepared for the wedding. He unpacked his custom suit, added a clean gray shirt, and knotted the black and silver tie around his neck. Other than the boutonniere, Mack called himself ready.

Sarge fussed in front of a mirror trying to get her makeup just right with unpracticed hands. At one point, she told him to stop watching her, possibly because her hands were trembling slightly as she tried to apply eyeliner. He gave her some space after saying, "You don't have to bother with that if you don't want. I've never seen another woman prettier without makeup." That seemed to settle her. She completed the ordeal, put her fancy foot into place, and dropped the glittering silver dress over her head. Setting the browband into place minus the feather as carefully as if it were a veil, she declared herself ready to marry him and insisted they get on the road so as not to be late.

They were early, plenty early, as they turned onto the road for the Wizard Academy. "Are you sure this is the place?" she asked.

"Yes, don't worry about it." They parked near what had been billed as an ancient walking trail that would take them to the chapel, and he presented his first surprise. Levon and Jenny Young waited for them with all four of their children dressed for the occasion. The two little boys tugged at their ties, clearly uncomfortable in their mini-suits. Their eldest daughter held the hand of the toddler and a basket full of dried rose petals to strew down the aisle. Jenny had dressed them both in white with a silver sash that matched her own gown.

"Oh, how good of you to come all the way here at a minute's notice. I'd cry, but then all the goop on my face would run, and it's hot enough out here to melt already." Sarge settled on giving Jenny a fervent hug. "I thought I wanted to do this alone, but I am so glad you're here."

"When Mack called, I left a message that I'd be missing team meeting to help out a friend. If they fine me, I'm okay with that," Levon said. "Stop fussing with your ties, boys. You can take them off after the wedding. Jenny whipped up those sashes on her sewing machine late last night. We piled the kids in the van, and they slept most of the way. Then, we changed at the hotel."

"That's why they are so clean," Jenny added.

"If you need my help anytime, day or night in the future, call me," Mack promised.

A truck drove up and parked next to them. A slim man in artistic black and sporting a short goatee got out and hauled a camera bag from the cab. "I'm Josh Ware, your elopement photographer." He handed over a business card. "Let me make sure I have all the info on where to deliver the proofs."

"There is such a thing as an elopement photographer?" Sarge failed to hide the amazement in her voice.

"Certainly is. I do lots of work with Chapel Dulcinea, three weddings yesterday, but only you on a Monday, our slow day. Having lots of good photos helps make it up to families, I believe. We should get started. It's a bit of a walk. Love your dress, dear, very original, but I've done some where the bride wore jeans."

"You mean we could have gotten away with jeans?"

"Hush, you're beautiful." Mack held out his arm. "Let's do this."

An arrow pointed the way. The photographer

dodged ahead, snapping pictures while walking backward. Once he had enough of the bride and groom, he let them go ahead, and filmed the two little girls who joyously began strewing their rose petals early. "You look great. We'll get some family pictures before the kids get into the cake."

"There will be cake?" Sarge asked.

"Yes, and sparkling cider," Mack said, very pleased with himself. "After we'll all go to a family restaurant. My treat."

By the time they reached the chapel on its small hill, most of the rose petals had blown away in the wind to become part of the Texas landscape, but enough remained for the short walk down the aisle where the officiant waited, a solemn woman dressed in black, eyes framed by glasses, and owning a very reassuring voice. Briefly, she spoke on the theme, Marriage is More than a Piece of Paper before reading the vows from a large, white book. "Do you, Susan Katherine Kozac, take his man, Mack Coy Christopher Billodeaux..." That fast it was done and sealed with a kiss. Simple, lovely, just the way they wanted.

The photographer snapped plenty of shots of the dark wood arches of the chapel with its plain plaster walls and tile floor as a setting for the bride and groom. Outside, he posed them under a cupid peeking from the eaves and beside a sign that made a very good point: Many adventures await you upon the road of life. Enter this gate and take your first step.

He captured the Young family in front of the bell tower as a group and then as the wedding party. After a few singles of the little girls he declared, "Adorable, simply adorable" and added in some of the boys being naughty. "Charming."

Escorted to a small, attractive room where a high white cake nestled in flowers and topped with a heart that read "Sarge and Mack," they posed again before feeding each other a tidbit. Mack leaned over to remove a smudge of icing beside Sarge's lips with the tip of his tongue. "May I call you…"

"What? Messy? Sloppy? Scrumptious?"

"Mrs. Billodeaux."

Sarge gave him a radiant smile he'd never seen on her face before this moment. "Always and forever."

Chapter Forty-Two

Almost back to the ranch after driving for six hours and Mack wished Sarge had been sitting beside him all the way in the Jag. However, she couldn't be persuaded to sell the Jeep in Austin, saying, "You don't throw something out for being a little beat up." He guessed that applied to both of them, too. Besides, they had the luggage to consider, very practical, though they could have had it shipped.

Yet he wished she'd been there when his agent finally called. "You knew I was being cut and didn't give me a heads up," he'd accused.

"Look, Mackie, you were a hotshot player right out of college. I got you a great deal, but you slacked off during your second season. I've seen that happen over and over again. You didn't play enough your third year to show you'd matured. How am I supposed to sell a player with a bum leg and a bad off-field reputation?"

"You're not—because you're fired."

He'd like to have had Sarge squeeze his hand after that bold move for a little reassurance he'd done right. No agent, no job, taking his bride home to live with his parents—and he knew she wouldn't care.

Last night after changing into casual clothes and going out for pizza with the Youngs, he joked again that she was a cheap date to which she'd answered, "Pizza was a luxury in my family. Having it anytime I want is priceless." He knew she meant it.

On their wedding night as he watched her change into the pink silk pajamas and remove her fancy foot, he'd toyed with the plume that had floated out of the garment bag when she'd replaced her dress and shoes. One of the silver sashes sewn by Jenny, lost along the trail on the way back to the parking area, plucked from a cactus, and stuffed into his pocket lay on the bed.

Sarge shifted to the center of the mattress and lay back. "I think we need more practice on what we did last night."

"I think I don't know you well enough yet. For instance, are you ticklish and where?" He leaned forward and unbuttoned her top to expose her breasts, drew down those silky bottoms to her knees, and quick as he was with his hands on the football field, gathered her wrists and tied them together with the silver sash.

"Don't' you dare," she said.

He dared, circling each pink nipple, running the feather lightly down her ribs and up again, crossing her cheek, her lips, her eyelids, tickling the inside of her ear with the very tip. She writhed, she struggled, she laughed, she giggled, and when she couldn't stand anymore, snapped her wrists apart, drew up her legs, and shoved him off the bed.

"You really thought that puny knot would stop me? Next time, you'd better use zip ties on my wrists and ankles—and I'd still escape and do this." She rolled as he attempted to regain the bed, landed squarely on top of him and his arousal. "Prepare to die the little death."

She rode him hard and long, stopped suddenly and began again until he cried for his release and after she had hers. They both staggered from the floor to the bed, satiated.

Before drifting off to sleep, he said, "I feel we are really getting to know each other."

"You think," she answered.

In the middle of the night, he felt something crawling up his spine and tried to swipe it away. Scorpions weren't out of the question in this area of Texas. But his hands didn't move to his command, tied together as they were with a silver sash and unbreakable knots. Sarge knelt over him with the feather in hand. She soon found his most vulnerable spot in the groin area.

"Playing dirty, are we?" He attempted to snap out of his bonds as she had. They didn't give.

"Knots class—how to subdue the enemy if you don't have zip ties." She tickled his genitals once more.

He did not kick her off the bed, but in a classic wrestling move, trapped her in his muscular thighs and twisted her under his torso. He didn't bother to fight the knots. She'd left him enough room to draw his arms over her head and pin her arms. When he entered her, she proved her readiness by drawing him in deep with her legs over his. They both came fast.

In the morning, they needed two cups of coffee and more for the road to get going straight on I-10 and home to the ranch. Still light as they arrived at the gate, and he used his fob to enter with Sarge right behind returning to the place where she'd told him she had been the most happy in her life despite her stern demeanor. He'd grown up here, knowing he was privileged and yet not appreciating it. Sarge had opened his eyes to what a wonderful life he'd had compared to hers. And he knew another way to make her happy.

His mom ran out to greet them with hugs. "So glad you brought her home. Sarge Kozac, we missed you."

"Wrong name," Sarge said, trying hard to keep a straight face.

"Oh, sorry. I thought you preferred Sarge to Susan."

"I do. It's my last name that's wrong—because now it's Billodeaux like yours." She showed her slim gold band, and Mack covered it with his.

Standing behind the women, his father nodded his approval. "You know how long it took for me to convince your mother to marry me? Fast work, son."

They moved indoors to a quiet house with Corazon gone for the day and both Edie and T-Rex back at college. Nell dabbed at her eyes. "But I wish we could have been there."

"We'll have tons of pictures and maybe another ceremony someday to appease Mawmaw and the Kozacs. She wanted plain and simple, and I gave it to her."

"But it was beautiful, you'll see. We didn't have to pay for the use of the chapel either."

"Well, I did tell them to keep the deposit and added on another two-hundred to help with the next wedding," Mack admitted.

"Should you be doing that since you are out of work?" Sarge questioned, genuinely concerned. "I mean I'll get a new job, but..." From her expression, she did not understand why the others laughed.

"Thanks to my dad's insistence, I didn't blow all I had on fast cars, faster women, and the penthouse. I still have two million tucked away and more invested. We won't starve, Mrs. Billodeaux."

"Most people could live on that for the rest of their lives," she told him, absolutely serious words, but a small smile curved her lips at the use of her new name.

"Yes, but we won't have to. Some team will give me a chance."

"I eloped with Joe first time around, private jet to Vegas, big ring. Only Connor Riley and the Rev and their wives came with us. Actually, the chapel was kind of tacky, but Stevie made it all look so nice in her photos that I cherish the memory. So, I can't shake a finger at what you've done. Now, you must be tired and hungry. What can I get for you?"

Over roast beef sandwiches and milk as they'd had plenty of caffeine, they considered Mack's future. His father had been working on his behalf. "Prince Dobbs did announce his retirement. That leaves a big opening for a top-notch wide receiver. I didn't see one among the recruits when I sat in on camp, at least none as good as you. I believe they'll let you work out with the team to see what you've got. Then, your agent can negotiate a contract if you get an offer."

"I fired my agent on the way home." Sarge gave him an affirmative nod.

"Good, he wasn't doing the job. I'll ask mine to take you on, though if you want to consider other offers elsewhere, I understand."

"The Sinners are the best if I can get on with them. I'll give them my all."

Sarge rummaged in her duffle that hadn't made it upstairs yet and drew out her laptop. "This might help. I have all his records and stats on here. I also filmed his training sessions in Dallas. None of his performance in camp, though. I'll send it to you."

"Wonderful. I'll see it gets to the right people." Joe clapped his hands once as if dismissing the meeting.

"One other thing I want to ask. I haven't discussed this with Sarge, and the possibility is way off in the future, but I wondered if we could build a house on the ranch like Teddy did, maybe next to his and near the woods. For now, we'll need somewhere to stay in New Orleans if I get on the Sinners team, but I want a special place to be our permanent home. I know Sarge says she's happy here."

His mother's eyebrows shot up. "I did not expect this coming from the kid who always wanted to get away from home and do his own thing. But that would be fantastic. It's a little lonely here since everyone has moved back to New Orleans for the football season. Xo took her children down last week. Jessie is still here, and we have Lizzie and May often to give her a break, but Teddy is on the road of course. I miss the bustle once Camp Love Letter closes and the others go back to the city."

Sarge put her hand over Nell's. "I'd like to be here every year to help with the camp. I'm still not sure I want children after having to raise all my siblings, but I think there are handicapped children, kids like Teddy who need a home. When we build, we should keep that in mind."

"Whatever she wants," Mack agreed.

"It's happened, Joe. He found the right woman and grew up." His mother's brown eyes filled with tears again, joyous tears.

Joe's arms went around Nell and held her close. "You were right as always."

Chapter Forty-Three

Billodeaux help came in abundance. They debated where to stay while Mack proved himself to the Sinners, the commute from the ranch being too distant. All of his brothers and sisters offered temporary housing, but he considered the number of children in each household and eliminated those. He didn't want to place Sarge in the spot of being a convenient babysitter. Jude's small apartment would be quiet, but he'd have to suffer her comments on his failures. Tom and Alix had room in their condo and seemed to be the best bet until an offer came from an unexpected source.

Jock Brown clapped him on the back and offered the downstairs unit in his building. "I know I'm not your favorite mate, but Lorena is your favorite sister. I bought our building with my new signing bonus as an investment. Now, it isn't as big as our place because of the space the parking takes up on the first floor, only two bedrooms and baths. The windows are around the sides and back and look out on the garden. Right now, we let Brody crap there, but we can stop doing that. You'd have all the privacy you want, and we're just above if you crave company. First month's rent free until you know how things are going to go."

The deal stung, but wasn't entirely charity. As Lorena said, Mack and Sarge qualified as family. She added she felt grateful not to have to be a bridesmaid again, and would help Sarge get the place furnished if she wanted as she showed them both their apartment and the downstairs rental. Mack eyed the Alaskan king bed. "Be sure to get one of these," he prompted Sarge who turned even paler at the cost.

"Hey, we'll be using it for the rest of our lives," he rationalized.

Once settled in, Lori invited them upstairs to watch the second pre-season game along with Trinity and Josee. She'd laid out a nice spread of sliders, stuffed potato skins, and deluxe nachos from Mariah's Place, cold drinks in the fridge. Like most pre-season games, it left plenty of time to talk. The consensus was Mack could outplay the other wide receivers striving for a permanent spot on the team. Dean and Jock played only a half, and Mack gave credit to the Aussie as an outstanding tight end.

"He certainly has one," Josee remarked and drew a "Hey!" from her non-athletic husband and Lori. "But I wouldn't trade you for the world, dear man." She hugged Trinity hard.

"Say, Mama Nell told us all about your line dancing lessons, and we've seen the Charleston contest on YouTube. If you want a side hustle, Mack, we could run with that idea about your doing instructional video line dances. Have you demonstrate and then get members of the family to join in, Sarge, Joe and Nell, even Corazon which would add to the fun and popularity. I have a studio and the equipment we'd need to make that happen," Josee offered, always the businesswoman.

"We can do this if you'll accept a percentage of the profits to pay for making them."

"Deal. Don't think about taking this idea to Shark Tank."

"If I get on the team, it will have to wait until the offseason."

"Not having married a football player, I forgot that playing season rules all, but fine. Whenever we have the time."

The Sinners won their pre-season game, but not by much. The team really did lack great wide receivers though they had Jock at tight end and Matt and X-avier Hopkins as outstanding running backs. Mack would continue to show them what he had to offer and hope for the best.

That night as he and Sarge lay in their Alaskan king bed on sheets so expensive she had balked about getting them, they discussed the house they'd build at the ranch: two stories but with a small elevator, gently curving ramps between floors, both walk-in baths and showers and of course, large windows with a view over the pastures to the bayou and the cane fields beyond. For now, only a dream to sleep on.

Chapter Forty-Four

The offer came through just before the first regular season game—against Dallas.

A one year $1.5 million contract with a meager signing bonus of $600,000 and containing a cancellation clause concerning his off-field behavior, Mack considered it a bargain-basement deal. Even Jock Brown, an Australian who'd never played NFL football, had gotten more last year. Having proven himself invaluable, Jock's second contract had been excellent. Swallowing his humiliation, that's what he'd have to do, become invaluable.

His father laughed. "I used to have a clause like that in my contracts, but once I met your mother, they didn't need it anymore. Take the deal. Suck it up and give it your all. Next year, they'll be begging you to stay."

"I guess."

Telling Sarge went harder. He'd failed her again.

"What?" she said. "That's more than two million dollars. I could stretch that forever—but you might have to eat grits for breakfast." She'd made a joke of it and forced him to smile.

Now, his wife sat in the fifty-yard-line box with his dad and Lorena, the rest of family and all the kids up in the sky box of the Super Dome, all waiting to see his performance. Talk about pressure.

He didn't play the first or second quarter, went into the locker room at the half with his red and black uniform unsullied when he knew he could catch Dean's passes as if the ball were made of metal and his hands contained magnets. The other two wideouts had dropped one pass and fumbled another, but both Matt and X-avier ran in two scores. Jock rose up in the end zone for a third to tie the game. On the other side, Levon had put two on the board. He wanted his chance so badly he salivated for it.

Coach Buck, known to be tetchy, had reamed the team about sloppy play, his eyes focused on the two wideouts. As they returned to the field, Mack sidled up beside the grumpy old man. "Put me in, Coach," he begged like a high school senior at the homecoming game who wanted to impress his date.

"Humph, okay. You're in and butterfingers Larrabee is out. Don't fail the team."

"No, sir."

Getting into the game was one thing, making plays another. Dean shot two short passes to him, and he'd gained some yardage with both before being forced out of bounds. Neither resulted in a touchdown. The second half became a battle of field goals as the staunch defenses held up, but the offense tired. Tom and the other kicker unerringly put up six points each. Still tied when the two-minute warning sounded, he hadn't proved himself in the way he wanted.

In their last timeout with only fifteen seconds to go, Dean called for three receivers in the backfield fanning out to give him a choice: Mack on the left, Jock in the center, and the wideout who'd previously fumbled the ball to the right. He raced to his position through a hole in the line made by Jock and turned to be ready to receive. Dean, always steady in the pocket, scanned his options: Jock with three men guarding him, no one paying much attention to the guy with the supposedly bad leg.

Dean flicked his head toward Jock, but Mack, practicing with him over and over recognized his brother's signature fake. The ball would come his way. Dean stepped out of the pocket and threw the ball seconds before being sacked. The football sailed through the air, one of Dean's long, long spirals. Mack rose up and snatched it, pivoting the second his feet touched the ground, tucking the ball in tight, and digging in to run. The coverage on the field shifted his way. Again, he heard the thunder of a pursuer on his heels and a dark shadow approaching from his right. He tried to quell the urge to slide and save himself from injury, but it grew stronger and stronger. He'd gained enough yardage to put Tom in easy field goal range, but they might not have time for another play.

The huge form on his right shouted over the crowd noise, "Run, mate. I got your back." Jock took out the pursuer with a satisfying thud and shoved another coming up on the side to the ground. Mack found his highest gear and sped, going all out across the goal line. He raised the ball into the air, still clutching it with both hands, refusing to make the rookie error of celebrating too soon and fumbling. The refs signaled touchdown, only two seconds left on the clock.

With not enough time for a second play and not bothering with the PAT, the Sinners swarmed the field in celebration. Jock clapped him on the back, and he found himself forgiving the man for the injury that had brought Sarge into his life and now allowed him to be the hero of the game. Other teammates knocked against his helmet, grabbed his arm for a second. He still hadn't released the ball. Only one person deserved to have it.

He made his way through the crowd, only pausing to shake the hand of Levon Young who said, "Good game. You were great at the end. Oh, and the best family pictures we've had taken in years. We're still on for dancing anytime."

In the box on the fifty-yard line, his dad and Lorena stood tall, cheering and hooting. Sarge sat in her seat, tears running down her pale cheeks, her fingers held up in the form of a heart. He'd made her cry again, but this time in a good way. Mack offered the ball to her, cupping it in both hands as if it were a golden egg that contained their future together: his career, the house they wanted to build, their children or those they adopted, even the line dancing tapes they'd do together. She smiled through those tears and accepted it.

A word about the author…

Once a librarian, now a writer of romance, Lynn Shurr grew up in Pennsylvania Dutch country. She attended a state college and earned a very impractical B.A. in English Literature. Her first job out of school really was working as a cashier in a burger joint. Moving from one humble job to another, she traveled to North Carolina, then Germany, then California where she buckled down and studied for an M.A. in Librarianship.

New degree in hand, she found her first reference job in the Heart of Cajun Country, Lafayette, Louisiana. For her, the old saying, "Once you've tasted bayou water, you will always stay here" came true. She raised three children not far from the Bayou Teche and lives there still with her astronomer husband.

When not writing, Lynn likes to paint, cheer for the New Orleans Saints and LSU Tigers, and take long trips nearly anywhere. Her love of the bayou country, its history and customs, often shows in the background for her books.

You may contact Lynn at lynn.shurr@yahoo.com, www.lynnshurr.com or visit her blog—lynnshurr.blogspot.com. She would love to hear from you.

Thank you for purchasing
this publication of The Wild Rose Press, Inc.

For questions or more information
contact us at
info@thewildrosepress.com.

The Wild Rose Press, Inc.
www.thewildrosepress.com

www.ingramcontent.com/pod-product-compliance
Lightning Source LLC
Chambersburg PA
CBHW050036030726
47506CB00001B/296